MW00748485

ABOUT THE AUTHOR

Born on the Big Island of Hawaii, Savannah
moved to Oregon with her family, where she
still lives with her husband and three children.
She passes her time with her head in the clouds,
her nose in a book or pounding away on her
keyboard.

Blog: http://savannahhartley.blogspot.com/

Email: Savannahhartley@ymail.com

DEADLY

SECRETS

DARK KINGS OF ETERNITY,
BOOK 1

SAVANNAH HARTLEY

Published by Silver Publishing
Publisher of Erotic Romance

If you purchased this book without a cover you should be aware that this book is stolen property. It was reported as "unsold and destroyed" to the publisher, and neither the author nor the publisher has received any payment for this "stripped book."

SILVERPUBLISHING

ISBN 978-1-61495-461-3

Deadly Secrets

Copyright © 2012 by Savannah Hartley
Editor: Monty Shalosky
Cover Artist: Reese Dante

All rights reserved. Except for use in any review, the reproduction or utilization of this work in whole or in part in any form by any electronic, mechanical or other means, now known or hereafter invented, including xerography, photocopying and recording, or in any information storage or retrieval system, is forbidden without the written permission of the editorial office, Silver Publishing, 18530 Mack Avenue, Box 253, Grosse Pointe Farms, MI 48236, USA.

All characters in this book have no existence outside the imagination of the author and have no relation whatsoever to anyone bearing the same name or names. They are not even distantly inspired by any individual known or unknown to the author, and all incidents are pure invention.

Visit Silver Publishing at https://spsilverpublishing.com

NOTE FROM THE PUBLISHER

Dear Reader,

Thank you for your purchase of this title. The authors and staff of Silver Publishing hope you enjoy this read and that we will have a long and happy association together.

Please remember that the only money authors make from writing comes from the sales of their books. If you like their work, spread the word and tell others about the books, but please refrain from copying this book in any form. Authors depend on sales and sales only to support their families.

If you see "free shares" offered or cut-rate sales of this title on ebook pirate sites, you can report the offending entry to copyright@spsilverpublishing.com

Thank you for not pirating our titles.

Lodewyk Deysel
Publisher
Silver Publishing
http://www.spsilverpublishing.com

DEDICATION

To my family, friends, and everyone on FF, AFF and LJ who have stood behind me every step of the way in the making of this book. And also to my editor, Monti, for dealing with all my crap in getting this story worthy of SP. Thank you.

Trademarks Acknowledgement

The author acknowledges the trademarked status and trademark owners of the following wordmarks mentioned in this work of fiction:

Fight Club: Fox and its entities
Stargate Atlantis: Metro-Golden-Mayer Studios, Inc.
Fifth Element: Gaumont Film Company
X-Files: Ten Thirteen Productions, 20th Century Fox Television, X-F Productions
Ghostbusters: Columbia Pictures Industries
Versace: Gianni Versace S.p.A.
Gucci: Gucci America, Inc.
Keebler: Kellogg North America Company
Scooby: Hanna-Barbera Productions Inc.

PROLOGUE

Hi, my name is Jamie Dexson. First off, I want to say how stupid I feel introducing myself to my own journal, but my mother's 'friend' Catherine says—and my mother agrees!—I need to open up more, that I'm disconnected from everything around me and there's repressed anger within me...

Of course I'm disconnected from everything around me! I'm a twenty year old boy who's pretending to be a twenty year old girl!

I've never said anything to my mother about how much I hate dressing up as a girl. I didn't argue when four years ago I was told I had to trade in my tools and motorcycle magazines for pantyhose and lip gloss. I didn't throw a fit when I had to shave my legs and underarms. I didn't make a fuss when I was told to grow my hair out, or bellyache when my mom or Catherine put little glittery flower pins in my hair.

No...

I never said one word to my mother about how I hated having to become a girl...

Until Catherine forced me to keep a record of my feelings.

I'm not one to show my displeasure. When Catherine and my mom told me I would be dressing up as a girl, I shrugged my shoulders and said 'fine'. Not a normal thing for a guy to say. I said nothing of the unfairness of changing my gender—in appearances only, of course. And because I've never voiced my anger in having to change my life to become a girl, in any way, my mother's lover suggested I start keeping a journal. I didn't want to. Writing about my feelings is just as bad as talking about them, but when it came down to talking about my feeling or writing about them, I chose writing.

I'd stayed quiet this whole time because I

don't want to give my mother any more problems than I've already caused her due to my existence. Years of watching my mom cry when she thought I wasn't around, which is why I caved, and why I'm writing in my new journal right now.

...So, no matter how stupid I feel, I'll keep writing in this tablet to make my mom happy. If anyone deserves happiness it's my mother.

I was born a healthy baby boy on the 23rd of October, 1990 and had blond hair and green eyes.

Yes, had.

Four years ago, I began dying my hair a dark brown and started wearing brown contacts.

The horrible part is I'm able to pull off being a girl. I'm a sad height of five feet two inches, and I look like my mother. Now, when I say I look like my mother, I mean I really look like my mother. I get my hair and eye color from my father but my face is a mirror image of my mom's. Every boy's dream, right?

In essence, I appear more female than male.

Hell, if I wore boy's clothing outside, people would probably think I was a girl trying to be a boy. My voice hasn't deepened enough for anyone to question what sex I am... and as of yet I still haven't been able to grow any stubble on my face.

Pathetic.

Anyway...

How does a twenty year old man, disguising himself as a girl begin his daily life?

Mornings:

1. Use the toilet. Brush my teeth. Wash my face. Typical morning stuff.

2. Put in my colored contacts.

3. Change from my boxers to panties— special panties my mother created to 'smooth out the lumps'.

4. Wear a special bra my mother made

so everyone can see that I have boobs. I have a large selection to choose from... my mother's really into inventing these kinds of things for me... yay...

5. Get ready for the new day. Normal things everyone does to get ready in the morning except, I wear skirts more than pants.

6. Apply a light amount of make-up. It's a sad day when a boy knows the difference between a liquid eyeliner, eye pencil, and soft eyeliner crayon...

7. Eat breakfast and spend my day making damn sure no one finds out I'm a boy.

8. Come home and take a bath, which washes more of the homemade brown dye from my hair.

Note: Because I have to continuously dye my hair, it came to the point where my mother started to make it. I was surprised how easy it was... but because my hair dye is made from berries and other natural stuff, it washes off very quickly. Every other day I have to reapply the color. Funny, but it makes my hair very silky and shiny. I wonder if I should be happy about that.

9. Go to bed and repeat the process the next day.

"Jamie, sweetheart! You need to wax your legs, so don't shave them when you take your bath, okay? Jamie? Sweetheart, did you hear me?"

9. Climb out my window, wait until my mother is asleep, then sneak back in, go to bed, and repeat the process the next day.

One of the reasons I decided to keep a journal—besides getting Catherine's nagging ass off mine—is I thought maybe one day, when I'm old and gray, I'll read this and think, "Man, my life was interesting."

Or something like that.

Oh... and the reason I have to pretend I'm a girl and deceive everyone around me?

Simple...

Someone wants to kill us.

CHAPTER 1

August 28th, 2010

I was seven years old when I overheard my mother and Catherine arguing. I ran over from the schoolroom to show my mom the perfect score I received on my spelling test when I came upon their rising voices...

The day I discovered my mother and father weren't married. He, my dad, was married to another woman and she, my mother, his live-in lover...

At such a young age, I didn't know what mistress or bastard meant, but from the way they had angrily shouted I had the feeling it couldn't be anything good.

I realize now the way I grew up, many would not consider normal. I was raised in a big fancy house with servants, a nanny, and a chef who cooked five course meals for us. Catherine lived with us as my caregiver. I was homeschooled, never stepped into a real classroom until I was eleven.

I remember backing away from my mother's door and going to my room where I looked up the words "mistress", "lover" and "bastard" in the dictionary. Words Catherine said to my mother, I needed to know what they meant, and why my mother cried when Catherine said them.

Then I searched for the word "whore"...

To this day, my mother thinks the first time I found out about her and dear ol' dad is when I turned twelve, and I let her continue believing that. What good would come out of her discovering how old I really was when I found out?

She's been through enough...

* * * *

School... the bane of every young adult...

Walking down the hall, Jamie smiled blandly at the giggling freshmen who waved in greeting to him. To them, he was one of the girls in the college he was forced to attend everyday…

Jamie sighed as he shifted his pink purse on his shoulder. Making sure he had his required books he needed for the day.

How many more years do I have before I can escape this crazy life pretending to PMS every month. Jamie took a small mirror from his purse, and looked at his perfectly applied make-up on his oh-so-obviously masculine face. Well, obvious to him anyway.

As stupid as it sounded, Jamie wished someone would come up to him and ask, 'Why do you dress like a girl? You're a boy, aren't you?' Or something like that.

As much as Jamie imagined someone pointing out his dick, he also pictured the utter chaos. What his family's life would become if something like that happened. Exactly the reason why Jamie took out a tube of strawberry flavored gloss, and applied another coat over his lips.

Once again, for another year, I'm walking through these halls as a girl. Jamie entered his classroom and sat in his favorite seat near the back. First to arrive to class, Jamie had the luxury of stretching his legs in a non-ladylike manner while gazing out the window. As he had done every day since the first day of his sophomore year, Jamie daydreamed of what he would do once he graduated.

He didn't imagine what kind of high profile job he might get with his snazzy Kegan State University diploma. He dreamed of the freedom the diploma would give him. The conclusion of the promise he had made to his mother.

Being homeschooled nearly all his life, his mother wanted him to have the experience of sitting in a classroom, of being taught by teachers and such. To enjoy what it would be like to walk across the stage in a school gymnasium or football field dressed in a stupid hat and robe and receive a piece of paper saying he was on his way to adulthood...

What crap.

In a few more days he would be twenty-one... it was hard enough having to dress as a girl, but faking he didn't already know everything he was learning made his ordeal even worse. Eight more months of knee-high socks, neck breaking high heels, short skirts, and make-up. A long, nerve-racking eight months before summer came and he'd be free for three months.

Then... then he would have to suffer another nine months of school... and another until he was free to run as far and as fast as he wanted. And, most importantly, going anywhere he dreamed to live his life as a *man*. Where no one had a clue who his father was... where he could disappear, and the ones lurking in the shadows would follow him, leaving his mother alone so she might finally stop living in fear. They wanted him, not her.

"Jamie, I swear, if I was a boy I could have been kneeling and looking up your skirt, at your panties, the way you sit and space out."

Jamie peered up and smiled. "Morning, Tiff," he said and sat up properly in his seat, crossing his legs and tucking his skirt around his thighs.

"Do you do that on purpose?" Tiffany asked, standing in front of Jamie with her hands on her hips, frowning down at him. "Come to school early so you can gaze out the window? If you are, then you need to knock off the 'I'm not getting a boyfriend until I graduate' crap and get one. You don't understand how pitiful you look every morning, but if you get a man and get laid, it'll save me from going nuts watching you for another year while you look out the damn window!"

Jamie rolled his eyes. Trust the daughter of an actress to be dramatic so early in the morning. "I'm not getting laid nor am I going to get a man simply because you can't stand the fact I like looking out the window."

"Why! I mean, come on with the chastity crap already! There are so many guys who are hard up for you! Why don't you go out with any of them? The year's only just started, and you've gotten... like, what... four love confessions?" Tiffany asked.

In a lower tone, so the students who just came in the classroom wouldn't hear him, Jamie whispered, "You remember my mother's rule..."

"Yes, yes, the 'no boyfriends and no sex' rule. Still, do you know how many girls have those kinds of rules with their parents? All of them! When they were *sixteen*! And not a single one of them followed it! Besides!" Tiffany said. "You're old enough to make your own decisions about your sex life."

Jamie laughed at the pigtailed redhead. Nodding as if he knew exactly what Tiffany was talking about. Did mothers and fathers from *normal* families have no sex rules with their daughters? He'd just made the whole thing up to stop Tiffany from setting him up on any blind dates.

"Sorry, Tiff, but I'm not budging. I think my mother has a valid point, which is why I haven't broken her 'golden rule'. Besides there aren't any boys I've found remotely attractive enough to begin lying to my mother in our nightly ritual of 'Have you found someone you like?' talks we have before dinner," Jamie sighed.

The no sex or lover rule was his lie to tell every boy that took an interest in him and stocked up enough courage to confess to him. Jamie always felt guilty when a nervous guy walked up to him, another shattered look on the poor boy's face when Jamie rejected him.

The only truth Jamie told the plucky redhead was his mother did have a little ritual of asking him if he found anyone yet... only because she worried his charade as a girl made him miss out on all the pretty, sparkly romances... duh.

The only option Jamie had as a girl was a boyfriend. Sure, he could act all lesbo, but acting like a lesbian came with a whole new set of problems. Like how he didn't have the correct parts to back it up if said girl partner wanted to get down and dirty. And getting a boyfriend? Yeah... nothing would say 'I love you' like a stiff schlong pressed against the dude who's under the belief you're a chick. His mother, on the other hand, didn't seem to understand that to keep his secret of being a boy, there would be no doe-eyed glances between him and the opposite sex... or same sex.

"Ahh, hello? Earth to Jamie! You're spacing off, sweetheart!"

With his perfectly, pink polished acrylic nails, Jamie tried to shoo Tiffany away, like he'd tried to do every morning for the past two years. Since the moment he stepped on campus and the girl latched to his side, declaring him to be her "best-est friend in the whole wide world", Tiffany acted as she did every morning— ignoring him and sitting in the seat next to him.

"You know what I love about you, Jamie?" Tiffany said, smiling sweetly.

"… The fact I'm not rich enough to be a threat to you? How I'll never show up wearing the same Versace dress? That I won't have a better Gucci bag than you? Or how I'll never steal your boy toys, and, let us not forget, how I allow you to copy all my homework?" Jamie brightly asked.

"Well, yeah, but that's not the reason."

"You mean you don't love the fact I'm a good friend in those areas? Hell, if you don't like that about me, I can always change… let's start with the homework part," Jamie teased.

Jamie already knew what the voluptuous, perfectly painted redhead was talking about, and sighed. Glancing at the group of guys who walked in, Jamie waited for Tiffany to begin her daily act.

With his head tilted dutifully back, Jamie closed his eyes when the future Academy Award winner stood from the desk she had been sitting on and cupped his face.

"The best thing I love about you is that you don't flake out when I wanna get attention by kissing you."

"Hurry up, Tiff, class is going to start soon," Jamie mumbled, listening as the excited voices of the males in the class as Tiffany slowly lowered her lips to his. The kiss was nothing super dirty. No deep tongue tangos or lewd moans. No panting or boob rubbing. Just a long kiss with tightly closed mouths, enough to get the boys hooting and shouting out for more.

"Alright, Miss Stafrin, Miss Dexson, break it up, please."

Jamie smiled up at Tiffany when she lifted her head from his.

"Aww, Mr Miller. I was just getting started!" Tiffany playfully complained.

Shaking his head at Tiffany, who

flounced away, Jamie opened his book to the assigned page written on the whiteboard and began reading even as his peppy friend continued to playfully argue with their teacher.

"Umm... ahhh... J-Jamie?"

At the sound of his name, Jamie looked at the boy seated next him. "Oh, hey, Asa." Jamie smiled politely at the pretty boy, trying to ignore the freshly made cut at the corner of his lip. One would think the schoolyard bullying would have ended already. Poor kid looked like he needed a break from life.

"I... could I share your textbook? I forgot mine..."

"Sure," Jamie said, giving Asa a kind smile. "Bring your desk closer to mine."

It was strange, the relationship Asa and Jamie had. They weren't friends, study buddies, or... anything. The more Jamie thought about it, while Asa moved his desk, he realized he knew absolutely nothing about the boy, other than the first time Jamie saw Asa in their freshman year, it was of Asa being picked on by a group of guys. Jamie had to stop himself from reaching out to protect the kid. He'd stood back like everyone else. Jamie remembered wondering why the boy hadn't done anything to protect himself. Asa was five or six inches taller and ten to fifteen pounds heavier than him, and while Asa was on the slim side, he physically hadn't looked like a weakling.

Jamie liked him... not *like*, liked him but if his situation were different he would have wanted to be friends with Asa.

"Tell me, Asa... what's a good looking guy like you doing single? Why don't you have a girlfriend?" Jamie suddenly asked, and smiled when the boy's face turned a bright red.

"Please, Jamie... please don't pay any more attention to me than necessary..."

Curious, Jamie looked in the direction Asa's eyes darted, and saw his loudly spoken question had caught the attention of everyone in the classroom, including the instructor.

"My father receives reports of how I'm doing in my classes. If the professor tells my father I've been talking in class…"

Jamie narrowed his eyes at Asa's words. Looking down at the boy's bowed, dark brown-haired head, Jamie tsked under his breath.

"Wow, your father is extremely strict," Jamie said. "All we're doing is talking. The instructor can't complain about you just for speaking to me. And I pay attention to you because I like you." Jamie's eyes widened. "I-I mean I like you as a person, not in a romantic sense." Jamie groaned and covered his eyes with his hands, completely embarrassed.

Soft laughter reached his ears.

"I like you to in a non-romantic way as well, Jamie…"

Uncovering his eyes, Jamie gave Asa a smile, and nodded in approval when, over the boy's glasses, Asa's hazel eyes finally met his.

"Miss Dexson. Mr Jacobs. If you both are done gazing into one another's eyes, I'd love it if you would follow along with the rest of the class and turn your textbook to page fifty-three."

"Yes, Mr Miller..." Jamie muttered to the irate teacher as he tapped his foot, but continued to smile at Asa and pushed his book in-between their adjoined desks so the shy boy could follow along to the day's lesson.

* * * *

This is the part of my day I hate the most, Jamie thought, pulling his shirt over his head and folding it neatly, putting it in his locker followed by his plaid skirt. Why he ever agreed to work out after classes with Tiffany, he didn't know. He'd been told by his mother that girls liked exercising together, and to appear like a *normal* girl he should do it.

Squeals of feminine laughter echoed through the locker room as Jamie stood in his bra and panties, pulling out his sweat shirt and pants and setting them on the bench behind him.

Yup, this is definitely the part of my day I hate the most. Jamie sighed. He stood in his girly underwear, which hid the fact he had a dick, and sports bra with squishy mounds artfully sewed into them to make him look like he had breasts. They even had nipples...

Another boy being in the girls' locker room and seeing half naked chicks running around would consider it a dream come true. Jamie felt... nothing.

No deep blushes when an especially sexy top ten figure girl strutted by, shaking her stuff and zero hardening between his legs, which would make him run to hide his erection. No tingles or shivers when one of those girls came up to him and absentmindedly touched his body, commenting on how pretty his skin looked... absolutely no reaction down south.

Of course, being gay, Jamie didn't expect a reaction from his lower extremity. "Seeing my mother and Catherine making out when they think I'm not around has effectively killed any kind of sexual awareness I might have for women," Jamie mumbled, looking at himself in his small mirror on his locker door.

The fact he stood in his underwear, unconcerned someone would suddenly scream, "Oh my God! You have a dick!" showed how comfortable he'd become. Even if it depressed him that no one looked at his body and thought, "That's not the body of a girl."

"Jamie, Jamie!"

Closing his locker, Jamie turned and smiled at Tiffany as she ran up to him. "You're a little too excited just to work out, aren't you?" Jamie mused, stepping into his red sweats, pulling them up to hug his slim hips.

"I swear, Jamie, looking at your body pisses me off. I've seen how you eat! How the hell do you stay so skinny?"

"Yoga and pilates." No body building for him, Jamie snickered.

"Your boobies are huge, too!"

Jamie smacked Tiffany's hands away

when she reached out to grope his thirty-eight B cups. "No touching the girls, there aren't any guys around to drool over you fondling me. My breasts aren't that big. Not big enough for you to shout out loud about," Jamie muttered.

"For your height they are."

Gritting his teeth, Jamie grabbed his shirt from the bench. He hated when people commented about his height. "So, what has you running over to me?" Jamie asked once he'd put his shirt on.

"Oh! Come quick! You've got to see this!"

Jamie grunted when his overly energetic friend dragged him out of the locker room, and toward the crowded open double doors to the indoor basketball court. A stream of giggling girl's blocked the way and Jamie yelled out, "I'm sorry" and "My bad" when Tiffany laughingly used him to shove them up to the front of the herd.

Rubbing his stomach from a stray elbow

that nailed him in the gut, Jamie dispassionately watched the game being played by a group of guys.

"Can you believe all this eye candy? And Aidan has his shirt off! Oh my God, I could die happy! Ahhh, isn't he dreamy?"

Aidan Alexander Christopher Rowan Montgomery the Sixth... or was it Aidan Christopher Rowan Alexander Montgomery? Jamie yawned, but he had to admit the guy did have a killer body. Like Brad Pitt's when he acted in the movie Fight Club, except taller and better looking. Jamie groaned in disgust, hating himself for the envy he felt at the sight before his eyes.

Maybe he also hated the guy because like all the other girls gathered around, he too had a crush on the boy.

"Yo, Jamie!"

Jamie waved to Ethan as he ran past them with the ball.

Ethan Bartholomew Martins, the second

'hottest' guy on the campus Jamie's mother spent an ungodly amount of money on so he could get the education she strongly believed he deserved and become smarter than she was.

His mother dropped out her junior year of high school year, and regretted her rash decision and all the opportunities closed to her for never finishing high school. She didn't want him to make the same mistakes she did in her youth, aka his father.

Jamie winced at Tiffany's high pitch squeal.

"Why is he saying hello to you anyway?"

I sooo don't want to deal with this crap today. Jamie glanced toward the snippy voice behind him and forced himself to smile. The second part of his day he hated. Running into the viper tongued brunette standing behind him. "Hey, Janis…"

"So? Are you going to answer my question? What makes you so special that Ethan would acknowledge you out of all of us?" Janis demanded.

Us or you? Jamie shrugged. "I don't know. Maybe he knows I'm not thinking thoughts like 'Oh, my God! He likes me and wants to be my boyfriend'! You know, those kinds of annoying things. Ethan knows I'm not looking for a BF, and I'm not planning on hooking up with anyone until I graduate." Actually couldn't hook up would be a better reason why Jamie didn't have a lover. All the girls thought he was one of them, and all the boys wouldn't like what they found if they saw what Jamie hid under his clothes. Wouldn't exactly be what they were hoping for.

Janis glared. "What a load of shit. I bet you're just pretending you're not looking, but you're really scheming to get him between your slutty thighs."

"Fuck off, Janis. You're just jealous because Ethan treats you like you have the plague. Maybe if he hadn't caught you sucking the captain of the football team's dick, he might talk to you. I mean, there's nothing like an STD to halt any kind of conversation, right, Jamie?" Tiffany said, stepping in front of Jamie, blocking the other girl's view of him.

Jamie tried to stifle his laugh but failed.

"Besides, why would Jamie go for Ethan when she could land Aidan in a heartbeat? Look, he's even checking her out right now," Tiffany said smugly.

Jamie looked out over the court. Sure enough, Aidan stood to the side looking in their direction.

"Oh, please! Jamie land Aidan?" Janis laughed. "I don't think so. Someone like her hooking up with the heir to the Montgomery empire? Never going to happen. My father said unless you have a minimum of forty million dollars in the bank, Aidan won't even look at you twice."

"That shallow, is he?" Jamie joked, trying not to squirm when he saw the tall stud continued to watch him.

"Don't call him shallow!"

"For crying out loud, Janis!" Tiffany said. "Will you show some class and keep your voice down to a more ladylike volume? It's no wonder everyone calls you 'Janis the Shrieking Shrew'."

Jamie played his female part well, covering his mouth to hide his smile, like a girl would. Trust his best friend to get the voluptuous brunette all riled up.

"They do not call me that!"

"Yes, they do! And by the way, someone like Jamie, even though she's poorer than a church mouse, can't afford designer clothing, and might only be able to get by as a rich man's plaything, is ten, no, twenty times better than the likes of you. Why don't you take that and shove it up your ass, or is there no room with that huge stick up there?"

"Thanks so much, Tiff," Jamie dryly said.

He *loved* how Tiffany talked about him as if his white collar family were a bunch of beggars. With insults like hers, Jamie wondered how he and Tiffany continued to be friends. Stupid girl.

"No problem, baby. You know I always got your back. Especially when being attacked by the zombie bitch, Janis."

Jamie had just enough time to jump between the two girls before Janis gave a shriek and rushed his plucky redheaded friend. Jamie shouted for the two to stop fighting.

From the time he had donned the petticoats and painted his face, the rose-tinted glasses were ripped away from his eyes when it came to women.

When he and his mother first ran away and he still walked around as a boy, the girls he met were all wonderful, dainty, and oh so gentle... but once he became one of them, he stepped into another universe.

The viciousness of females opened his

eyes. The backstabbing, hair pulling, overall cruelty of girls had been so shocking Jamie had wanted to take his bra off, and go back to being a boy. Not that he thought all girls were mean, but Jamie knew there were many who said one thing and did another once his back was turned.

Any other boy would be delighted to be in my place right about now. Tiffany's breasts rubbed against his back and his face was smothered by Janis's large C cups.

"Stop, you guys!" Jamie shouted as the pushing and pulling became more and more aggressive, to the point Jamie started to get worried. Being considerably smaller, and shorter, than the two girls determined to rip each other's hair out, he ended up trapped. Stuck, Jamie had no way to escape, and whenever he tried, he was pulled back in.

Squished between them, Jamie didn't notice the shouting and cheers from the other girls around him quieted until someone yanked him away, by the arm, from between Tiffany and Janis. Stumbling, Jamie fell into a hard body. Looking up Jamie flinched and tried to back away only to be stopped short by the large hand wrapped around his wrist.

"Stay."

Fuming at the command, Jamie stopped moving but still twisted his wrist, trying to get Aidan to release him. "Let go of me!" Jamie hissed to the sandy-haired Greek god towering above him.

"I just saved you from getting trampled on, and this is the thanks I get?"

Jamie barely stopped himself from growling at Aidan. Swallowing his pride Jamie gave the larger boy a tight smile. "Thank you... now, please let go of my wrist, so I may leave?"

"No."

More embarrassed and angry at himself than the arrogant boy, Jamie just wanted to find the nearest exit and run away. To be rescued from a girl fight, even if he was pretending to be female, stung. Sure, if Jamie could be himself, if he was dressed as a boy, then getting in this predicament wouldn't have happened... he probably also would be dead or running for his life if he was still dressed like a boy.

Then again, it wouldn't matter whether I'm a boy or a girl. Looking at Aidan's hand, completely wrapped around Jamie's wrist to the point Aidan's thumb covered, and even went over, the first knuckle of his index finger, Jamie noted the depressingly vast difference between Aidan and his own body.

Slowly, from his captured hand, Jamie's gaze trailed up Aidan's powerful forearm to his large and well defined bicep, trying not to show his jealousy over Aidan's muscles, broad shoulders, pecs or washboard abs.

Wait. Maybe I don't like the guy. I could just admire Aidan's body, wishing I had a bod like that, and, because I do, my mind's being fooled into thinking I have feelings for Aidan, when in fact I don't!

Licking his lips, Jamie ignored Aidan as

he spoke to Tiff and Janis. Thinking the guy probably would scold them for interrupting his game.

Tearing his eyes away from Aidan's jaw-dropping body, Jamie watched a group of boys play basketball on the other side of the gym. Jamie perked up when he saw Asa in the corner reading a book. Just like Asa to read while everyone else played sports. Asa's differences amused Jamie.

Their one class together had ended with a little more than a nod and smile in acknowledgment to each other, and a note from Asa ripped from the corner of Asa's notebook saying they would be secret friends. Jamie didn't want to be secret friends. Quite frankly, he had too many damn, frickin' secrets, but from the little bit of information Jamie discovered about Asa, the guy's father rated as a major prig, and wanted Asa to learn more than have friends.

Jamie wished his mother could be the same. Not the prig part, but not wanting him to have any friends. Instead of coasting unseen for his four years of college, Jamie had been spotted by Tiffany, and to be normal, his mother encouraged their friendship. The hope Tiffany's wealthy parents wouldn't like him because of his family's triple digit bank account was never realized.

Because of his childhood in such wealth, Jamie knew how to properly conduct himself in the presence the girls' parents, earning him their respect and, frighteningly enough, their approval of his friendship with Tiffany.

With money came curiosity. Attention. Something he didn't need, but no matter how hard he'd tried to chase Tiffany off, she wouldn't go away. After a while he'd given up. He'd never had friends, and besides a few annoying things Tiffany did, he enjoyed the redhead's company. Jamie just made sure never to go to her house or anywhere overly crowded with Tiffany.

His mother worried too, but instead of

helping him think of ways to get rid of Tiffany, she took him shopping where she embarrassingly picked out the most girly outfits for him to wear. To better help in camouflaging his gender if he were to go out with Tiffany.

I wish I could be like Asa. Jamie continued to watch the boy push up his glasses and try to hide his face deeper in his book. No one bothered him or crowded around him. Minus the bullying Asa received, the guy had the school life Jamie wanted.

"Jamie..."

"Huh?" Jamie looked up and tried not to stare stupidly at the insanely handsome face peering down at him.

"I asked if you were alright. Twice. However, you seemed more interested in looking at the boy sitting on the sidelines than listening to me."

"No, I'm not alright," Jamie said, smiling tightly, "because someone is cutting the circulation from my wrist." Lifting his arm,

Jamie pointed to his imprisoned wrist. "Do you mind?"

Jamie backed away once released, mumbling under his breath about steroids, and the harm users inflicted on innocent bystanders as he joined Tiffany in the hall, trying to control the wild beating of his excited heart.

"Holy shit. Jamie! Aidan—the Aidan—held your hand!"

"He didn't hold my hand, Tiff; he held my wrist, vast difference," Jamie muttered as he watched the sandy-haired god rejoin the group he had dismissed himself from.

"He is so totally into you!"

Jamie stared at Tiffany. "Excuse me? Why the hell would you think that?"

"Ah, heelloo? Maybe because the hot and sexy stud came all the way from across the court to save you?"

Confused, Jamie shrugged. "So?" Determined to ignore how his heart raced even more at her words.

"So? So, Aidan Christopher Rowan Alexander Montgomery the sixth, the richest guy in the frickin' world has never, ever, stepped in to help a girl before. I've seen him walk over a girl after she's fallen, leg bleeding, and he didn't spare her a glance! But you! You, he comes rushing over to save, and quietly, in that oh, so sexy voice of his, rips us a new one! He's so going to marry you, and you're going to, like, have a dozen of his babies." Tiffany grinned.

Jamie rolled his eyes. "If Aidan has any interest in me, it's only because I don't think he's hot shit like everyone else does." *You* do *think he's hot.* "I don't fall all over him and weep like the stupid biddies do here." *You do, but you make sure no one sees your longing glances toward Aidan.* Cursing at his inner voice, Jamie turned and began walking to the doors that would lead him to the running track.

"Where's Janis?" Jamie asked, just now noticing the feisty brunette was nowhere to be seen.

Tiffany shrugged. "Don't know. She probably ran off to cry in some corner somewhere when Aidan scolded her for starting the fight."

"What about you?" Jamie smiled at the mental picture of Janis's perfectly applied make-up in ruins from her tears.

"Me? Hell, I was so star struck I didn't hear a word he said."

Jamie laughed. One thing about becoming friends with Tiffany that Jamie loved was how everyday something exciting happened. There were no boring days at school with Tiffany around. From the make-out sessions in the mornings until his last class in the afternoons, Tiffany somehow made the day fun and took his mind off all of his problems.

Stepping outside, Jamie began stretching.

"Hey... Jamie?"

"Hmm?" Jamie waved to a few girls he

knew on the bleachers as he and Tiffany began running.

"I noticed that you and glasses boy got a little chummy in class this morning. The both of you were whispering all lovey-dovey."

"Who, Asa? Not really," Jamie panted as they ran down the track. "But so what if we were? Asa's a nice guy and I enjoy talking to him."

"Do you think it's a good idea? The guy seems like such a loser. We'd be disappointed if you and he got together."

"We?" Jamie shot Tiffany an amused glance.

"Okay, *I* would be disappointed if you dated him."

Jamie barked out a laugh. "You're shitting me, right? Come on, Tiff!" Jamie knew Tiffany to be a snob, but he never thought her snobbishness would extend to him and who he might or might not like.

All the times Tiffany pressured him to

go out and have fun, one would think she'd be happy he'd be interested in someone. Hell, it amazed Jamie that Tiffany didn't hold a sign above his head advertising his availability to the opposite sex... err... the same sex actually...

"I'm serious, Jamie! That boy is way below you, and you're the one with the greatest chance of getting it with Aidan."

Jamie stopped running, pulling Tiffany to the side to let the other runners pass them. "Tiff, chicky, you do realize Asa is the one who is, socially, higher up on the genteel ladder than I am, right? I mean. I'm a frickin' chambermaid compared to him."

"No, you're not."

Shaking his head and softly laughing, Jamie took his curvaceous friend by the shoulders. "Sweets... I'm poor. Not begging in the streets, panhandling poor, or lacking sufficient money to buy food or clothes, but enough that no mama would ever allow her all important heir, second son, or even third son to be tied to someone like me."

"Well… yeah, that's true… but as arm candy—"

"No, Tiff," Jamie said firmly giving the girl's shoulders a little shake, "I will never be any man's arm candy."

"This coincides with the 'No sex and no boyfriends' rule, huh?"

"Even after that, Tiff," Jamie sighed. The fact that Tiffany voted him to be Aidan's arm accessory was just too funny. He didn't like the guy *that* much… *God, graduation can't come quick enough.*

"… You won't change your mind about Aidan?"

Never in a fucking billion years. Jamie held firm even as a pesky little voice in his head whispered seductively for him to go for it, to get a taste of the stud.

"Sorry Tiff… I'm a one guy kind of girl." Jamie forced the words out of his mouth. "I can't see myself going out with someone knowing there would never be a future with them."

"Get out of the way!"

Suddenly shoved from behind, Jamie shot forward and slammed hard into the ground, gasping in pain when his left upper arm was scraped painfully from a broken branch protruding slightly from the grass.

"Janis! You stupid, jealous bitch!" Tiffany yelled angrily.

"It's okay, Tiffany," Jamie rasped, stopping the girl when she made a move to chase after the cackling, brunette wench. "Forget about Janis. She's just looking for attention, and I seriously don't want any of the drama she'll blow my way if we give her what she wants."

"The only reason Janis isn't doing it with so many people around is because Aidan said he didn't want to see you get hurt. The bitch knows you're not a talker, and you won't get in her face for all the crap she does, which is why she continues to pick on you."

Wincing, Jamie pushed himself up and sat in the moist lawn. "What about you? Why doesn't she think you aren't going to go after her?"

"Because we've played this game too many times already, and she knows you'll tell me not to say anything, and after a while I'll agree."

"Well, we are consistent in that regard, aren't we?" Jamie mumbled as he looked at the ghastly, angry scratch on his inner arm.

Jamie didn't need to look down to feel the cold water on his chest, which in itself was the problem... with his fake boobies, he shouldn't have felt anything on his chest. His real chest.

Pulling the soiled cloth away from his breasts, hiding the fact that one of his tits had sprung a leak, Jamie ignored the pain on his scraped knee and jogged backward. "I'm going to head back to the locker room and change, then go to the infirmary to get bandages for my cuts."

"You want me to come—"

"No! I'm good going by myself!" Jamie tried to run as fast as he could off the track.

Thanking whatever God was looking out for him when he wasn't spotted by anyone he knew, Jamie burst into the locker room and rushed to his locker. Even though he had told Tiffany she didn't have to come with him, Jamie knew the girl would follow. He was only grateful that Tiff was prissy about getting grass stains on her white running shoes, so she wouldn't be barreling across the field to catch up to him.

He shouted out a quick, "Hello? Anyone in here?" Hearing nothing, Jamie ripped his shirt and sports bra up and over his head then cursed when he saw the small tear in the undergarment.

"Fuck, fuck," Jamie whispered as his mind raced for a solution on how to fix the humongous problem.

A gasp filled the air, echoing throughout the empty room. Freezing, heart dropping in dread, Jamie turned his head and met the widened, shocked eyes of Asa Jacobs, then slowly looked down to his very flat, obviously male, chest.

"I-I w-was shoved in here by some guys... they tied my hands and gagged me, I got free, but they'd barricaded the door. I hid when you came in and was startled when you called out, so I didn't answer when you shouted... I thought to sneak away, but I had to pass you to do so..."

Jamie's mouth opened and closed repeatedly. He could only stand there with his leaking boob in his hands staring at Asa. Jamie faintly remembered kicking a board away from the entrance to the girls' dressing room, but his mind had been in such a panic he hadn't thought much about it... now Jamie wished he had.

"Jamie...?"

Asa's voice calling his name snapped

Jamie into action. Grabbing his clothes Jamie pulled his sweat pants down, but first put his sports bra back on and struggled into his white polo shirt. The "lump smoother", as his mother called it, in his underwear took care of his... well... lumps, so Jamie didn't care all that much about his skirt.

"Get me some tissue quickly!" Jamie hissed to Asa. "Asa!" Clapping his hands together, Jamie pointed to the dazed boy. "Go. Get. Me. Tissues! Now!"

"Y-yes!"

Stuffing his hand in his bra, Jamie pulled the Velcro that held the implant in the cup of the bra then lifted the boob out of its hidden pocket. Rummaging through his school bag, Jamie breathed a sigh of relief when his hand closed over the small little tube of superglue.

"Ahh... h-here Jamie."

Avoiding Asa's eyes, Jamie grabbed one of the coarse paper towels from the boy's hand. "Put them on the bench then get me a wad of toilet paper." Jamie ordered, quickly wiping the beads of water from the translucent bag, and then squeezed a healthy amount of super glue over the small tear. "Please God..." Jamie whispered as he searched for something, anything to put over the adhesive.

"Will this help? They put it over my mouth, so I couldn't call out..."

Surprised, Jamie nearly wept when he saw the small strip of duct tape in Asa's hand. "Yes, yes it will." Taking the silver seal, Jamie slapped it on, smoothing it over his boob a few times, then shoved it back in his shirt and sports bra. He had just finished securing the Velcro in place when the locker room doors opened and Tiffany came in.

"Damn it, Jamie, I got my shoes all dirty running after you! I can't believe you ran away so... fast... what the hell are you doing in here, Asa? And why aren't you wearing any pants, Jamie!"

Knowing he wasn't out of the doghouse

yet, Jamie grabbed Asa's hand and pulled him tightly to his side, digging his, pink, French-tipped acrylic nails into the taller boy's arm, making him visibly flinch.

"Hey, Tiff? Remember our little talk on the track?" Jamie's smiled hard and filled his eyes with warning when he looked up into Asa's panicked gaze.

"Yeah... what about—oh, fuck no... no, no, no, Jamie!" Tiffany shouted, stomping her foot.

Picking up Asa's arm, Jamie draped it around his shoulders. "Asa and I have decided to date."

"Huh? What about your golden rule? Remember them?"

"I remember. I'm not planning to have sex. Asa and I are only dating. He's not going to be my boyfriend." Jamie's face hurt from smiling so widely at the suspicious redhead.

"This is kind of sudden, isn't it? You just told me you two weren't all smoochy and now you're saying you're going to start dating? Something smells fishy here." Tiffany crossed her arms over her chest, looking from Jamie to Asa with suspicion.

"Nothing is going on Tiffany. I just wanted to keep my budding romance with Asa a secret." *Lord knows I'm good at keeping secrets.* Jamie continued to smile.

Tiffany threw her hands in the air. "Fine. But I just want to make it clear I don't approve, and if you think I'll be sweet to him because you're 'dating' then think again... Are you sure, Jamie?"

"Uh huh." To prove his commitment, Jamie wrapped both his arms around Asa's slim waist and hugged the boy tightly, painfully tight. "As of today, I plan to keep Asa by my side." Jamie bared his teeth when he smiled and looked up at the rapidly paling face of the poor boy standing frozen in his arms.

"I can't believe you would pass up being Aidan's candy for him."

"The heart wants what the heart wants," Jamie said, giving Asa's waist one last threatening squeeze before letting the guy go.

"Whatever," Tiffany muttered. "Anyway, this is the girls' dressing room, so Asa? Get lost."

"Asa," Jamie quietly called out, stopping the boy when he tripped over his feet in his rush to leave. "Wait for me at the entrance. We need to talk about our relationship."

"As in, don't go blabbing your mouth off about you and Jamie dating," Tiffany said, glaring at Asa.

"I won't say a word, I swear."

Jamie stared at Asa for a long minute before nodding. "We can trust Asa to keep silent, Tiffany. Right, Asa?"

"O-of course. I swear I won't say anything to anyone," Asa said.

"Good." Jamie smiled at Tiffany to reassure the girl. Hoping he wasn't misplacing his trust, and he could rely on Asa.

I pray to God I can.

Chapter 2

When I was eight years old I met my father's wife for the first time. I didn't know who she was at first.

My mother had been out doing something away from the house, and I'd run away from Catherine's annoying nagging, when I came across this pretty lady sitting alone on a bench in my father's garden.

I remember standing there, unsure of what I should do. I wasn't allowed to talk to strangers, but the woman appeared to be so lonely that even now I can recall the need to go to her and ask if she was alright.

My memory becomes fuzzy after saying hello to my father's wife, but when I think back, I know I spent the better part of the day with her. Two weeks later my mother, with a worried look on her face, told me my father wanted to see me at the main house... another clear indication something wasn't quite right in my life.

Normal parents didn't live apart from one another. Not parents who are supposed to love each other like my mother said they did...

My mother, Catherine, and I stayed in a cottage on the outskirts of my father's estate. Out of sight so not to be an embarrassment to my father's wife, but close enough he could visit my mother whenever he wanted.

Anyway... it seemed like my father's wife, who told me she was my aunt, had taken a liking to me, and wanted to spend some time getting to know me. She introduced me to her son—my brother—who was two years older than me... it had been the most uncomfortable day of my life, to say the least.

Incredibly, though, my brother and I hit it off and became good friends. I was invited over daily to play with him... almost like a paid playmate. I even went on trips with my father's wife and my brother.

It never occurred to me at that age how

much those trips scared my mother. To think about it now, anything could have happened to me. I was the bastard son of a powerful man, and a potential danger to the inheritance of the legal heir. Truthfully, if she had wanted to, my father's wife could have killed me on any one of those trips. She had the power and connections to get away with the crime.

Killing me would have been simple for her. I was born on my father's estate in my mother's bathtub in the little cottage we lived in. Catherine delivered me and I was also homeschooled... I mentioned that already. If I got sick, a doctor was brought to the house. When I asked my mother about my birth certificate, she told me she never received one... You can't report a missing person or murder if the outside world doesn't know you exist, can you?

Warning bell number two, right?

Once a month I used to meet my father and stand in the middle of his office while he reviewed my tutors' report on what I'd learned from them and what improvements I needed to focus on... I asked my father at one of those meetings about my birth certificate... and never asked again, not after he only coldly looked at me. It wasn't that he ignored my question, more that I had dared to speak out loud without his permission.

I still don't understand how my mother could have had an affair with such a cold, unforgiving type of man.

Suffice it to say, I never asked my father or my mother about it again. Besides, I could only imagine the pain I would feel if I saw under "Father's Name" on the birth certificate, nothing written there.

I had a lot of daddy issues back then.

I still do, but now they're all for different reasons...

* * * *

Staring blankly at the ceiling from his bed, Jamie couldn't stop thinking about yesterday's fuck up and what he would have to do to try and fix it. Telling his mother was out of the question. She loved the little three bedroom house they lived in, and she had finally stopped rushing into his room in the middle of the night to make sure he was still in his bed.

Well... his mother still checked up on him at night, but it was different... Jamie couldn't really explain, but his mother's nightly peeks were... normal... if that made any sense.

Jamie groaned and drew his blanket over his head.

Just as he had ordered, Asa waited for him at the entrance of the school. Not that it would have mattered if he hadn't. Jamie could easily find out where the boy lived and corner him at his house, but thankfully he hadn't had to go through the trouble of doing so.

Finding a wide open spot, so no one could sneak up on them, Jamie tensely asked, to the point of begging, for Asa to keep the fact that Jamie was pretending to be a girl a secret. Without saying so, Jamie made it clear it was a matter of life and death and not some sick game he was playing. Seriously, what boy would dress up as a girl for as long as Asa knew him? Hell, even gay guys had more pride than dressing up as a woman... unless they were transvestites, drag queens, fraternity members hazing their pledges or actors...

Whatever.

Jamie shook his head to clear his mind from that line of thought.

He didn't care what he had to do. Asa had Jamie at a disadvantage because, besides killing the kid, Jamie had no way of stopping Asa from blabbing his mouth to every single person at school. Anyone could stick their hand down Jamie's shirt to see he had no breasts, or really grab him between his legs, past the padding, to feel he had a dick.

Asa had all the winning cards. If he

wanted, he could have Jamie on his knees kissing Asa's feet, howling and barking like a dog, or ordering Jamie around like a slave...

Telling Tiffany they were dating had, in part, been a way to stay close to Asa in school, but another part had been to protect him. If Jamie hadn't said they were seeing each other, the girl would have made Asa's life unbearable. Not just in school, but out as well, and all because Asa had seen Jamie in his underwear.

Even now Asa's life would be hell, with only the popular redhead, socially powerful, and destined to be famous like her mommy and daddy, thinking they were going out. Jamie had started out as the girl's plaything, but as time went on, they had really become good friends. But Tiffany also liked having her way, and she wanted Jamie with Aidan, so Jamie knew Tiffany would relentlessly pick on poor Asa, and nothing Jamie said would stop the redhead.

Even so, to Jamie's ultimate surprise, Asa didn't try to blackmail him for his silence, but instead quietly listened as he had talked, and never once interrupted him. Just as Jamie had known all along, Asa was a great person.

"Jamie? Sweetheart?"

At the knock on the door and his mother's voice, Jamie sighed. "Yes?"

"It's almost noon. I know it's Saturday, but you haven't come down to eat breakfast yet."

"I'll be down in a minute, Mom," Jamie softly called out.

"Are you sure?"

"Yes. I'm okay, Mom. I'm just tired today. That's all," Jamie said when his mother didn't leave.

"If you have a problem…"

Sitting up, Jamie said, "Then you'll be the first one I'll come to talk to."

"Thank you, sweetie," his mom said.

Jamie heard his mom walk away. He didn't want to go downstairs, look into his mother's eyes, and lie to her face when he knew she would ask him again if everything was all right. What could he say? *'Sorry, Mom, I fucked up?'* That yesterday he had wished someone would find out he wasn't actually a girl, and alakazam, his wish was granted?

Jamie could just imagine Catherine and his mother's faces if he told them that over the dinner table.

"What happened at school yesterday?"

"What happened? Well, Tiffany kissed me in class like she does every day, then one of my boobs popped, and I got caught taking it out when I tried to see if I could fix it. Oh, and by the way, I was shirtless at the time, so now someone knows I'm not really a girl. Can you pass the peas, please?"

Jamie groaned again and fell back onto his bed, curling into a ball, pulling the covers back over his head. Yeah… he would never hear the end of it from Catherine if he said something like that.

"Jamie!"

Speaking of the harping shrew…

"What Catherine?" Jamie called out.

"Get out of bed! Your mother made you her famous, chunky tomato soup!"

"Yeah, yeah…"

"Jamie!"

"I'm getting up!" Throwing the comforter off the bed, Jamie sat up and glared at the door.

"I don't hear you getting up!"

"I said I'm up!" *You frickin' witch*, Jamie added silently.

"Then go eat! You're worrying your mother!"

"I'll be down in five minutes." Jamie grounded out through tightly clenched teeth.

"What?"

"I said I'll be down in five frickin' minutes!" Jamie shouted, throwing his pillow at his closed bedroom door.

"Do not swear at me, young man!" Catherine yelled.

"Frickin' is not a curse word!" Jamie's

anxiety over Asa forgotten, his blood began to boil due to Catherine and their shouting match.

"It is when used the way you are using it!"

"Go away, Catherine! The longer you stand in front of my bedroom door bothering me, the longer it'll take me to come down!" Jamie felt like pulling his hair out whenever he talked to the pinched-faced woman. He didn't know how his mother could put up with her.

"Just hurry up and come down to eat."

Jamie snapped his mouth shut. If he talked back, he knew he and Catherine would never stop going at it with one another. He hated to cave, but the two of them had, more than once, yelled for over two hours, which had his mother laid up in bed with a splitting migraine for the remainder of the day.

Throwing on a white tank top and tan cargo shorts, Jamie stepped out of his room and stomped down the stairs toward the kitchen. Silently, from the doorway, Jamie watched his petite mother hum a sweet tune under her breath, his earlier annoyance fading as she puttered around the stove. Only two inches shorter than he, Jamie grinned when his mother stood on the tips of her toes, to reach a cup far back in the cupboard.

"You're going to hurt yourself if you keep straining like that." Jamie chuckled.

"Oh! Jamie, don't sneak up on me!"

Skipping into the kitchen, Jamie hopped onto the counter and grabbed the coffee mug his mother had been reaching for.

"Thank you, my son."

Jamie grinned and leaned down, allowing her to give him a gentle kiss on his forehead.

"You feel a little too warm. Are you feeling alright?"

Dodging his mom's hand from touching his forehead, Jamie shook his head. "I'm not sick, Mom. Don't worry so much."

"Are you sure? You didn't look so good

when you came home from school yesterday."

Jamie winced. "Just a rough day, that's all. But I feel all better now."

"Are you—"

"Mom!" Jamie laughingly yelled. "It's the weekend, and I don't have to wear my boobs, put make-up on, or put on restraining panties. Believe me when I say I'm fine; more than just fine, wonderful."

"Sorry, sweetheart. I'm smothering you, aren't I?"

Sliding off the counter, and once seated at the kitchen table, his mother placed a bowl of her famous "For Jamie, chunky tomato soup" in front of him.

"Eat every last drop. I know you said you're fine, but you still look too pale for my comfort."

Jamie gave his mother and exasperated look as he dipped his spoon in the thick red, liquid. "It's cold." Jamie grumbled after the first bite.

"Sorry," Mom said, giving him an apologetic shrug. "You took too long upstairs. I would have heated it up, but I know how much you hate it when I put it in the microwave."

"Mm…" Jamie made a face as he ate another spoonful.

He chewed quickly and swallowed. Eating another bite, Jamie pushed the bowl away from him.

"Eat everything, Jamie," his mother scolded.

"Thanks, but I'm not very hungry." Jamie smiled.

Standing, he got a soda from the refrigerator, opened it, and chugged the whole can down to wash the taste out of his mouth.

"Child, you need to get over your aversion of eating the soup cold already. Your mother and I will be going out of town for a week, and that's what you'll be eating for dinner for the next seven days," Catherine said, appearing in the doorway.

Wiping his mouth, Jamie glared at Catherine. "Yes, Catherine. I know."

Seriously, Jamie didn't know why he and the pinched-face shrew didn't get along. He'd be in a good mood one second, and be angry the moment he saw Catherine for no apparent reason. He didn't hate the woman's guts. Well, not much anyway. Maybe because Catherine had been his nanny, and to this day, treated him like a three year old. The moment they were in the same room, they immediately tried to go after each other's throats.

"Then stop complaining. Once we leave here, you won't be able to contact us."

"Once again, Catherine, I know," Jamie said calmly, trying to keep a cool head.

He didn't want to start a fight.

"Catherine, we've been going on our trips for a couple of years now," Jamie's mother said. "Jamie knows how to take care of himself."

Jamie looked smugly at Catherine.

"I'm not saying he's incapable of being by himself," Catherine replied.

"Then please don't fight. For once, just be nice to one another." Mom sighed.

"I just worry about him, Mary... I get scared when I think about us leaving him, and I want to make sure he'll take care of himself when we are gone..."

Uncomfortable at the tender look Catherine gave him, Jamie shifted from foot to foot not knowing what to say.

"Of course, if he had grown taller and didn't act like a two year old, maybe I would treat him like an adult." Catherine reminded his mom.

"Of all the things you could have made digs about, and you go after my height." Jamie fumed.

Sensitive, Jamie reacted defensively whenever anyone said anything about his vertical impairment. Tease him about wearing boobs, shaving his legs, whatever. But, not about being short, and Catherine knew he hated it.

"Not everyone can be a damn bean pole like you, Cather—"

"Stop!"

Catherine and Jamie snapped their mouths shut at his mom's shout.

"I said I don't want you to fight!" Mom said.

"We aren't fighting. Just talking loud," Jamie lied. "We are just playing around. It's nothing to get worked up about."

"That's right, Mary. Jamie and I... this is just the way we communicate," Catherine said.

Jamie sighed. "I think I am hungry after all," Jamie said after a few moments passed and the three of them stood in silence.

"You're still hungry?"

Jamie didn't really want anything to eat, but telling his mother he's still hungry, Jamie hoped, would take her mind off about his and Catherine's constant bickering for the time being.

"Sit, sit. I'll make you a sandwich."

Jamie did as he was told, and even held back his groan when Catherine followed and sat across from him.

"So, how was school yesterday, Jamie?" Catherine suddenly asked.

"Fine," Jamie muttered.

"Really? Nothing interesting happened that you want to tell us about?"

"Nothing comes to mind," Jamie said slowly, after thanking his mother for the sandwich.

"No problems we should be aware of?" Catherine asked.

"No..."

"What about the busted implant I found in the trash, which looked like you tried to fix with duct tape and glue?" Catherine asked.

Jamie choked on the bread and sliced lunch meat. How the hell did she find it?! When Jamie came home, he wrapped the ripped tit in an old shirt, put it in a paper bag, and then threw it away outside.

"Little boy," Catherine said tauntingly, "you know I double check everything that leaves this house. *Everything.* This includes the garbage outside, before it's taken away. And what did I find when I did my search five minutes ago?

"You did a bad job of hiding the thing. What if someone dangerous were watching, suspecting who we might be, and were to search through our trash? They would have found the implant and all our hard work of hiding would have been laid to waste."

The sandwich became unrecognizable, clenched in Jamie's fist. "You're right," Jamie said tightly, the words tasted sour on his tongue. "I should have disposed of it properly. Cut it up in pieces and spread it throughout the neighborhood. Not put the whole thing in our trash where 'they' are more likely to find it. I'm sorry. My mind was elsewhere and I didn't stop to think."

"You should be thinking about it every second of your life. Do you want to die? Do you want your mother to be without her son? Because if you're not careful, and you screw up *again* like this, then that's just what will happen."

"Kitty Cat…" Mary started.

"No, Mary. The boy needs to remember *why* he can't mess up. And why exactly did you hide the fact the implant tore? Why didn't you come to us?"

Jamie uncurled his fingers from the demolished little hoagie, and wiped his hand clean before placing it in his lap. "It was a stupid accident. Nothing serious to inform you about, so I didn't."

Pinned down by Catherine's disapproving, blazing brown eyes, Jamie unflinchingly stared back. His mind filled with Asa finding out about him, and the fear of what would happen if the boy didn't keep his mouth shut, on top of the stress of deciding to keep the fact that his secret had been discovered... Jamie hadn't thought about what could happen if someone had been watching.

"Jamie... did someone find out about you in school? Is that why you tried to hide it?" His mom asked.

Jamie continued to hold Catherine's gaze.

"It's a simple question, Jamie. Did someone find out you were disguising yourself as a girl?" Catherine demanded.

Jamie's palms stung as his nails cut into his flesh from how tightly he clenched his hands closed.

"Your silence tells me yes, someone did find out you've been pretending to be a girl. I should congratulate you for carrying on the charade for this long," Catherine said.

"Jamie... you should have told us right away," His mom said.

"I've taken care of the problem." Yeah,

he knew he should have spoken out about being discovered, but Jamie didn't want to. Even if in the next city he might go back to being a boy, Jamie liked it here. This city was the closest Jamie could call a home, the place they'd lived the longest, and Jamie didn't want to leave. He went to school and had friends. Granted, he was deceiving all of them into thinking he's a girl, and they would want to string his ass up in a tree if they found out, but he still wanted to stay.

"We'll begin packing immediately. We can't take a chance the person who found out won't keep his mouth shut. One careless word to someone else, and before we can scream, they'll have us, and if you're lucky Jamie, you won't suffer when he kills you."

Jamie gave Catherine a look of loathing; he hated her for saying such things in front of his mother. Jamie didn't care if what she said was true. To continuously go on about how he'd get killed, Catherine knew better than to bring that topic up. Especially since his last run in with his father, he'd come back bleeding.

His father was the one they were running away and hiding from and he had power. They'd been found a handful of times and—with the exception of Jamie's last confrontation with the man—there'd been a light shining down on them, giving them the miracle of escape, unharmed.

Where they were now, had been the longest they had ever been in one place. A place that they had planted roots, and even though Jamie planned on ripping himself away from the roots they planted here, he didn't want to tear himself away just yet.

"No," Jamie said firmly. Looking up into his mother's frightened face, Jamie gave her an apologetic glance, before turning back to Catherine's disapproving gaze. "I know I screwed up by not disposing of the boob properly, and yes, I did get caught. But the only reason why I tried to cover it up is because I like where we are. I don't like the fact I have to carry tampons in a pink purse to pretend I'm menstruating, or that I need to wax my legs, or the many, many other things I need to do just to live here. I didn't tell you because the person that stumbled onto my secret... I really think he won't say anything..."

Jamie frowned, thinking back at what Catherine had said earlier. "Wait... you said we can't take the chance if the person who found out won't keep *his* mouth shut... how did you know it was a boy?"

"Why aren't the both of you going crazy?" Jamie asked. All the times they'd been found in the other places they'd tried to hide, Catherine and his mother dropped everything they'd been doing, panicking and rushing to get the car packed, so they could speed off and find another safe haven.

"You can come in now," Catherine called out.

Whipping his head around at the sound of a polite cough, Jamie paled when he saw Asa, with a wobbly smile on his flushed face.

"Um… hi, Jamie…"

"This young man met me outside after I finished destroying your implant the correct way. He stumbled when asking if you were home. Asked for *he* rather than *she*.'" Catherine said smugly. "When I heard you in the kitchen, I told him to wait and not come in until I called out to him."

"All he knew is that I dressed like a girl! What have *you* done?" Jamie said, glowering at Catherine.

"You decided to trust him, so he needed to understand that you aren't dressed like a woman because you're sexually confused, but because it is a matter of life or death," Catherine said calmly.

"I'd already handled it!" Pissed, not understanding what Catherine's goal could be, Jamie jumped to his feet. Grabbing Asa by the arm, Jamie dragged him backward to the stairs. "We're going to my room!" Jamie shouted.

"We aren't done talking about this Jamie!" Catherine yelled.

"Later!" Jamie yelled, as he forced Asa to run up the steps to his room.

* * * *

"Catherine…" Mary worried, watching her son drag the taller young man away. "You told me I could always trust you, but…"

"And you can," reassured Catherine. "I treat and speak to Jamie like he's a small child, but I know he is not. No matter how much I wish differently."

Catherine gently patted Mary on her slim shoulder. "We can't stay next to him forever, Mary. Talking to Jamie—exposing the extent of the danger surrounding him—was the quickest way to get the other boy up to speed with our situation. Jamie needs someone strong to watch his back."

"And you think this boy is that person?" Mary asked doubtfully.

Catherine smiled. "He may look

helpless. I thought so too when I first saw him. But he's special. If all goes well, when we return from our trip, we will take Jamie to the side and tell him the truth of who he is. I'll also talk to Asa and with luck I can begin training him to be Jamie's guard."

"So we wait?"

Catherine nodded. "We leave them alone. Jamie naturally draws people to him. However, the large percentage of those people are bad. We just need to give Jamie time to work his natural charm on the boy. And by the time we return, I'm positive Asa will be on our side."

CHAPTER 3

August 30th, 2010

Have you ever felt like you were living a dream and scared of waking up? Scared that all the wonderful things in your life would disappear once you opened your eyes?

If you did, then you would know how I felt when I was a kid, only my life was the opposite of that.

I was scared my life really was as bizarre as it seemed. That it wasn't a dream, and I would never wake up from it.

A little over a year had passed since I met my father's wife and his other son. At first everything was great. Trips around the world, getting just about anything I asked for, eating anything I wanted without being scolded by Catherine.

It was wonderful. For a while.

I was a couple of days away from my

tenth birthday and, once again, I ended up at a luxurious hotel with my 'aunt', and 'cousin'. My half brother's birthday and mine were only a day apart, and I was allowed to celebrate it with him.

Gracious of them, wasn't it?

At the time, I was so blown away. I didn't think about my mother or what she felt when I took off with my father's wife. I didn't give a second thought about not going, when I was asked if I wanted to have my tenth birthday in Hawaii. Sand, sun and beaches. Even at ten, I knew how big that was.

But I must be a magnet for discovering secrets. Hell, I should be a detective for all the taboo shit I've stumbled upon. Finding out I was a bastard, and my mother was my father's mistress, was just the batter of the cake mix. Meeting my father's wife and having a sibling was nothing.

The strange thing about memories is that they fade over time, but for me, they haven't. Not one bit.

One of those memories is the day I found out my father's wife hated me. I clearly remember waking up to the smell of the sea, the heat of the morning sun shining down on me through the huge windows of my hotel room. But most of all, I recall the hushed voices from the room adjoining mine. The door had been open slightly, enough that I could hear my father's wife speaking to an unknown person.

After a few visits, I got a strange vibe from Lisa, my father's wife. She was always nice to me, and smiled and laughed when I was around, but her happiness seemed fake, like maybe she didn't welcome me with open arms. The wonders she had shown me, the outside world I had never been allowed to see with my two eyes, had wowed me, and those visual delights must have muffled the warning bells going off in my head about the woman.

The gift of having a brother and being able to interact with him, to have a friend close to my own age... I purposely closed my eyes to the dangers, and yes, I know I shouldn't have, but I was also a little kid. I was young and didn't think about death, or myself ever becoming intimate with it.

I have nightmares about how stupid and trusting I was back then.

I remember sneaking up to the door in the hotel and listening, thinking I was eavesdropping on Lisa's plans for the party for Joey and I...

If only it had been that.

Have you ever overheard someone you thought was your friend, talking bad about you behind your back? Sucks ass, right? Yeah, well, add that feeling and times it by a billion and that's how it feels to hear someone say they wanted you dead.

Feels awesome.

Thousands upon thousands of miles away from my mother, I ended up stuck with a psycho who wanted to off me. Not exactly the *kind of present I'd hoped for, hearing how disgusting my 'aunt' thought I was or how I couldn't be gone soon enough.*

What a great happy birthday, right?

The most unexpected of heroes arrived in the form of my father, who decided to surprise me and Joseph by coming unannounced. I always wondered if my father knew his wife had been planning on killing me, or if he had come because she was acting too quickly for his tastes. But thankfully, because of his interruption, I lived to see my tenth year.

* * * *

Once inside his room, Jamie shoved Asa's hesitant ass farther in so he could close his bedroom door.

"I'm so sorry, Jamie. I—"

"Why are you here, Asa?" Jamie growled. "Didn't we agree we would never meet each other outside of school?"

"I know and I'm sorry, but—"

"But what, Asa?" Jamie tried not to yell, he really did, but remembering the smug look from Catherine made it really hard to control his temper. "You show up at my house, and fuck up by calling me a 'him'! You know what could have happened if it hadn't been Catherine you asked?" Jamie began to pace.

Flinching, Asa backed away from Jamie. "I didn't know. You didn't say—"

"Of course I wouldn't tell you because it's a frickin' secret!" Jamie bellowed.

"I get that now. I mean. I knew it was a secret before… I just… didn't think it was this kind of secret…"

Jamie counted to ten and tried to calm down. Yelling at Asa would be pointless. He couldn't change what already happened, and truth told, his head hurt from all the drama.

"Why did you come to my house, Asa?" Jamie tiredly asked, flopping down on his bed.

"I, ahh… I know I have no right to ask you this, but… could I sleep over for the weekend?"

"You're shitting me, right?" asked Jamie in disbelief. "You come over, get that harpy on my back because you wanna have a sleepover?" Jamie fell back on his bed and laughed. "Oh, this is rich."

"Please, Jamie. I don't have any friends besides you. I'll do anything you want... but please let me stay over? My father is on a business trip... and it's just me and my stepbrother. My father comes back on Monday, so if I could stay until then..."

Something in Asa's voice had Jamie sitting up. He noticed the rumpled quality of Asa's shirt and narrowed his eyes. "Is that blood on your collar?" Standing, Jamie reached out to touch the red stain only to have the boy jerk away. Looking at Asa's face closely, Jamie saw the beginnings of a bruise forming on his cheek, and that the cut on his lip had been re-opened.

"Dude, what happened to you?" Jamie asked softly.

"My stepbrother and I don't get along very well. I got home late yesterday, and he got angry…"

Jamie's brows furrowed. "Yesterday after school? As in, when you and I talked?"

"Yeah."

"We spoke for maybe half an hour." Jamie didn't want to think that because of him, Asa got hurt.

"I know…"

"I didn't mean for you to get into trouble with—" Jamie watched as Asa winced when he touched his shoulder. "Where else are you hurt?"

"Nowhere. I just got a slap, that's all," Asa replied.

"Don't lie, man. Tell me where else you are hurt," Jamie demanded. "If it was only your face then you wouldn't be grimacing in pain when I slightly touch your shoulder."

"It's nothing."

Pursing his lips at how stubborn Asa

acted, Jamie grabbed Asa by the ear, and yanked his head down to eye level. "Take off your shirt and show me how bad it is… or I'll drop your ass and take it off myself." In all his travels, and watching people, Jamie noticed time and time again with meek guys, that if someone considerably shorter threatened them, they grew a pair and stood up for themselves.

Unfortunately, taking such actions toward Asa didn't work, and only gave Jamie a rush of guilt when he released Asa's lobe and the guy's trembling fingers went to the buttons on his rumpled shirt.

"It's just a small cut on my shoulder," Asa mumbled.

"Just show it to me." Jamie shoved Asa on his bed so he could examine the damage to the boy's partly uncovered shoulder. "Take off your whole shirt," Jamie ordered.

He could see slight bruising where Asa's neck and shoulder met, but from the chaste way Asa exposed the mark, Jamie couldn't see more than what Asa allowed him to see.

"… Does it really matter? I have a few cuts and bruises, but nothing that needs care," Asa grumbled.

Jamie might be an asshole, but he wanted Asa to remove his clothing, because it could be the only thing he might be able to use against the guy. It didn't matter anymore about trust. Jamie had only so much faith in people. If Asa got hurt badly enough by a family member to come running to him—someone whom he didn't really know—then Jamie wanted to know what lurked in Asa's life.

Jamie *needed* to know what kind of secrets Asa had, and would continue to harass the guy until he spilled his guts to him. "Take off your shirt."

"No," said Asa firmly. "I don't want to take my shirt off."

Ahh, it's gotta be big, if the docile kid is showing some fight. Jamie smiled kindly. "If it was just a little tiff with your bro, then you shouldn't feel so self-conscious about showing me, right?"

"Yeah… but even though I know you're a boy, and you're not w-wearing your breasts. It's still embarrassing for me to undress in front of you."

Seeing how Asa fidgeted, Jamie felt bad forcing the guy. However, a little guilt wouldn't stop him from digging around for Asa's secret. Tit for tat and all that shit. Jamie needed leverage more, and couldn't afford to be understanding toward Asa's feelings.

"Come on, Asa. We're both guys. It's not like I don't have the same thing you have." Jamie snickered. "I can do it for you, if you're too shy."

"I don't want to," Asa pouted.

Jamie rubbed his hands together. "Then I guess I'll do it for you." Pouncing on the bed, Jamie laughed when Asa shouted out a girlish squeal, and tried to get away. Tackling the taller boy, they both tumbled off the bed onto the floor.

Straddling Asa, Jamie smacked the guy's hands away when they tried to fight him from unbuttoning his shirt. "Stop moving. I'm not hurting you, Asa." Jamie wickedly grinned.

His amusement faded, when he revealed the extent of the abuse on the teen's chest, sides, and stomach. "Asa…"

"Jamie! I heard a loud bang—"

Jamie and Asa stopped moving when Catherine and Jamie's mother burst into his room. Jamie froze. He understood very well the image he and Asa made to the two women. Asa's shirt practically ripped off his body, Jamie sitting on Asa, holding him down. It didn't help Jamie's cause when Asa struggled to get out from under him. It looked like Jamie had attacked Asa.

"Did you really have an accident which resulted in you popping your implant, or was it because you both were fooling around, causing the tear?" Catherine asked.

"I told him to stop, that I didn't think it would be alright to do this type of thing in his room, with you so close… but he wouldn't take no for an answer," Asa whispered.

Jamie's jaw dropped at Asa's lie.

"Jamie and I are going out. If you don't believe me, then you can call and ask Tiffany."

"I think it's time we had *the talk* again, Jamie," Mary stated.

Jamie stared at his mother in horror. "No… oh, God, no." Jamie turned and glared at Asa when his mom pulled out his desk chair and sat down.

* * * *

"My mom found a dirty comic book a kid in my class gave me once. The girl in the comic had huge knockers and ninety percent of the time she was topless. My mom decided I must be getting interested in the opposite sex and sat me down for a conversation. Do you know the trauma I received when she gave me the sex talk about what to expect when I lost my virginity to a girl?" Jamie asked, giving Asa a dirty look. "No? Well, that was fucking nothing compared to the sex talk she just gave about me losing my cherry to a boy!" Jamie fumed, sitting on his bed, brushing his long hair.

Jamie made it through an unbearably long hour while his mother chatted embarrassingly to him about the wonders of sex. When she finished and left the room he and Asa sat in stone silence for another minute before Jamie could move. Going to his dresser, Jamie dug out his biggest shirt and shorts for Asa to wear to sleep.

"I was sitting right next to you when she gave that talk, Jamie," Asa said.

"Were you? Because from the look on your face, you had run off somewhere far away in your mind, while I, on the other hand, had to repeat everything my mother said just to convince her I was listening!" Jamie couldn't believe the amount of detailed information which came out of his mother's mouth. One would think a mother would be devastated to hear or suspect her only son was a homosexual. But with his mother that wasn't the case. Being in a gay relationship herself, it would be kind of hypocritical of her if she were to get angry or disappointed in him for liking the same sex.

Jamie never discussed the lack of attraction he felt toward women, or how, when he fantasized, he pictured a guy in his head. He found some of the boys at school very attractive, but none gave him a physical response. Well, one guy made his member twitch, but only a little. Jamie hadn't had an opportunity to confirm where his 'tastes' lay, but after years of seeing naked women in the locker room and getting no wood from being close to their near nude bodies, it was maybe a little safe to say females didn't turn him on. However, 'it' *did* stand in attention for the most obnoxious prick in the whole universe, one Aidan Montgomery.

Go figure.

"I said I was sorry," Asa sulked.

"Yeah, yeah, you've fucking been saying that a lot today." Jamie still couldn't believe the boy had the balls to say they were dating. "My mother fucking gave *you* a box of condoms. You! Like it was impossible for her think I would be the one to take you!" That had been the snapping point for Jamie. He might be smaller than Asa, and had to look like a girl, but did his mother automatically have to think Jamie would be the one to 'accept'? Hell, having his mother give him condoms made Jamie sick.

"I didn't think I had much choice. I couldn't—I *can't* go back home. Not right now."

"What happened to make you decide to come running to my house, Asa?" Jamie threw a pillow at Asa when he clammed up. "Look, shithead, I had to listen to my mother on the proper way to care for my body after doing it with another guy from a print out she got online, and on top of that, they set up your bed in my room, so you better start talking."

"It's noth—"

"I swear," Jamie said, ready to chuck the brush he had in his hand at Asa, "if you say it's nothing, I'll make you holler out so loudly my mother will think that I'm the dominant one in this 'relationship'."

"I… ahh…"

"Spill, dude."

"There isn't all that much to tell. My father remarried five years ago, and with his new wife came an older sister and brother. My stepsister lives on her own and I hardly ever see her, but my stepbrother lives with us… and he hates me."

Jamie watched Asa fidget on his inflatable bed, twisting the corner of his blanket. He could see how the whole thing upset Asa, but he didn't care. Okay, he did care, but at the same time Jamie couldn't let Asa not tell him why he showed up, not after what Asa made him go through today. "*And*? I hope you don't think I'll be satisfied with just 'He hates me' and no further explanation. I want fucking details, not the PG-13, bunny version."

"Do I have to? I don't like talking about it... Actually, you're the first one I've ever talked to about this... I don't feel comfortable."

Jamie gave a little hoot. "Sure, I'll respect your wishes and leave you alone—aw, but wait... you just stood there, not letting me know you were listening, while Catherine spilled my secret." Jamie gave Asa a look that suggested he start spilling his guts. "I think I deserve the NC-17 tale of why your ass decided to come to my house."

Jamie felt for the kid, he really did, but he needed a hold over Asa, something to make Asa think twice about talking about Jamie and his 'little disguise'. Catherine scolded him for being careless, yet did nothing to stop the mayhem from unfolding. If digging into Asa's painful past got Jamie what he needed, he'd do it.

"You won't tell anyone?"

"I plan to shout it out on the rooftop the first chance I get," Jamie said sarcastically. "Of course I won't say anything! That would be kinda stupid of me, wouldn't it? You just found out I'm a guy and there are people out there who want to kill me." Jamie shook his head in wonder.

"Just tell me your story, *and* I promise I won't tell a soul," Jamie swore, putting a hand over his heart. "You promised me yesterday you would keep my gender hush-hush, so I'm going to do the same with whatever you tell me."

"Blood oath?"

Startled, Jamie stared at Asa. "What?"

"I want to make a blood oath with you. An exchange of blood between you and me, and exchange vows we will never speak about anything that goes on in this room."

"No!" Jamie coughed, trying to hide his embarrassment at the high pitch of his voice. "Um, I mean. I don't mind saying vows to you, but I'm not good with blood. I get... well, I'll just say it's not pretty."

"Oh, okay... I didn't know..."

Jamie sighed. "Yeah, I know you didn't know. Which is why I told you."

"So you have a type of blood phobia? What's it called? Hemophobia?" asked Asa.

"I don't—you know what? It doesn't matter. I just can't stand looking at human blood." Jamie felt exhausted talking to Asa.

"Does that include your own?"

"No, just when I look at everyone else's." Jamie frowned. "Why the hell am I telling you this? We're supposed to be talking about *you,* not me."

"Hemophobic people... don't they have a fear of all blood? Why do you have just a fear of everyone else's blood?" Asa continued his questioning.

"I never said I feared blood, only that I have a *thing* about seeing it and— why are we still talking about this? I think you've learned more than enough about me for one day." Jamie gave Asa a stern glare. "Don't think pissing me off will keep me from grilling you."

"You were much nicer when I thought you were a girl. You didn't swear either."

"Yeah, well, life's a bitch." *And then you die... hopefully not too soon*, Jamie silently added. "In any case, it's your turn, and don't try and change the subject. After the talk Mom gave us," Jamie shuddered, "you owe me."

"This and that are two different things!" Asa exclaimed.

"Not in my book they aren't." Jamie went back to brushing his hair. "You've been pulled into my world now. Let this be a lesson to you. Next time, don't listen to anything Catherine says to you."

Jamie paused, lowering the brush. What had Catherine been thinking? Why would she drag Asa into their nightmare? Jamie peered at Asa and saw nothing more than a tall, brown haired guy with glasses. What could have prompted Catherine to trust Asa?

What is she planning? "Did Catherine say anything to you, other then for you to wait until she called out to you?" Jamie asked. "Did she touch you? Smell the air around you?"

Jamie ignored the weird look Asa gave him. "No... or at least I don't think so..." Asa said to him.

"Are you sure?" Jamie insisted. "She said nothing else to you?"

"Well... she stared at me in a strange way, and then invited me in. Besides telling me to come in the house and wait until she called me, that was all she said to me."

"You're not lying to me, are you?" Jamie demanded.

"Me?" Asa said. "I'm the only one in this room who's been nothing but honest."

Jamie made a dismissive little noise at Asa's complaint.

"Don't start with me about lying to you." Jamie pointed to himself. "Hello? I've got everyone believing I'm a girl. Lying is a good friend of mine, and I don't feel any guilt with doing it either, so don't even think about giving me a lecture."

"Don't you have any pride?" asked Asa.

"Sure I do, but I also have to give a whole shitload of it away when I slip into pantyhose, and don't get me started on all the other female crap I have to do." Jamie rolled his eyes. "There's shit I have had to do to stay alive, Asa, and if lowering myself helps me keep breathing then, fucking shit, I'm going to do it. I'm not ashamed of the things I've done."

What Jamie said, he meant wholeheartedly. That didn't mean he'd whore himself out or anything, only when it came to *bending the truth,* he didn't feel a single twinge of guilt, unless he was lying to his mom, of course. He got a kind of sick enjoyment seeing his little white lies get eaten up like candy.

"I would never say you should be ashamed of the things you've done. I... I myself have done things to keep myself safe... I understand. Well, I will never fully understand where you're coming from, nor will you understand where I'm coming from, because both of our situations are completely different," Asa stated.

"Are they? So far, I've heard nothing that would make me think so. You've still refused to say jack shit about what your problem is, so how would I know what makes you sympathetic to me and mine?" Tired and wanting to go to bed so he could put the day behind him, Jamie put his brush on his nightstand and pulled his shirt up and over his head.

"W-what are you doing?"

"I'm going to go to bed." Jamie grinned. "Why are you blushing? Did you think I was going to do something else?"

"No, but... It's still strange to see you without..."

Jamie raised his brows. "Without what? My shirt on? No boobs?"

"Both…"

Jamie snorted. "Yeah, well, I only have the weekends to be free from wearing bras and dresses, and that's if I'm not forced to go out with my family or to the store, so forgive me if I don't put them on just to make you feel better." Standing up, Jamie drew the covers down so he could crawl in between them, just in time for the expected timely knock on his door.

"Come in," Jamie called out, already knowing who was at his door and smiling when his mother peeked in.

"How are you two doing?"

"Fine, considering you know we are going out, and you put the both of us in the same room with a box of condoms." Jamie gave Asa a fiendish grin. "I think your sex talk this afternoon may have given Asa a little bit of performance anxiety—" Jamie laughed when Asa jumped on the bed and frantically covered his mouth with his hand.

"Thank you for letting me stay over, Mrs

Dexson, and I'm very humbled you've accepted my relationship with Jamie, but I was brought up to never disrespect or insult my host and to-to try and deepen Jamie's and my l-love for one another under your roof... I couldn't do such a thing here. It has been instilled in me since birth, to not do such a thing," Asa insisted firmly.

Oh, nice one, thought Jamie.

"I just want you to know that I support you, regardless of where your relationship takes you. I'm so happy Jamie has finally found a lover, and if you need me for whatever reason, I'll be here for you."

Jamie wanted desperately to see what Asa would say to his mother's reply, but when the boy froze, Jamie had to step in.

Pulling Asa's hand away from his mouth, Jamie said, "Thanks, Mom, but I think Asa and I can take care of things from here. If we have questions, I'm sure we can figure it out together." Jamie grinned and lightly tapped Asa on the cheek. "Isn't that right, Asa? If we have any questions of an intimate nature, we can hold hands and find them out together."

"Are you sure? I don't mind answering them if you have any now," his mom reassured.

"I'm sure, Mom," Jamie said dryly.

"Okay."

Jamie allowed his mother to kiss him on the forehead, then snickered when she did the same to Asa.

"I know tomorrow's Sunday, but please don't sleep all day. And I need you to go to the store for me, sweetie. Catherine was called in to work so she won't be able to do it," Mom said.

"Not a problem, Mom." Jamie shoved Asa off of him and off his bed once his mother left. "Will you turn off the lights? I want to go to bed already." Lying down, Jamie covered his eyes with his forearm, and kept it over his eyes even as he heard the light switch being flicked off.

Listening to Asa get onto his inflatable

bed, feeling the weight of the darkness pressing down upon him, Jamie couldn't stop the thoughts filling his head. Asa's questions about him fearing blood had Jamie remembering things he wished he could forget. Thinking about blood before he fell asleep didn't count as one of Jamie's favorite things.

"Can I ask you a question?" Asa asked.

Jamie sighed. "All you've been doing is asking me questions."

"True."

"Go to bed." Even though Jamie wanted to sleep, he found himself turning and staring at the wall.

"Why doesn't your mother go to the store herself? I noticed earlier when she wanted the newspaper she had to ask the other lady to get it for her... it was just a few steps outside the front door..."

Jamie stayed silent for a while. "My mother is scared of going outside..." he lied.

Asa might already know people were out

to kill Jamie, but he didn't want to fully explain his mother's face would be the one they looked for the most. "Once a month Catherine takes her on a vacation, for seven days... they go to a place that helps people get a handle on their fears... Monday they'll be leaving for one of those trips..."

"Oh... I'm sorry."

"Don't feel sorry for her," Jamie said. "My mother is a strong woman, and doesn't need your pity." *With everything she has to deal with me, she's had to be strong...*

"I don't know her, but from what I've seen, I think your mom is a very courageous woman," Asa quietly said.

They were silent for a long time, but Jamie was still awake; still staring at the wall in the dark. From the neon red glow of his alarm clock, Jamie saw only a measly twenty minutes had passed. Determined to ignore the demons that normally haunted him during the night, plus those reawakened because of Asa's talk of blood, Jamie closed his eyes and tried to sleep.

"When I was sixteen my mother passed away..."

Jamie opened his eyes.

"... My father remarried two years later. His new wife is a very nice lady... I was happy for him because my mother and he... they didn't have a very happy life together..."

Staying as still as he could, Jamie did nothing to indicate he listened, knowing instinctively if he said anything Asa would stop talking.

"I was happy at first... my new family came with a sister and brother, and I was so ecstatic when I heard she had a son just a few years older than me... I was lonely after my mother died..."

Which meant you had been ignored by your father, Jamie thought sadly.

"My stepsister was considerably older than me and Jake, my stepbrother, and she was already on her own. For a few months everything was great… until my father and new mother left on their delayed honeymoon. That's when I found out Jake wasn't as happy as I was about our parent's marriage…"

Jamie didn't like where Asa's tale headed. The tension in the air grew thick enough to cut.

"I came home ten minutes late from school on a Friday, the first day they were gone… Jake was waiting for me, and… and he wasn't pleased. The look on his face as he held me down and hit me. Afterward, all he said was to clean myself up, and never come home late from school again…"

Jamie had planned on not saying anything, but couldn't stop the questions from coming out of his mouth. "This started when you were eighteen? After your dad's remarriage? So when we both entered Kegan State, that's when it began? Your brother beating on you?" He hoped he didn't scare Asa from continuing to talk.

"Yeah..." confirmed Asa.

"So for two years you've been letting this prick beat on you? Why didn't you tell your father? I've seen the wounds your brother leaves on your body. I'm amazed he didn't break something." Pissed for the guy, Jamie couldn't help but also be angry at him.

"I did tell my father... when they came back, my face was a mess. I told him everything..."

"You obviously didn't tell him everything if that fucker is still kicking your ass!" Jamie said. Not even he would tolerate that kind of shit from anyone.

"When Jake hurt me the first time, he told me my father didn't care about me... he said I was unwanted baggage my father was forced to drag behind him... he was right... And I *did* tell my father *everything,* Jamie. I told him, in detail, how Jake hit me. I told him the things Jake said to me, and how he had threatened to kill me if I told him or anyone else... I told my father I was scared and needed his help. Do you know what he told me?"

Jamie forced himself to hold his tongue and listen.

"He told me I was old enough to solve my own problems. He couldn't keep protecting me from every little bump in the road. He said I was just pissed he got remarried and looking for a little attention."

Jamie didn't know what to say. He couldn't impart any wisdom to the guy on daddies, since his father wanted his head on a stick. He also couldn't give him any advice on the mindset of siblings either, because his half-brother probably wanted him dead just as badly as their father.

"I'm trapped at the house. Jake doesn't do anything if my father and his mother are around, so I'm relatively safe when they are home."

"Relatively…" Jamie whispered.

"… It doesn't completely stop him from

coming at me when they're home, but it's not as bad…"

Jamie sat up. "What about his mother? Does she know?"

"She knows…"

"Then—"

"She knows, but she doesn't do anything about it. Her first husband wasn't a nice person, so she won't do anything because she's scared of Jake."

"She's scared of her own son?" Jamie turned his face away and closed his eyes. Hearing those words hurt his heart in more ways than Asa would ever know.

"I'm stuck in that house. I'm twenty. In June, on the seventh is my birthday. I'm of age to leave now, but my mother left me a considerable sum of money in her will when I turn twenty-one. One of the requirements is I can't leave my father's household, but in another year I'll be financially free from him and that house. I just need to hold on until then…"

Jamie got out of bed and walked over to where Asa lay. Without saying anything, he climbed under the covers, back to back, giving Asa comfort as best as he could without making a big deal about it. Jamie and Asa fell asleep in that position.

* * * *

Waking up to the sound of someone taking a picture had to be one of the main reasons people have heart attacks and die.

Eight o'clock on the dot, Jamie's mother came and woke them up for breakfast. It was as if they were going to the prom, or if they were a couple of celebrities caught getting down and dirty, the way his mother snapped shots off left and right with her camera. Asa and he might have fallen asleep back to back, but by the time morning came, they'd been all over one another. The embarrassing part was it was *he* who'd been snuggled up against Asa. His arms and legs wrapped around the guy in a way that would make a porn star jealous.

"I'm telling you, I think she posed us in some of those photographs. There's no way I was sleeping like that," Jamie complained, as Asa and he walked down the road to the supermarket.

"It did seem a little…"

"Whore-ish? Porn-starry? I had one of my arms under your shirt, and my leg around your waist. I was wearing boxers, but from the way the blanket was covering us, it looked like I was buck ass naked." Jamie scooped up a rock and threw it farther down the empty sidewalk. "In every picture you never once saw my chest. It was always covered by my arm or yours. Don't you think that's a little weird?"

"Yes… but your mother seems to be a very good person. I know I only met her yesterday, but she doesn't seem like the type to do something like that," Asa said.

"You're right, but her harpy beanpole

lover would, so my mother could take pictures."
Catherine would do anything to make my mother happy, Jamie thought. As excited as she'd been last night about the fact that he had a 'lover', and how badly his mother wanted him to get closer to another person, Jamie had no doubt Catherine would fuck with him in his sleep, just so his mother would find them like that.

"They weren't raunchy though. The way she took them was very tasteful."

Jamie gave Asa a sideways glance. "You're not offended by the fact you got your pictures taken in a compromising position? If, for whatever reason, those pictures were ever to go public, and if it was ever discovered I'm a dude, then your carefree days of getting the crap beaten out of you every *other* day at school will disappear quicker than you can say 'hit me, I'm gay'. There will be no breaks in your ass beatings like before."

"Thanks, Jamie. You really know how to comfort someone," Asa said sarcastically.

Jamie gave Asa a little salute, and chuckled when the guy pushed up his glasses with his middle finger. "Good to see a little spirit in you. If you're going to be spending time with me, and my family, you'll need it."

"You were so much nicer when the wool was still over my eyes, and I thought you were a girl. Your mouth was cleaner too," Asa replied. "In my house swearing is the same as stealing."

"Aw, am I hurting your sensitive sensibilities by uttering curse words? Suck it up. This is the real me, so take it and like it." Although Jamie gave Asa attitude, he actually enjoyed not having to watch his every word. Even at home he couldn't fully be himself, not with his mother and Catherine watching him like a hawk. He found it… refreshing.

Finally reaching the supermarket, Jamie halted their conversation, and immersed himself in his role as a girl. He smiled politely, speaking in a softer tone of voice, and most of all made sure not to swear. Nowadays, people didn't look twice if they saw a pretty girl, but a girl throwing out curse words that could make a sailor blush did leave a lasting impression.

It stuck in people's minds more than it did if a boy said them, and the last thing Jamie needed was for any of the many people shopping to remember him and go home or to work and say, "Hey, you should have seen it. There was this girl in the supermarket that said bleep, bleep, bleep."

Not a good thing for someone trying to hide in plain sight.

Jamie was thankful Asa had to come with him. He liked the taller kid and enjoyed his company, and, even if he didn't show it, Jamie was glad Asa had been the one to find out about him. There was something about Asa he couldn't put his finger on. A strange connection he felt when he was around the boy. Nevertheless, even though he was happy Asa came with him, he also noticed everyone watching the both of them as they walked down the aisle.

"People are staring at us," Asa commented.

"Just noticed that, too, did you?" Jamie mumbled. "Probably because I've never come to the store with anyone who wasn't my mother or Catherine."

Rushing to get everything on the list, Jamie tossed the last item into their little basket and hissed at Asa to go to the checkout counter. Jamie, feeling paranoid, suspected everyone who was talking on their cell phones as being a potential rat calling his father and reporting their finding for the reward money. Jamie knew he had to get out of the store, or he'd end up doing something stupid, like being a dumbass and saying or doing something which would bring unwanted attention in his direction.

Paying for everything on his list for tonight's dinner also became some kind of test of Jamie's willpower, when the only clerk on duty turned out to be the owner's mother... his very *old* mother. With pursed lips, Jamie bit his tongue to keep from shouting at the elderly woman when, with shaky hands, she tried to scan a bag of carrots... carrots they'd put in translucent thin plastic produce bag themselves.

Twenty minutes later, Jamie briskly walked out of the store, and took a deep breath of crisp morning air.

"Jesus fucking Christ, I thought we would never get out of there! It took her forever to ring up ten items," Jamie said once they were far enough away not to be overheard.

"She's old. To her, she was probably going as fast as she could," Asa said.

Jamie and Asa started walking back to Jamie's house, Asa carrying all the bags, since it wouldn't look good if Jamie carried them, being a chick and all. Jamie laughed, but shrugged and let Asa take everything. Jamie didn't want to lug it around anyway, so he wouldn't pitch a sexist line if the guy wanted to be chivalrous.

"Let's go to the park and swing on the

swings before we head back," Jamie turned down the well worn dirt path, a short cut, to a small abandoned playground a few houses away from his own.

"Are you sure? Isn't your mother expecting us back soon?"

Walking backward, Jamie gave Asa an amused look. "My mother gave me two hundred dollars to rent a room at a love motel so you and I could have some "cuddle time" away from prying eyes." Laughing when Asa stopped, a stunned look on his beet red face, Jamie swung around and continued down the path.

"I can't believe your mother gave you money to take me to a love motel."

"And four condoms," Jamie called out. "Mother Mary is a firm believer in having safe sex. She said you looked like a virgin, and she knows I am one as well, but she said it's best to learn to practice safe sex from the very beginning... you know, when you're about to engage." Jamie stopped long enough to make a few crude thrusting motions with his hips.

"Wait! If we don't go back immediately, then she'll think we really did go, and she'll think we had sex!" Asa said when he caught up to Jamie.

"That's the point." Jamie snickered. "If we come back just a little late, then she'll think we 'did it', and she'll be happy. And while she's preoccupied I'll slip the money back in her hiding spot. We can't afford to part with this much cash."

"But we're boys…"

Jamie halted in his tracks. "It doesn't matter to her." Turning his head to look at Asa, Jamie tried to express why his mother didn't care who his partner was. "You know the barest of what is going on in my life and why I am the way I am now. To my mother… she thinks by making me dress as a girl, she's taken something away from me… so she's just happy I've found someone, be it, a boy or a girl."

"So, if Tiffany had been the one who

found out that you were a boy? Would Mary have been happy?"

Jamie smiled and shook his head. "If Tiff had been the one who had found out about me, then we wouldn't be having this conversation right now. My family and I would have already been packed up and in the next city."

"Then why—" Asa started.

"Let's go to the park first. Race you to the playground!" Taking off, Jamie ran down the path until they reached a small clearing. Overgrown with weeds, there was only a rusted metal jungle gym and swings.

"This place doesn't look very... safe," Asa said.

Jamie agreed, and that became the reason he loved coming to this place. A little oasis for him to run to when he needed to be alone and away from everyone. "A year ago, two girls were kidnapped and taken from here," Jamie said softly as he made his way to the swings. "Their assailant raped and brutally murdered them."

Sitting down on the swing, the black rubber groaning in protest, Jamie kicked off and sailed into the air. "You should know about that. It was the biggest news to hit the papers, since the person they caught was a big shot in our school."

"Jonas Camzins... they found his DNA on the girls' bodies..."

"Yup, but his parents hired a big shot lawyer, and the prick got to walk, over a small mistake the cops made when collecting evidence." Jamie smiled cruelly as he swung his legs back and forth to get higher. "Everyone knew he did it, but because of a tiny error, he was able to walk free... for a while anyway."

"I remember... he was killed a few months later. His body was found in the exact spot those girls were killed..."

Jamie leaned back, not caring his hair dragged in the dirt. "Killed by a wild animal, the police said. His throat ripped out, and parts of his body eaten. An appropriate ending for someone like him, wouldn't you say?"

"Yes."

Pulling himself up, Jamie looked at Asa in surprise. Of all the responses he thought he would receive, having Asa agree with him hadn't been one of them. Considering how many times Asa brought up his cursing, Jamie expected Asa to give him a little speech of how killing would always be wrong. "You also think he deserved what he got?"

Jamie remembered the day the girls' bodies were found. They'd been pretty, quiet, nice girls from hard working families. However, at their college they were nobodies; just poor kids who'd gotten scholarships. Innocent, fresh-faced girls who shouldn't have had their lives stolen in such a horrible way.

"I do think he deserved his ending... I think about them from time to time. I still think about how everyone mourned *his* lost life and not the lives he stole," Asa said.

"But for those girls? Nothing. It was as if the school wiped their existence from the school registry." Jamie felt saddened at the memory of the poor girls who were victims of Jonas's crime.

"I'm happy he met his fate the way he did, and I applaud whoever sicced their dog on him, ending his life," Asa said.

Jamie watched Asa for a few long minutes before nodding his head. "Take a seat beside me, Asa." Jamie beckoned the boy over to the empty swing next to him. "You and I will be good friends; I can tell."

Asa gave Jamie a shy smile and lazily pushed his swing back and forth for a few minutes before standing and grabbing up the bags. "We should head back or the meat will spoil."

Jamie nodded and fell into step beside Asa, wondering if he could one day trust all his secrets to the boy. He'd grown tired of keeping everything to himself, and thought maybe fate or even destiny had sent Asa to discover one of his lies.

Jamie was tired of being alone, and he really did need a friend...

CHAPTER 4

August 31st, 2010

Fear is a funny thing... as in, I don't fear very much. That's not to say I'm not scared of anything. Only, the things I'm frightened of, I don't necessarily have a fear of... It makes sense to me.

Anyway.

Being afraid of something and fearing something are two different things. Like when I was ten and found out my father's wife wanted to pick out my burial plot. After that I was scared of her... well, not scared, more like wary, but the point is I didn't fear her.

Strange, right?

What I do fear? Hurting my mother tops the list. My rock. My source that keeps me connected to everything and everyone; the person that keeps me human.

My second and last fear is my father...

Anyway, enough about that. I should talk about my father's wife.

As stupid as it was, I didn't fear Lisa, or the fact she wanted me dead. I didn't even tell my mother what I overheard. Instead I kept it a secret—I'm good at secrets.

I remember being scared Joseph was in on it with his mother, but the need for human contact was strong, so I kept seeing him. Sure, there were other people I saw and talked to, but they weren't anyone whom I could really converse with. They were employees of my father's, and it was their job to talk to me, but only to see if I needed anything, and nothing else.

From the time I turned ten, and my father's presence put a stop to the first attempt on my life, I kept my eyes open fully to everything Lisa said or did when I was around her. I also made damn sure I never went anywhere with her again. I'm not that stupid.

That didn't mean the threats on my life

went away. But knowing what was on the dinner plate, I could avoid eating it.

By the time I successfully reached my eleventh birthday, there had been four near misses... and I never told my mother about any one of those. If my mother knew about them, we never talked about it. I still don't know why I didn't say anything. My mother is a gentle soul, yes, but she also has such inner strength it would make a man envious. It wasn't because I didn't think she couldn't take the news that her lover's wife was trying to off the bastard kid.

Wherever I went, I was careful to watch out for Lisa and every step she took. Whenever I knew she was at the main house, I would stalk her and listen when she talked on the phone. I watched and I waited, trying to figure out her next move...

And it seemed like I wasn't the only one...

Three months after my eleventh birthday, I was hiding in a little cubby blocked from view by a huge potted plant. I was sleeping over at the main house because my half brother, Joseph, would be coming the next day, and Lisa didn't want to wake me up and get me from my house to bring me over. So as not to inconvenience her or my mother, I slept over. Suspicious be thy name.

I hid there because I knew she would be planning something, and I ran from my room to sleep somewhere she wouldn't find me. No way would I just let her kill me off. I may have been young, but I could... well, I could hide like a pro.

I picked my spot because I could see downstairs and everything and anyone coming... my mistake.

I could see, but I couldn't hear anything. Well, I could hear voices but couldn't understand what they were saying, or maybe I blocked it all out. Who knows? I saw my mother come in and begin arguing with Lisa, who may have been searching for me... I remember how

loud they were and how their voices echoed.
Lisa hit my mother... then I saw my father...

I saw my father kill her.

He killed Lisa; his own wife.

I remember watching her blood splatter
and pool on the white marble floors... I watched
and listened as she screamed and begged for
her life, and I watched as he... as he tore her
apart as if she were nothing but paper...

Fear...

In that moment, I began to fear my
father, and that fear kept me in my hiding spot.
Kept my mouth glued shut from crying out in
terror. Filled my body when my father dragged
my mother into another room.

I stayed where I was, frozen.

I couldn't move a muscle...

I remember tears falling from my eyes as
I stared at Lisa's mutilated body, stared at the
crimson pool spreading from her still form. The
only time I cried out was when I heard my
mother start screaming, and the sound of glass

breaking and what might have been furniture being thrown against the walls.

I was finally able to move when I saw my mother rip the door open and race up the stairs to come get me... she had blood all over her... Lisa's blood. My father murdered her right next to my mother, and it was smeared all over her arms and face, my father's handprints marring her neat appearance when he grabbed her and dragged her into the room.

She had been crying... hell, I was crying...

My mother picked me up and ran out of the house.

However, before we left, I saw my father... his hands, all the way up to his forearms, had been the deepest shade of red I'd ever saw... he smiled at me before the door slammed shut...

He had smiled and licked some of the blood off his fingertips...

He had smiled at me.

As I said before... I fear very little, and I may fear hurting my mother... but my father... my father is the monster in the dark that parents tell their children about to keep them quiet at night...

* * * *

Walking onto campus with Asa racked Jamie's nerves.

In Jamie's head, he heard whispers and felt stares from every person standing around. His imagination ran wild when a student stopped and pointed in their direction. Paranoia made Jamie think they were all talking about him and Asa.

But of course people didn't know Asa and he were 'going out'. The only ones who thought they were an item were his mother, Catherine, and Tiffany. Jamie very much doubted his mother would say anything, and Tiffany had her reputation to think about; it wouldn't do if her best friend hooked up with someone the majority of the student body thought was a loser. As for Catherine... well, Jamie wouldn't put it past his ex-nanny to do something like that, but she wouldn't come to his school just to tell people he had a 'boyfriend'.

"I feel like everyone is watching us... I told you we should have left the house at different times," Asa whispered.

Jamie nodded. "I know and I had agreed, remember? It was my mom who wouldn't allow us to leave separately."

"I'm nervous... what if I accidentally refer you as 'he' instead 'she'?" asked Asa.

Jamie grabbed the guy's arms and turned Asa toward him. "If anyone starts asking you questions about me, and they will, just remember this." Jamie grabbed Asa, bringing his head down to him, and slammed their mouths together.

When the other boy gasped, Jamie stuck

his tongue in his mouth, kissing him deeply, before pulling away.

"Now," Jamie said, slightly breathless, "when you think about me, think about this kiss, and what someone will think if you call me a boy. This is the same as if someone found those pictures my mother took. Just think about the crap talk you'd be subjugated to if anyone found out I was a guy." Not the brightest idea Jamie had, considering he should be trying to keep himself under the radar, but the only thing to come to mind to keep Asa's lips shut.

"I can't believe you did that in front of everyone! Tiffany looks like she's about to kill me!" Asa shrieked.

Sure enough, Jamie's redheaded friend was shooting daggers at the both of them from the entrance doors to the school. "Don't worry about her. The important thing is... did you feel anything?"

"What?"

"Did. You. Feel. Anything?" Jamie

looked pointedly down at Asa's crotch.

"No!"

Jamie tilted his head. "Really? Not even a twinge?"

"No! Wait. Why? Did you?"

Sadly, Jamie shook his head. "Nope, nothing. That's a good thing though. It means we can remain friends. If you felt anything, then I would have to kick your ass. I told you I like you, but my 'like' has nothing to do with wanting you physically, or wanting to pick out tuxedos and pairing rings."

"You want to be friends with me?" Asa asked.

Jamie gave Asa a little tap on the cheek. "Take that look off your face, Asa. You look desperate and that's a little sad." Mostly because it was probably the same expression he had on his own face.

"Shit! Don't look now, but Tiffany is coming and so is Ethan," Jamie whispered, releasing Asa's arms but remaining by his side.

"Morning, Tiff!" Jamie called out to his enraged friend as she stormed up to them.

"Good morning?! What's so good about it! I thought we would be keeping your *relationship* a secret!" she hissed.

"Relationship? Oh, ho, ho! So you didn't kiss Asa just to fuck with his head? Damn girl, what happened to the 'no boyfriend' rule you had?" Ethan asked.

"Good morning, Ethan," Jamie said to the handsome, extremely tall boy. "And yes, Asa and I are dating. We were going to keep it under wraps, but I felt it was wrong to do that. I don't want anyone to think I'm ashamed of my hot lover," Jamie teased, pulling Asa's arm and squeezing it between his fake breasts.

Tiffany glared at Jamie. "You and Asa and this *thing* you have with one another was supposed to be kept a secret! Don't you know how to keep a secret? But now! Now everyone knows you're dating!"

Jamie's lips twitched, and he tried not to

grin at Tiffany's question. "Just because Asa and I walked side by side when we came to school... because I'm acknowledging the fact Asa happens to be a human being—not some insect to be stepped on—*that* is the main reason you are in a frenzy... not because me and Asa are dating."

Even so, because of paranoia's seductive words whispering in his ear, making him believe it was the cause, he'd kissed the guy in front of everyone. And now everyone knew they were going out... crap.

"Who gives a rat's ass about that? Hot damn, Asa, my man! I can't believe you hooked up with Jamie!" Ethan exclaimed.

Jamie grunted when Ethan pulled Asa away from him, and threw his large arm over the boy's shoulders.

"Boy, you are so totally screwed when the male population of this school finds out you're nailing Jamie. Hell, you'll get shit from some chicks, too. But don't worry; I've got your back." Ethan grinned.

"I'm not *nailing* Jaime," Asa whispered, embarrassed.

"Have you ever been in her room?" Ethan asked.

"That doesn't mean any—"

"Oh, so you have!"

"Yes, but—" Asa tried to protest again.

"Have you slept in the same bed?" Ethan then asked.

Jamie would have loved to watch Asa get playfully picked on by Ethan, but he would have to put a stop to it before the poor kid let something like, "Nothing happened! He's a boy!" slip out from his lips.

"Stop teasing him, Ethan, before I maim you." Jamie laughed when Ethan threw up his hands, and slightly stepped away from Asa.

"Don't get all pissy with me for wanting to get a few more details from the little guy."

"Pissy? You haven't seen pissy yet." Jamie wanted to continue, until he saw how truly distressed Asa had become.

It didn't seem to be from the joking around but the close proximity of Ethan. Asa even shot 'help me' pleads to Jamie with his eyes, silently begging Jamie to get the jock away from him or vice versa.

"Ahh, Asa… why don't you and me head on over to our first class?" Jamie asked.

"Hell no, girl! I'm taking Asa, and we are going to have a little talk with the boys. We want to know *all* the details about the both of you and how you hooked up."

"Wait, Ethan!" Jamie watched helplessly as the larger kid dragged Asa away, while Asa looked over his shoulder at him in desperation. Jamie couldn't see Asa's eyes because of the glare from the boy's glasses, but Jamie could feel the panic pouring out of him.

Cursing, Jamie started after them only to have Tiffany stop him.

"Hold up there, missy."

"Missy?" Jamie looked Tiffany up and

down. "What era are you from?"

"Don't be such a smart-ass, Jamie," Tiffany huffed. "Leave them alone. Ethan will protect your little love interest, although I don't know what the hell you find so interesting about him."

"What I see or don't see about Asa is my business. I need to make sure Asa will be alright with him," Jamie said.

Trying to pass Tiffany, she stopped him. "Don't you know? Ethan is all up into charity cases and has always protected Asa's skinny ass. I don't know why, but he has."

Jamie didn't care if Ethan pitied Asa. The only thing concerning Jamie would be if Asa opened his damn mouth… and okay, maybe a little of that worry involved the guy himself, but only a little.

"Besides, Asa can take care of himself. I may not like the fact he somehow got you so wet to the point you would publicly tie yourself to him, but from the amount of times he's gotten bullied, it's obvious he can take a couple hits. Not that he'll get in any fights while he's out of your sight. He'll be fine with Ethan," Tiffany said.

"Are you sure?" Jamie forced himself to relax.

He didn't know Ethan very well, never thought to get closer to the guy, so it was hard not to go running off to 'rescue' Asa. Doing so would also bring more attention to the both of them than he foolishly had already.

"Take my word for it. Asa will not be harmed," Tiffany reassured him.

Jamie eyed Tiffany. The girl delivered more insults than compliments, so her trying to comfort him came as a surprise. "Are you trying to make me feel better? Why, Tiffany... how *kind* of you." Jamie couldn't let something like that pass by.

He couldn't help himself from ribbing Tiffany about it, reminding her she had a soft spot, a heart.

"Shove it up your ass, Jamie. The only reason I told you is because I don't want you to create a scene by running after him. *And* because I know the kid can literally take a hit. This one day I watched a group of guys picking on him. They took his glasses and broke them, ripped up all this textbooks and assignments; you know normal bullying stuff. But he didn't bow down to them… it was a sight to see. I shit you not. When he wouldn't beg, they started to beat on him, and he had this look on his face that was like 'What bitch? That all you got?' It totally withered those bullies' wood."

"Is that when you stepped in?" Jamie didn't know Asa got picked on to such an extreme; then again, they weren't bff's and he hadn't spent any personal time with the kid, not like how he planned to do now.

"Why the hell would I wanna step in? No, I watched the whole thing and, baby, it was one kick-ass fight. He impressed me. Asa really can take a beating. I've watched bigger guys get kicked down into the dirt with some of the blows Asa was given by Mick and his gang of numb nuts, but Asa took it and asked for more."

Probably from his brother constantly beating on him. Jamie also got annoyed as hell that the punk just took it like a bitch. "Did he fight back at all?"

"Nope, but it was the look on his face... this 'go fuck yourself' look that impressed me."

"So you just watched as he got beaten?" As much as Jamie liked Tiffany, it was talks like they were having now, the 'you're an ant, and I'm the kid with the magnifying glass' attitude of Tiffany's, which made him want to clock her, to try and knock some sense into her brain.

"Don't get all vexed at me, girl. What did you want me to do? Jump in and rescue him? Yeah, that would have panned out *real* well for him. Having a chick save him would be like saying, 'yes, I'm a pussy so please fuck with me some more'. Didn't I say I was impressed by the dork? Jeez, Jamie, follow the line of conversation, will ya?"

"So what happened then?" Jamie grew impatient with Tiffany.

Another thing he hated about Tiffany. She had to go around the block and then back again, before she got to the damn point. "Hurry it up, too; class will be starting soon."

"Aw, what's the matter? Don't like the fact that your lover boy was getting picked on?"

Jamie flipped Tiffany off. "Just tell me already, Tiff. Are you trying to be a bitch on purpose?"

"Yes! Because you broke your promise to me! As punishment, I'm making you suffer by making you drag it all out of me, one word at a time."

"Tiffany!" Jamie moved toward the girl threateningly.

"Okay, okay! I didn't do anything because I didn't need to. Ethan came out and beat the shit out of those guys."

"So Ethan and Asa really are good

friends?" Even as Jamie uttered the words it didn't sound right.

Asa didn't look like he was pleased Ethan had, in essence, kidnapped him. Asa looked more terrified than aggravated by being alone with the hulking jock.

"I don't know. Why don't you ask your *boyfriend* the next time you see him?"

Jamie rolled his eyes and turned around, entering the school. Just as they turned the corner Jamie's good humor disappeared when he saw Aidan waiting at the bottom step of the stairs that he and Tiffany needed to take to reach their class.

"Looks like Aidan found out you've got a beau." Tiffany giggled.

Jamie swatted Tiffany away from him. There could be many reasons why the Greek god would be standing there—in his way— Jamie just wished that he would go somewhere else and stand. Those freaky pale yellow-green eyes of his gave Jamie goose bumps. They made him feel like they saw right through his deception, and was waiting for just the precise moment to expose him.

"Hey, Aidan. What brings you here to this side?" Tiffany asked as she skipped past Aidan.

Jamie glared at Tiffany when the girl, behind Aidan's back, mouthed the words, "*he wants you*", before ditching him and running up the stairs. Scratching his cheek, Jamie looked at all the girls, and even boys, as they stared at Aidan's god-like perfection with either lust in their eyes or envy.

Don't worry ladies; I can tell you now he doesn't want what I got, so you all still have a very big chance at trying to bag him for yourselves. Jamie gave his audience a wink... unfortunately, his wink came off mocking, and he received many dirty looks.

"So, I hear you've got yourself someone?"

Jamie shivered at Aidan's deep tones that

seemed to caress every inch of his body. He'd deep-tongued Asa with no response down south, but hear this guy talk and Jamie could feel himself 'rising' with each syllable. "News travels fast," Jamie said nervously.

"When it comes to you, it does," Aidan replied, smiling.

Jamie's face heated at Aidan's beautiful smile.

Jamie lowered his eyes or he'd end up stuttering like an idiot. "Because of my rule, right?" Jamie tensed when Aidan came closer to him.

Jamie's heart beat faster when he got a whiff of Aidan's wonderful scent. However, Jamie also began to feel crowded. The larger guy moved too close to him and Jamie felt cornered.

"One could feel insulted by the fact you started going out with him, just when the rumor of you and I becoming an item had started."

Refusing to look up into Aidan's jeweled

eyes, Jamie instead stared at Aidan's chest... his clearly defined chest that strained against his black shirt. Not knowing what to say, Jamie stayed silent.

"Tell me... did you do it on purpose?" Aidan asked.

"Do what?" Jamie croaked, backing up a few steps.

"Did you pair up with Asa Jacobs just to spite me?"

Jamie snorted. "No, I did not. Asa and I have been an item for a while. I thought it was best to speak out about our commitment to one another, once I realized how set Tiffany was in pushing me toward you." Sweat beaded between Jamie's shoulder blades when Aidan leaned close to his ear.

"Really? Then why does it smell like you're lying to me?"

Feeling Aidan's hot breath on his neck, Jamie shuddered.

"Or are you just with him to force me to

run after you?"

Mentally slapping himself to get it together, Jamie barked out a strained little laugh. Everything he'd learned about pretending to be a girl, Jamie used on Aidan. One person already discovered his secret, and instinctively Jamie felt if Aidan found out about him it would be bad.

Stepping away from Aidan, Jamie smiled kindly. "Look, Aidan... you and I... well, we don't fit. People talk about you, and I'm the kind of girl that doesn't like to be talked about. You're flashy, looked at, and I'd get stressed if I'm in the spot light. I can't even do an oral presentation in class, so just thinking about being engaged in small talk with your friends... I think it's best if we not... do *this*." Jamie motioned between the both of them and how close they were as well as what they were talking about.

"You want me to leave you alone?" Aidan asked, with an amused smirk.

"It's for the best, I think." Jamie silently crowed at the flash of anger on Aidan's face. But Jamie's glee became short lived when Aidan continued to stare at him with those strange yellow-green eyes. If Jamie had known Aidan would come to speak to him when he got himself a boyfriend, then Jamie would have never kissed Asa... although it hadn't been on purpose. Besides exchanging pleasantries, he and Aidan never spent any time together, and if they found each other alone then Jamie always found an excuse to leave.

He couldn't help being attracted to Aidan... but there had always been a sense of danger surrounding Aidan, making Jamie wary of him.

The feeling of peril intensified at the sudden rage Jamie saw glimmering in Aidan's eyes. It scared him. But, why the hell would Aidan be pissed at Jamie for supposedly finding someone else? If Aidan wanted Jamie for himself, then wouldn't he have done something already? He'd had over two years at Kegan to do so. Why get angry now?

A long tense moment passed between them, before Jamie breathed a sigh of relief when Aidan backed down, stepping away.

"You're right... I shouldn't be affected by the fact that you've found someone. Not when there is someone waiting for me," Aidan said.

"Like... what? You already have a girlfriend?" Jamie shouldn't have been shocked to hear Aidan had someone, but he was.

With a face like Aidan's, it wouldn't be surprising if a girl—or two—hung on his arm. Yet, never once had Jamie seen Aidan with a female companion... maybe why Jamie felt unsettled by Aidan telling him such a person existed...

"What I have is more than just a 'girlfriend'. This person was chosen by me to become mine. Even so, you... you've made my decision waver from the moment I met you.

Your innocence, the purity I see in you, pulls me to you."

Holy crap, this guy's rose tinted glasses are a tad darker than most dudes. He thought Jamie innocent and pure… Jamie would laugh if it wasn't a little depressing. He didn't know how to respond to… Aidan's confession? *I need to get out of here.*

Tucking a lock of hair behind his ear, Jamie said, "If you chose this person, then she must have appealed to you greatly. I would concentrate on her, and not iffy feelings you *think* you may have for me." Jamie edged away from Aidan, toward the stairs. "I'll see you around Aidan…"

Swallowing hard, Jamie slowly climbed up the stairs. He could feel Aidan's eyes on him, and it freaked him out. It always did whenever he felt those pale yellow-green orbs focused in his direction.

"I'll be talking to you later, Jamie," Aidan called.

Jamie stumbled on his way up the steps, trying to trample the thrill he felt at Aidan's words. At the landing Jamie was stopped by, God forbid, Janis and all her raging perfectly styled hair. Peeking over his shoulder, he saw the spot Aidan had occupied was empty, his reflection was still visible in the windows. Aidan had only stepped out of view when Janis showed up.

"I heard Aidan was talking to you, and I had to see it for myself," Janis snootily said.

Hoping what he was about to do wouldn't backfire on him, Jamie smiled cockily at Janis. "Oh, you heard right, Jan, hon. *The* Aidan came to see little ol' me because he heard that I was going out with Asa... just as I planned." If Aidan was drawn to him because he thought him to be pure and innocent, then maybe he could make him think he wasn't.

"*Just* as you planned?"

"Ahh, hello? Me go out with a nobody like Asa? Please, girl. For almost two years I've been watching Aidan and thinking of the best way to trap him. I've got him on my hook now, and what a pretty little fish he is." Jamie threw his head back and cackled. "Soon he'll come crawling to me, and when that happens," Jamie slammed his hands together with a loud crack. "I've got him for good. Play the innocent school girl, tell him 'No, no, I can't go all the way' and then once I've got him in my bed, all I need to do is get myself pregnant," *yeah like that could ever happen*, "make a fuss so big his family will be forced to marry us or at least pay me a shit load of money to make me go away."

Sneaking a peek at Aidan's reflection, Jamie inwardly cringed when he saw Aidan's murderous expression captured clearly in the glass. Aidan hating him didn't sit well in Jamie, but allowing Aidan to get closer to him was impossible. *It needed to be done.* If only it didn't feel like his chest was being crushed, then Jamie would've been just fine.

"You bitch. I'm going to tell Aidan

everything you just said!" Janis said, glaring at him.

"Go ahead." Jamie laughed, pretending perfectly like he didn't care. "He won't believe you. He thinks I'm all pure and innocent, and you? Well, everyone knows how much of a jealous, spiteful bitch you are. Who do you think he'll believe?" Looking discreetly again, he caught the edge of Aidan's back as he turned and left, and felt like crap.

Holding back his sigh, Jamie gave Janis his full attention. "If you run after him like a bitch in heat, and tell him, then maybe he'll believe you."

Suddenly tired, Jamie told Janis to "run along" and dragged his feet to class. Jamie had a nagging feeling he'd just opened a box that should have been left closed, that pissing Aidan off had been a bad idea, even though turning Aidan against him was the fastest way to keep the guy away from him. Jamie was so preoccupied with his thoughts he didn't notice the silence that filled the classroom when he entered.

"Well, well, thank you very much, Miss Dexson, for joining the rest of the class. Now, would you please take your seat, so I can continue with my important announcement?" The teacher asked when Jamie fully entered the classroom.

"Sorry, Mr Miller," Jamie mumbled, embarrassed to be the main focus of attention. Walking down the rows of desks to get to his seat, Jamie shied away from Tiffany's glare, no doubt the girl heard he'd rejected Aidan, and winced when students bowed their heads to the person next to them, behind them and in front of them. It wasn't hard to figure out they were whispering about the scene many of them had witnessed between him and Aidan. News traveled fast in their school. The day just started, and Jamie already wished it was over so he could hide at home with his head buried under his bedcovers.

"What happened with Ethan?" Jamie whispered once he got to his seat next to Asa.

"Nothing... he wanted to know about us and when we started dating... and if we had done it," Asa whispered back.

"And?" Jamie moved his desk closer to Asa's. "What did you say?"

"I told him the truth... kinda. I said we started seeing each other on Friday, and how I slept over your house last night... Ethan kept pressuring me to tell him until it just slipped out."

Jamie froze. "What slipped out? You don't mean you told him I'm..."

"No! What slipped out was me telling them we slept in the same bed!" Asa quickly whispered.

"Mr Jacobs! Miss Dexson! Please pay attention!"

"Sorry, Mr Miller," Jamie and Asa mumbled, both sliding down in their desks as everyone turned around to stare at them.

"We'll talk about this after class," Jamie muttered.

"Okay, class. Wake up and put your cell phones away. This morning we received a call informing us, the faculty, to warn our students there have been six attacks on young girls ranging from the ages of sixteen to twenty-five," the teacher said.

Jamie sat up straight in his chair and listened intently.

"From the report emailed to us by the police department, the assailant has been described as roughly being five feet ten inches tall, weighing a hundred and sixty to eighty pounds, dark hair, eyes, and from the surviving victim, this criminal has a web-like scar on his neck. We are cautioning all the girls not to walk home alone, to stay in groups. This also applies to those who live in the dorms."

"Mr Miller, what's the chance this jack-ass will come to this side?" one student asked.

"Has he killed anyone?" another

questioned.

Jamie held his breath as he waited for the teacher's answers.

"Someone fitting this man's description was last seen in the city only a half an hour away from the school," Mr Miller said. "So I'd say the chances are more than fairly high. Furthermore, yes, he has killed, hence the reason why I said 'surviving victim'. Remember to never walk alone, always have someone with you and, lastly, don't be stupid. If you see this man or someone who could fit his description, call the police. I have flyers with a police sketch for you to look at."

Slumping back in his seat, Jamie's hand shook when he reached up and took the flyer from the teacher as he handed them out. Jamie looked down at the picture and his stomach tightened painfully.

"Jamie… Are you alright?" Asa asked.

Jamie began to nod then stopped and shook his head. "I feel sick." Jamie needed to get out of the stuffy room.

"Do you want me to come with you?" Asa asked, concern written plainly on his face.

Jamie smiled. "Nah, its okay, Asa… I just need to get something to drink." Getting out of the class as fast as he could, Jamie rushed through the hall to the main lobby of the school where the vending machines were.

As if his luck didn't run bad enough today, when he rounded the corner, he found Janis… leaning against the wall next to the soda machine.

"What are *you* doing here?" she asked.

Jamie sighed. "Shouldn't I be asking you that question?" Digging into his purse, Jamie withdrew his wallet. "Skipping class?"

"Obviously, stupid."

"Awesome…" Not what Jamie needed, to be in the presence of the chick he'd pissed off not even ten minutes ago. "So what are you doing here?"

"Getting something to drink, why else

would I be here? Not so bright, are you?"

Grinding his teeth, Jamie shoved his sixty-five cents in the soda machine, and selected his drink. "I hate to inform you, but this isn't a pill dispenser. They don't stock the Morning After pill here." Bending over, Jamie reached to grab his soda.

"Good one. I need to talk to you," Janis said.

Jamie gasped in pain when Janis jerked him around to face her, something sharp caught his skin from inside the machine. A small pea-sized glob of blood pooled on the back of Jamie's hand from the ragged cut, and before he could get something to wipe it off, the brunette seized his hand and sucked the blood off.

"What are you doing?" Jamie shouted, yanking his hand away from the crazy girl.

"What? Are you disgusted with me for licking the blood off your wound?" Janis smirked, wiping her mouth.

"Disgusted? More like scared shitless.

Who the hell knows where your mouth's been!" Soda forgotten, Jamie stormed off to the restroom a short distance away.

Entering, Jamie walked straight to the sink. Turning on the faucet, Jamie stuck his hand under the water.

"Don't be such a cry baby, Jamie." Janis laughed.

Jamie glared over his shoulder at the stupid girl who'd followed him. "Shit, my first thought had been I would need a tetanus shot, but now I'm debating whether to chop my whole hand off due to the fact your slimy tongue touched it."

"Don't be such a whiny bitch," Janis huffed.

Angry, Jamie turned off the water and scowled at Janis while scrubbing his hand with a paper towel. "What do you want, Janis? Did you catch up with Aidan after I left you on the stairwell? Going to gloat, and tell me the gory details of how you succeeded in convincing

Aidan how much of a two-faced whore I am? You have the same classes as he does, don't you?"

"I told him to meet me here. I couldn't very well tell him what a cunt you were in front of the whole class. Aidan doesn't like scenes," Janis said, rolling her eyes at him.

Shit! The last thing Jamie needed was to be anywhere near Aidan.

"If you think confronting him with the truth while I'm here is good, then you're digging your own grave. He'll just think you're jealous." Jamie looked at the cut on his hand, and pressed a paper towel on the wound. "I need to get out of here," Jamie whispered.

"Here."

Jamie caught the box Janis threw at his head. Band-Aids. "What…?"

"Keep it. Don't want your cut getting infected. There's some disinfectant ointment in the box, too. I want you nice and healthy so you'll be here to see me walking around with

Aidan on my arm." Janis smugly smiled. "He'll need someone to comfort him when he discovers his perfect little princess is nothing but a greedy gold digger."

Why is Janis talking to me like Aidan and I are a couple? The longest conversation we ever had happened this morning...

Jamie mentally gave a shrug and smiled. "Good luck, and remember it's your responsibility to tell all your bed partners you have an active sexually transmitted disease," Jamie called out as Janis spun around on her heel and walked out the door, but not before she flipped him the bird.

Truthfully though, the small amount of time he spent with Janis, as unpleasant as it was, gave Jamie enough time to calm down from his teacher's announcement. A killer was in the neighborhood... Jamie squeezed his eyes and shook his head to try and clear the memory that played behind his eyes.

"Why would Janis give me bandages?

And the whole box of them to boot?" Muttering to himself some more, Jamie slapped a bandage on his hand, and shoved the box in his bag.

More importantly, he needed get home now and tell his mother and Catherine about the killer running around too close to home... or did he?

Whoever this criminal happened to be, it had nothing to do with Jamie. His father's people would never do something stupid as harm strangers just to see if those violent acts would frighten them into running, thus flushing them out into the open.

But the thought of a killer being in town filled Jamie with anxiety... his mother would be leaving tonight. What would be the harm in not telling her...?

Jamie looked at himself in the mirror, and with shaky hands turned the faucet back on, splashing cold water on his face. *Should I tell Catherine?* Jamie's heart raced. *But if I tell her, they'll cancel their trip, and they* need *to go... I can control it...*

Yeah... I'll be okay. This has happened before. Jamie winced. Yes, this little attack of his happened before. A year ago... and he'd failed. If not for his—with Catherine's help—quick thinking they would have had to move.

Breathing deeply, trying to relax, Jamie tried to shake off his anxiety... and his hunger. He needed to go home and have his mother make him some of her tomato soup. Nasty as it might be. Cold or not, he'd eat it. Have Catherine tie him up and force it down his throat if he had to.

Taking one last deep breath, Jamie patted his face dry. Did a little touch up on his make-up, and then combed his fingers through his hair until he looked presentable. Hopefully Jamie wouldn't meet up with anyone he knew, wanting to leave as quickly as he possibly could. Luckily, Jamie couldn't hear any foot traffic in the halls, meaning classes were still in session.

Exiting the restroom, Jamie came to a dead stop. In his path were Aidan—Greek god Aidan—and Janis—I fucked your boyfriend, twice—making out. One of the brunette's long shapely legs wrapped around Aidan's waist and her hands under Aidan's shirt, running them up and down his back.

Jamie flinched when Janis moaned, wanting to look away but unable. Not until Aidan lifted his head away from Janis's.

His chest tight, Jamie cleared his throat, loudly, and directed his smile to Janis's dazed, lust-filled, pissed off eyes. "Ah, yeah... sorry to interrupt, but you're in my way. I can't get by you... so could you..." Jamie made motions with his hands, asking them to please move to the side.

"That smell..." Aidan turned his head and pinned Jamie with a piercing stare.

Jamie shivered at Aidan's husky voice. "Umm... teen spirit?" he joked, then sobered when Aidan's pale yellow-green eyes narrowed at him.

Those eyes frightened Jamie. But Aidan's intense gaze didn't shake Jamie to his core, but what he saw *in* those amazing eyes did.

"I don't smell anything… I-I need to go." Jamie pressed himself to the side and tried to slide past the two lovers.

"It's coming from you… not her," Aidan commented.

Startled, Jamie backed into the restroom again when Aidan suddenly pulled Janis's arms from around his neck, and took a step toward him. Jamie clenched his bag close to his chest, feeling cornered and helpless as Aidan's huge body came closer.

"Let her pass. She's nothing to you. Remember what I told you, what she said?" Janis hissed, pulling Aidan back by his arm. "Who cares if she smells?"

Jamie didn't stick around, but took the opportunity Janis gave him and rushed past them, running his ass as fast as he could to the exit.

He needed to get home; nothing else mattered but getting home.

CHAPTER 5

August 31st, 2010

The night I saw my father kill his wife, we ran away—my mom, Catherine, and I. There'd been no one at the front gates, so no one stopped us from leaving. I'd always wondered why, but never voiced my questions.

If I'm such a threat to my father, why allow us to leave? If he wanted me dead, why did he kill Lisa when their goals were the same? Why would a bastard son be worth all this trouble...?

Maybe I should have asked... because then maybe I would stop thinking about them.

But I won't, because with those questions came the memories. The smell of blood all over my mother. Remembering how it smeared onto me when she touched me and carried me away from the main house... Remembering how scared I'd been.

I still can't get the image of my father licking Lisa's blood off his fingers and smiling at me as he did it... freaky shit that would make a kid wake up screaming in the middle of the night.

The first place we tried to hide ourselves had been in a town far from everything... yeah... that didn't work out very well for us. We thought we could disappear in a small town, but we learned how naive we were after a week of living there.

The thing about small towns is the people living there wanted to get out, not stay in. From the moment we drove past 'Welcome to 'blank', Population, Two Thousand', you could feel the eyes of every person who called that place home. It took my father less than a month to find us, but just like when we escaped the house, a shining hand came down, and we were able to get away.

We drove for days upon days before Catherine, my mother, and I found a slightly larger town than the last to hide in... I still remember how I'd stayed quiet in the back seat of our 'borrowed' car. My mother was on edge, and I didn't want to make her cry by saying something like 'Wasn't the first town, and what happened there, not enough for you to learn your lesson about small towns?' Some smart-ass sarcastic remark like that from my mouth, and I knew I would be seeing her eyes filling up with tears. Especially since the reason why we left the last town had been my fault.

Actually... every town and city we'd been forced to flee had been my fault...

We'd been on the road for weeks and even though a town wasn't the best choice to rest, we were low on funds, and we didn't have the option to keep driving. In the new place, the whispers hadn't been so bad, and we were able to live there until I was almost twelve. I got to be a normal kid who went to school, made friends, and even tried out for the JR baseball team. I'd begun to enjoy my life in that town.

A month before my twelfth birthday, our happiness was shattered. The day the police found a dead body close to the entrance of the town. The corpse was identified as the stranger who'd cornered my mother, roughed her up, stole her wallet, and her car.

They found him sliced to ribbons, mutilated, inside her car...

Reporters came and started asking questions, taking pictures... we left once the townspeople began pointing in our direction, pointing to the 'new people', telling them to talk to us, because it had been my mother's car he'd been found in.

We never lived in another town again.

However, that didn't mean our problems ended once we left there. Lady Luck must have been on a break, because after we departed in haste from the town my father found us in the next three locations we thought we could rest, and all three times we ran we left a dead body or two behind us...

For six years, we ran from city to city, state to state, and every time my father found us, and every time there was one or more dead bodies of strangers who were left behind...

It wasn't until Catherine and my mother devised a plan to keep us safe and hidden. A plan perfectly executed on my sixteenth birthday. I began dressing like a girl.

We created a whole new identity for ourselves and once I turned eighteen we faked my high school exams to get me the scholarship to Kegan State University. And while pretending to be a girl has dropped a whole new set of problems onto my lap, it's because of this plan I finally found a measure of peace.

Dressing as a girl and hiding my sex gave me a sense of freedom I'd never had before...

* * * *

It was almost five before Jamie finally

made it close to home, even though he'd left the school at eight.

Earlier his hunger pains had him going to a family restaurant, but when Jamie got there… nothing appealed to him. He'd sat there in the booth staring at the menu forever before walking out. Shakily, Jamie had wandered around. Went to the mall, to the arcade, the movies. Wandered around aimlessly, trying to keep his mind off Aidan, Janis, Asa, and most importantly, the killer.

Until the hourly chimes of the mall clock struck four and snapped Jamie out of his dream-like walk, then he began to panic. Mom and Catherine were leaving in two hours to go on their trip. He wanted to tell them goodbye, to be careful, and have a safe drive.

Jamie's urgency faded the closer he got to his house. If he spoke to them, they'd know something was wrong with him. They'd delay leaving and he'd crack and tell them about the killer. But if he didn't go home, just called them to say goodbye, then everything would be fine.

Even if he did do something... would it really matter? This was a stranger; a wanted criminal. No one would miss the guy if...

"Jamie!"

Stumbling to a stop, Jamie blinked in surprise, and waved at his elderly next door neighbor. He hadn't realized he'd reached home.

"Hi Mrs Davis." Jamie waited impatiently as the old woman hobbled over to him from her front door. "I need to get going, Mrs Davis. My mom—"

"Oh, they left very early this morning, around eight thirty."

Jamie's bag dropped from his numb fingertips. "They left? But... they weren't supposed to leave until six-thirty tonight... why would they..." He forgot his cell phone at home, so they couldn't call him.

"Oh, sweetheart, I'm sorry. Your mom came to me asking, if I was to see you, to tell you their reservation at the hotel made a mistake with their check-in time. If they didn't leave this morning, they would have given their room to someone else, and they would have had to cancel their trip," Mrs Davis said.

So it wouldn't have mattered if he had come immediately home after skipping school. They would have been long gone by the time he got back...

"Your mom wanted me to also tell you she left soup in the refrigerator for you, but sadly the whole block, as well as the next one over, has been without power since Mary and Catherine left. There was a huge accident and a few power lines came down."

It was still bright enough out so he hadn't noticed the houses around him didn't have their lights on. "Thanks, Mrs Davis," Jamie mumbled as he picked up his bag. "I'll see you later." Smiling his goodbye, Jamie walked up the driveway.

Unlocking all the dead bolts, Jamie slipped into his eerily silent house and headed straight to the kitchen. His stomach felt hollow. He needed to eat.

Opening the fridge, Jamie gagged at the smells that assaulted his nose.

Eight and a half hours without power... close to nine hours with a refrigerator that leaked out its frosty air. The milk and everything else was wet, due to their cold contents warming. Fruits and vegetables were fine, but the individual containers his mother left him for dinner were ruined.

All the precious remaining cold air drifted out, curling around his bare legs. With the lids on, no one would have noticed the smell, but Jamie did. Unlike Saturday morning when his mother served him the soup cold... this was worse. He could have forced himself to eat it cold, but not spoiled. This was beyond what he could stomach.

Taking out all seven containers, Jamie closed the refrigerator and placed them on the kitchen countertop.

What can I do... Jamie numbly let his gaze wander from the containers to the outside through the window above the kitchen sink. *There were other things in the house I could eat, can goods, but... nothing which would do anything to help me.*

Turning, taking off his sweater, Jamie draped it on the back of one of the kitchen chairs, along with his long sleeved shirt, until he wore nothing but his short skirt—which Jamie hiked up a little higher. His undershirt tank top showcased his slim waist and fake boobs.

Walking out the back door, Jamie looked up at the darkening sky. There would be no moon tonight. These days of the month Jamie hated the most—the absence of the moon's calming soft glow, just darkness when the lovely silver, glowing disc disappeared to sleep, three days of worrying, three days of praying until it came back.

Jamie shivered when the beginning of the October night's slight chill whispered across his bare skin. Darkness came faster as he stood there. Jamie desperately wanted to call Catherine—the only time Jamie willingly ever wanted to talk to the woman—and ask for her advice, but he couldn't call them, and even if he could contact them, doing so while hungry wouldn't be smart.

His jaw and teeth hurt. His fingernails…

It's more dangerous being next to me then whatever headhunter is out there looking for us right now.

Looking at the gate covered in shadows from the moonless night, Jamie walked over, opened it and stepped out.

Walking away from the house, Jamie took only the darkest paths. The pale glow of candles from the power outage lit the windows of the homes he passed by. The more Jamie walked, the darker it got.

Nothing but sweet darkness all around him.

Soon Jamie heard footsteps behind him.

Glancing over his shoulder, Jamie's breath caught in his throat when he took in the description of his sidewalk partner. Quickening his steps Jamie dashed to the right, down the dirt path that would lead him in the direction of the old playground he took Asa to on Sunday.

Jamie heard the man chasing after him and picked up his pace, running faster. He just made it to the play structures when he was tackled from behind and rolled over. Striking his fist up, Jamie caught the man on the nose and heard him curse.

"Stupid bitch. Fuck it. I plan on getting out of the city tonight so a little bit of blood on your body won't matter much."

Jamie couldn't feel the man as he squeezed his fake breasts, but being so close to his face, Jamie could see the blood on the stranger. The man attempting to rape him. Jamie blinked when those black droplets fell on his face, and breathed in its coppery scent.

Fresh blood dripping on him…

"You bitches think it's alright to dress like whores and walk around as if it's nothing. It wouldn't take nothing more than a strong burst of wind for your skirt to flutter up, and I'd see your ass. Chicks like you beg to be treated like this."

Hands ripped Jamie's tank top and reached under his bra to feel the flatness of his male chest, the same time as a drop of his would-be rapist's blood dripped into his gasping mouth.

"What the fuck? You're a bo—"

The man didn't get to finish his outraged sentence, as Jamie overpowered him. Permanently silencing him and his discovery.

Screams of terror turned into ghastly wet, gurgling sounds piercing the night before even they were cut off.

* * * *

Running, Asa checked his wristwatch,

bringing it close to his face so he could see it clearer in the rapidly darkening skies.

It was almost twenty minutes to six. His father should have just made it home from his trip, and he didn't want to be late welcoming him back, even if his father couldn't have cared less if he was there to greet him or not.

When he'd opened up to Jamie, Asa hadn't told him the full truth about his situation at home. Oh, he told him a good amount of it, but not everything. Asa heard the unspoken questions the pretty petite boy wanted to ask. Like would it be worth staying for the money his mother left him, and why he didn't call out to someone other than his father for help... but strangely Jamie hadn't asked. Of all the things Asa had stumbled on about Jamie, the boy hadn't pressured him to tell him *all* his secrets.

Secrets... Asa wasn't new to them. As a child, he had kept a secret from his mother. His father had been having an affair with the very woman he was married to now. The only reason it took so long for them to get together was because she had been joined in matrimony to another man. And from the things Jake said to him, her kids knew all about his father, just as Asa had known about their mother.

Asa couldn't just up and run away or go to the police, because of the conditions his mother had placed in her will—the main being he had to live under his father's roof. If he broke any of them he'd lose all the money and continue to be under the mercy of his father, trapped in that house until he graduated from college and found a job...

His mother stipulated his father would be forced to take care of Asa until he completed school, and if not, even Asa's father wouldn't get one cent of her money. Every last dime would be turned over to various charities.

But if Asa held on, kept his head low he'd receive his inheritance in less than eight months. Asa tried balancing a part time job before. Tried to save money should he need the funds to run if things got worse. His stepbrother's orders to be home right after school got Asa fired, ending his plan.

Asa hated his father's actions. The man basically signed over his parental responsibility to Asa's stepbrother. Jake controlled so much of Asa's life already, but his father still paid attention, if only to complain about Asa's grades. Asa hoped his father never completely turned away from their relationship, because that meant Jake would take full advantage of his power if Asa's dad abandoned all authority. Asa stumbled at that frightening thought.

Anger filled Asa as he picked up his pace again. His childhood had been bleak. No affection from this father, and his mother showed him she cared only when his father hadn't been around to see. The pathetic amount of love caused Asa to stay close to his mother, and in doing so cemented the impression with his father that Asa was weak like his deceased mother.

Her will had been a blow to Asa's pride, because her conditions begged Asa's father to acknowledge him. However, his father would never do so, and all she succeeded in doing was caging him, chaining Asa to a family who didn't want him.

Asa saw disgust in his father's eyes whenever the man looked at him. He didn't understand why his father hated him, a feeling Asa had felt for as long as he could remember.

Unwanted, unloved, Asa could care less, or a least Asa tried to convince himself he didn't care. Yes, being rejected so openly by his father hurt, however, time dulled his pain.

Asa dealt with the cold shoulders, the dismissive glances, and the passing hurtful comments used by his father when comparing Asa to his mother… but to ignore what his new stepson did to his own child hurt most of all.

Asa told Jamie about getting beaten by his stepbrother, which hadn't been a lie. If he ended up being more than a minute late, Asa would get the shit kicked out of him. But his stepbrother did try not to hit his face. Asa risked running to Jamie's house after Jake put his hands on him only because his father would be returning tonight. Jake's abuse stopped when their parents were home.

Reaching his house, Asa checked his watch again as he bent at the waist to catch his breath. Five minutes until six. His father should have only been home for a few minutes. Smoothing his windblown hair back and pushing his glasses up firmly on his face, Asa opened the front door and walked in.

"Hello? Dad?" Asa called out. The entry hall was dark. No luggage or sounds of his father or stepmother talking... just silence. "Dad?" Asa called out again as he slowly made his way into his house. A bad feeling passed through Asa when his calls went unanswered and he began to back up, retracing his steps back to the front door.

"Leaving so soon, little brother?"

Spinning around, Asa's heart felt like it wanted to run away from him with as fast as it pounded in his chest. "Jake... w-where's dad? He came tonight, didn't he?" Asa asked his stepbrother, who blocked his way to freedom with his big body.

"Clark? He came home a few hours ago; came back on an earlier flight." The corners of Jake's lips lifted in a cruel twist of a smile.

"Did he already head off to bed?" Asa asked, the bitter, but familiar, taste of fear filled his mouth and sent his body trembling whenever he saw Jake. "Is he upstairs?" If his father was in the house then Asa would be safe from his stepbrother.

"He left," Jake said.

Asa began to back away. "Really? T-to where?"

"Well, if you'd been home right after school like you were supposed to be, then maybe you would have found out our *father* was called away with mother to go back overseas."

Jake matched each step of retreat he made with one of his own.

Asa didn't mean to be late. Ethan had been waiting for him after his last class, and had taken him somewhere private, and cornered him. Ethan wanted more details of his relationship with Jamie, not having bought the lies Asa told him that morning. The strange 'friendship' Asa had with the posh, too-handsome-for-his-own-good jock wasn't really a friendship he'd ever been in before. Asa didn't know what to call Ethan.

One particularly bad day, a couple months back, Ethan helped Asa with a few immature students harassing him. They'd dumped soda down his back and Ethan chased them off. Asa thanked him and escaped to the restroom to clean himself up.

Asa had just taken off his shirt and turned around to grab a few paper towels, when he saw Ethan out of the corner of his eye. Ethan had stood there looking at the damage done to

Asa's body from his stepbrother's beatings. Since then, Ethan wouldn't leave Asa alone. Always finding ways to be near him, touching him, and in most cases Ethan would kiss him. Like today, for the first time, Ethan—while Asa protested—gave him a hickey—

Asa gasped in pain, holding his hand on his throbbing cheek from Jake's slap. So caught up in the heat of his memory of Ethan, Asa didn't see Jake about to strike and didn't block the hit.

"Pay attention when I talk to you!" Jake shouted.

"Sorry," Asa whispered, wiping the blood from his cut lip.

Frankly, it was good his father never called him, never thought to inform him he'd be leaving again. Not that Asa wouldn't have appreciated a warning, so he could have steered clear of going home, but because Ethan had taken his cell phone.

"I called you."

Oh no. Asa fearfully looked at Jake, and what he saw made him turn and run to the backdoor, in the dining room. Asa didn't make it. Strong arms wrapped around him and threw him onto the dining room table.

"So who is he? Who the fuck answered your phone?" Hissed Jake.

A sad little whimper escaped Asa as he was repeatedly slapped across the face, but he fought when he felt Jake's rough hands begin tearing at his shirt.

"What is this shit?" yelled Jake.

Asa cried out when his head was yanked back, baring his neck to be better inspected by his stepbrother. Exposing the love bite Ethan had given him.

"So you have someone on the side," stated Jake.

"No, you're wrong," Asa gasped, his eyes tearing from the grip tightening in his hair. "He was just messing around, causing trouble for me."

Which was true; Ethan didn't know everything about the beatings or the rapes. Asa made sure to use the excuse of getting picked on to explain where he received his bruises if Ethan saw them, and asked.

"Did you like it?" Jake asked.

"Don't Jake," Asa rasped, as his stepbrother's hand reached down to his belt and began unbuckling it. "Stop, please, Jake!" Asa's struggles increased as his pleas were ignored, and very quickly his pants and underwear were pulled down his legs and his thighs were forced apart. "Remember what happened the last time? You beat me so badly you almost had to call an ambulance!"

Asa thought he would die that night. His life might be shitty, but Asa didn't want to die, so he learned quickly not to fight back when Jake came after him. Taught himself to take the beatings, because Asa knew he wouldn't get help from anyone, but from the look on Jake's face right now, Asa saw he was in for a hard night.

"If you harm me too badly then my father—"

"Clark has given me permission to deal out your punishments as I see fit. He wants nothing to do with you."

The pain Asa thought he could no longer feel toward his father stabbed at his heart. Flinching under the hot body laying over him, Asa cleared his mind and stared up at the ceiling as Jake ground his pelvis onto his bared lower half.

"Put your arms above your head and keep them there until I tell you otherwise," Jake ordered.

His face throbbing from the blows he'd received, Asa, trembling, did as he was ordered to do, and in the process his hand grazed over the decorative vase which normally adorned their dining room table, somehow saved from being knocked off when Asa was thrown onto it.

"Running off and spending the weekend

at a girl's house. Staying out past your curfew. Allowing a strange boy to answer your cell phone, *and* daring to flaunt his mark on your body to me, are all things I'm going to punish you for," said Jake.

When Asa tried to protest, Jake cruelly pinched the hickey Ethan playfully made on his neck making him cry out in pain.

"Do you really think Clark, or even my mother, would protect you from me when you returned?" Jake laughed cruelly.

Stretching slowly, Asa reached above him until his hands wrapped firmly around the vase.

"Before this night is through, you'll learn never to test me," stated Jake.

With all his might, Asa brought the heavy vase down over Jake's head, closing his eyes tightly to protect them as shards of glass flew around and on his face, and with a grunt from Jake, Asa suddenly became pinned down by his stepbrother's dead weight. Struggling to heave Jake's body away, Asa succeeded with much effort, panting as he pushed Jake off of the dining room table with a loud thud.

Groaning, Asa sat up. His battered body protesting with every movement. Peeking gingerly over the side Asa gave a half-sob, half-sigh of relief when Jake didn't move from the position where he crashed. Asa, mindful of the glass, got off the table and fetched his discarded pants from the floor, pulled them on, and pocketed his underwear.

Touching his face Asa hissed at the pain, and withdrew his hand to see blood on it.

"Asshole," Asa whispered as he jogged over to his school bag, picking it up as well as grabbing a jacket from the coat closet and putting it on to hide his ripped clothing.

Stepping out into the night, Asa began running toward the only safe haven he knew of—Jamie's house. The first time, when Asa found out where Jamie lived, he'd been shocked at how close they lived, and yet Asa never saw

Jamie around… not that Jake allowed him to leave the house after he got home from school, nor was he allowed to go out on the weekends.

The night so dark without the moon's light to shine down on him, Asa didn't see Jamie on the other side of the road coming in his direction until he passed him. "Jamie?" Asa gasped, trying to catch his breath when he stopped. "What is he-*she* doing?" The fool boy was walking around in a scandalously short skirt and a tank top. On a night like this Jamie had to be insane if he thought he wouldn't get assaulted, and with a lunatic killing women on the loose—

Asa narrowed his eyes when he saw a large shadow following not too far behind Jamie.

"Jamie!" Asa yelled, but Jamie didn't hear him, and Jamie actually looked over his shoulder at the man following him before he dashed into the bushes.

The stranger followed quickly after

Jamie.

"Idiot!" Asa hissed. Why would he run off into the bushes!

Running across the road, it took Asa a couple precious minutes to locate the path Jamie ran down in the dark. Thrashing through bushes and falling into dips in the dirt path, Asa stumbled and fell into the clearing of the playground.

Pushing his battered body up, Asa faintly made out figures on the ground near the swings he and Jamie had played on yesterday. Asa wanted to rush over, but the unnatural sounds coming from the figure on top of the other, the wet sucking noises and tearing made Asa's steps hesitant as he made his way forward.

"Jamie?" Asa quietly called. The closer he got the more he could see the person, the girl, who he'd been positive was Jamie when he chased after him. Yet, Asa couldn't be sure anymore... The girl, she had long blonde hair, not brown... but she was wearing the same clothing he had seen Jamie in when he'd taken off.

"Jamie?" Asa called again, only a foot or so away from the two people on the ground. The girl's body blocked whoever she sat on, but Asa could see the form under her twitching. But the sounds Asa heard... he'd read and watched too many shows not to know the sounds he heard were death rattles.

That alone should have been more than enough to scare Asa and send him running, but it was the growls which kept Asa frozen in his spot. Asa's last call out had stopped the girl from whatever she'd been doing above the man. Asa held his breath only to release it in a rush of relief when the face that swung toward his direction was Jamie's. However, his relief was short lived as Asa took in the sight before him.

Jamie's mouth along with a good portion of his face was covered in blood and his eyes shined back at Asa with a reddish glow like those of an animal.

Whatever Asa looked upon had Jamie's face.

Asa stepped cautiously backward when the blond spun around and snarled, crouching almost protectively over the man.

Breathing hard, Asa took another step backward then froze when Jamie's impostor crawled off the body and toward him. Blood covered the front of the girl's... male's chest... Asa's eyes shot back up to the blond's face. It was Jamie! But the Jamie who stalked Asa— wearing a feral expression and covered in blood—looked at him as if he didn't recognize him.

"Jamie? What's wrong with you?" Asa whispered, backing up faster. "It's me, Asa."

Jamie came at him even faster, and against better judgment, frightened beyond anything that ever scared him before, Asa turned and ran, and for the second time that night was taken down by force and flipped onto his back.

"Jamie! Jamie! It's me, Asa!" Asa

shouted.

Asa thought he had finally gotten through to the boy when Jamie paused above him, but that hesitation lasted only until Jamie's eyes zeroed in on the bleeding cut on his lip at the corner of his mouth. "Don't Jamie…"

Screams erupted from deep within Asa as Jamie snarled, and the blond struck. Asa choked as pain filled his body, felt teeth tearing into his flesh.

CHAPTER 6

September 1st, 2010

When I wrote and said I only feared two things, I lied.

I have a third fear. Myself.

I tremble in terror over myself more than hurting my mother or my father finding me.

In all those towns and cities we'd run from, it wasn't just because my father found us, but also because of me. I couldn't control the hunger that started when I was eleven, in the first town we tried to hide in.

The hunger... It started as just a twinge, a little voice inside you that says 'I need food'. I don't know how it happened, but when I saw my mother beaten, bloody, and in tears on a hospital bed because of the man who wanted her money, her car... something in me went crazy. My mother hurt in that kind of way, the woman saved me and stood beside me all this time, even though a mad man was after her because of me.

I didn't have trouble finding the carjacker. All I wanted to do was confront him and... and I'm not sure what I wanted. I don't even know how I found him in the first place, or why it'd been so easy for me to find him, but I had, and I'd lured him away from the bar he'd been about to enter.

It had been just my luck the prick had been a pedophile and one interested in doing sick things to little boys. I'd gotten into his— our—car. The day had turned into night and I remember how he'd driven me to the edge of town.

That's where I killed him.

There'd been no moon, just the beauty of the night, black as death, all around us. I remember how cold it'd been, only because of the steam from my breath. I didn't remember feeling it. All I felt was the burning in my gut, the hunger that had been rising within me.

I don't remember how I killed the

stranger. My mind consumed with making the howling for food stop, by the time I came back to my senses I found myself in the backseat of our family's station wagon, straddling the stranger, covered in blood... staring at the mangled mess under me... and noticing parts of the stranger were... missing.

The gnawing in my gut had disappeared by the time the man stopped twitching. It was only when I had begun licking my fingers clean of his blood that I'd realized what I'd done.

I was a monster.

I remembered how my father had done the exact same thing the night he'd killed Lisa.

My belly full of the man who had harmed my mother, who falsely thought he could harm me... I sat there and felt not one ounce of guilt for what I had done. Not about killing him or eating *him*.

I felt... nothing.

Covered in blood... I loved it, the feel of its warm stickiness on my skin, the sweet taste of *his flesh on my tongue. I loved it all.*

And it scared the shit out of me...

Under the moonless night I ran back to town with speed no normal human could run, and with eyes that could see in the dark just as well as if I were seeing in the day. I raced home and tried to sneak into our rental house, but got caught by Catherine. I'd been scared of what she would do. If she would condemn me, since it was obvious from my appearance I had done something seriously wrong.

But she didn't.

Catherine looked at me and told me she'd get rid of my bloody clothing while I took a shower. And when I was done, to come down to the living room.

I thought I was a freak of nature as I stood under the hot spraying water, watching the blood wash down my body and whirlpool down the drain, looking at my hands with nails that could only be described as claws.

Washing thoroughly, I quickly dressed

and nervously went downstairs as I was ordered to do, where my mother and Catherine waited, hands clasped in their laps. But instead of disgust, I saw... understanding...

What they said to me rocked the very foundation I lived and breathed on. They said outrageous things you would only read about or see in a movie; things that made me feel more alone than I ever felt before... but then they told me something else that floored me. Turns out I'm not a unique little freak after all.

Because there are more like me out there...

A lot more.

* * * *

"You bit me..."

"Could you please shut-up already? You've been repeating those same three words since I nipped you ten minutes ago. I told you I was sorry! Geez! Cut a guy some slack, would you?" Jamie mumbled.

He did feel bad for attacking Asa, but Jamie's guilt faded six 'you bit me's ago, "You know you're also to blame for this. If you hadn't interrupted me, called out to me, then I wouldn't have attacked you."

"You seriously cannot be placing the blame for *you* attacking *me* onto *me*!" Asa hissed.

Dropping the legs of the guy he just killed, Jamie put his hands on his hips. "I *said* I was sorry, damn it! Jesus Christ, how long are you going to continue complaining about it! I'm *sorry*, okay? I'm sorry I bit you," Jamie said.

"Not just bite," Asa said, as he struggled to hold onto the upper half of Jamie's victim. "You. Tried. To. Eat. Me!"

"If I tried to eat you, like you're complaining, then you would have more than teeth marks on your shoulder. Don't make me regret not finishing the job, okay? It was a mistake! I was in the zone when I went after you." Jamie leaned down and picked the dead man's legs back up. "Get over it already."

Asa stared at him in disbelief. "I caught you eating someone, and you want me to forget about it? Oh, and by the way, you totally looked like a chick with your hands on your hips just then."

"Shut up, Asa, and keep moving toward the trees," Jamie hissed. Weird, but Jamie wasn't overly concerned that Asa found out about him. Oh, he should be scared, and maybe, to a certain extent, he was… but after biting Asa, that fear of discovery had… disappeared. Jamie didn't understand why his fear of Asa knowing his biggest secret went away.

The first rule Jamie learned had been to never let anyone see him after he'd changed. Accidents happen, and he'd been seen in his true form before. Experience had shown Jamie that people tend to shit themselves and call the cops when they saw creatures like him, something obviously not human, or they start shooting—

something Jamie found out for himself one scary night after surprising a farmer in one of the small towns they lived in briefly.

What made Asa so special? Did Catherine see this coming? Did she know Asa would react like this if the boy saw him change? *Why the hell wasn't Asa freaking out?*

Jamie lived a strange life, and he learned the craziest things about himself that weren't normal, but the one solid thing which never changed—humans. Yet, Asa, and the guy's strange-tasting blood threw all of what Jamie thought he knew about humans out the window.

"So... what are you?" Asa asked him.

"A meat Popsicle," Jamie sarcastically replied, using one of his favorite lines from the movie The Fifth Element.

"Are you going to tell me?" Asa asked, slightly breathless.

"Now is seriously not the time, Asa?" Jamie said, cursing when one of the severed arms they'd poorly tied to the corpse, fell off the body.

"Stop! Don't kick it along! Pick it up!" Asa hissed.

Grumbling under his breath, Jamie kneeled and picked up the bloody arm, and slapped the limb back onto the mutilated torso.

"And I think now is a great time for you to tell me! Considering everything I've been through and seen *and* the fact I'm helping you get rid of the body!"

"Keep your voice down, stupid!" Jamie dug his clawing into the corpse's legs to keep from dropping them.

Hissing at Asa to stop, Jamie cocked his head to the side, listening to the sounds of the night. Heaving a sigh, Jamie glared at Asa after confirming the coast was clear of humans.

"I'm not asking *you* questions, am I? I'm not asking *you* why your face is all messed up or why your clothes are ripped. Why can't you give *me* the same courtesy?"

"I don't know... maybe because you

tried to *eat* me!" Asa snapped back at him.

Jamie halted Asa by a large tree surrounded by tangles of prickly bushes, a few feet from where Jamie killed the man. Far enough away someone walking past would never notice if the ground had been disturbed.

Hanging around the playground as much as he did, Jamie knew in the daytime the tree gave off an ominous feeling with its twisted branches and shadows, which made humans wary and unconsciously shy away from walking too close, making it the perfect hiding spot to get rid of the body.

With a little heave, Jamie and Asa released the dead man with a wet thud. Then leapt away when the severed limbs rolled off the corpse toward them.

Kicking the limbs out his way, Jamie glared at Asa. "I didn't try to eat you, damn it! I gave you a little nip on the shoulder. It's not like I took a chunk of flesh!" Getting on his hands and knees next to the corpse, Jamie began to dig the soft earth with his claws.

"This is not a little nip!" Asa exclaimed.

Jamie glanced up and flinched, noticing how large the wound was on Asa's shoulder. The guy's coat and shirt had been completely shredded by his claws. "It's not even bleeding anymore so why are you bitching?" Actually with his night eyes, Jamie saw how gruesome the wound really was. It should have still been bleeding, but wasn't. Another strange thing Jamie could add to his list about the boy.

"What if you've turned me into one of your kind?"

Jamie expelled a little 'piff' under his breath. "What the hell do you think I am? A werewolf? Do I look all fuzzy to you or have you seen me once howl at the… well, there is no moon, but you get my drift."

"Then what are you?!" Asa demanded.

Jamie stood up swiftly, a growl rumbling out of his throat, and he had to give Asa credit, because not once did Asa flinch away in terror from him. "You wanna know? Fine. My 'kind' come from a world far, far away and we landed here unknown to the human race hundreds of years ago. We were hungry. A group of travelers had awoken our hive ships on our world before the humans on other worlds we feed from had a chance to repopulate, so we began to starve. We normally feed by pressing the flat of our palms onto the human bodies, preferably their chests, but I was too hungry to do that. Satisfied?" Getting back onto his hands and knees, Jamie went back to digging.

"Satisfied? Sure, if you didn't just describe Wraths on the fucking show *Stargate Atlantis*!"

Jamie chuckled. "Dork. You know, I liked you better when you pretended to be a shy and *quiet* boy."

"Sorry, but nearly getting eaten has a way of freaking a person out, and makes them ask questions!"

Jamie threw a handful of moist black dirt

at Asa, catching him in the face and making him sputter. "Shut up! God, I can't take your whining anymore. Why don't you try helping me dig a shallow grave for this asshole so I can go home and take a shower! I may not be a girl, but shit, are you just going to stand there and make me do this all myself? What kind of man are you?"

"One that was almost eat—"

"Eaten. Yes, yes, cry more. You're beginning to make me regret snapping out of my feeding frenzy and not killing you." Jamie stared at Asa, who squinted his eyes in the dark, trying to stare back at him. "Well? Are you going to help me or not?"

"I can't believe I'm doing this," Asa muttered, kneeling next to Jamie.

"You are, so shut up and start digging." Aside from his annoyance, Jamie couldn't help feeling happy. Maybe because he was full for the first time in a long time, and the fresh blood and meat were making him stupid and lightheaded, but once again he was glad Asa knew about him and more importantly hadn't run off screaming after witnessing his dark need. But Asa's easy acceptance confused Jamie… and frightened him too.

"Why aren't you going crazy over this? I would have thought if anyone discovered my true secret they would be calling the FBI on me or something," Jamie curiously asked after five or so minutes of them digging in silence.

"I'm still in shock," Asa answered.

"I *am* really sorry I tried to kill you," Jamie said sincerely.

"Are you really a natural blond?"

Of all the things he asks about and it's this. Jamie shook his head, laughing a little. "Yes, I am, and I can show you my short and curlies if you want proof."

Asa rolled his eyes. "I think I've seen enough of your true self, thank you very much."

Jamie snickered. "Let's just get this done and get back to my house. I don't know how much longer it'll be before the electric company will get the power back on, but I, for one, do not want Mrs Davis seeing me like this and setting off the neighborhood alarm."

"Umm... can I spend the night, the next few nights actually, at your house?" Asa asked.

Stopping Asa from digging, Jamie got out of the hole. "Throw his arms in first," Jamie ordered, wiping the sweat from his brow with his forearm. "Then push the rest of him in."

"Why don't you do it?" Asa asked, grimacing at the bloody corpse Jamie motioned him to.

"You want to say at my place, don't you? Freeloaders shouldn't bitch, so grab his frickin' arms and throw them in the hole!" Jamie hid his face, not that Asa could really see him in the moonless night, but Jamie didn't want Asa to see how relieved he felt that Asa wanted to stay over. Jamie also wondered if he'd accidentally hit Asa on the head when he tackled the boy to the ground.

"Bitten, beaten, and nearly raped, and

now I have to grab your victim's dismembered body parts? You owe me big for this," Asa grumbled.

"I'll let you sleep on the bed tonight, how about that for helping me?" Jamie hadn't missed the 'raped' part of Asa's mini-rant, but pretended he did.

All joking aside, forcing Asa to do most of the work with throwing body parts in the grave wasn't to torment Asa, but because he was guarding the boy. If Jamie was right, then he wasn't the only predator out stalking the night for food.

"I need help with the rest of him. He's heavy," Asa panted, holding his wounded shoulder, and wincing in pain. "I can't do it by myself."

Scanning the area, Jamie nodded and quickly helped Asa drag his wanna be rapist into the shallow grave, then covered it up with the dirt they'd removed, added fallen leaves, branches, and anything else they could find, which included a smelly, dead squirrel to top the dirt mound.

"What if he's found? What if they find your DNA and stuff all over him?" Asa worryingly asked, dusting dirt off his hands

"Look," Jamie sighed, "there's nothing I can do about that right now, and it's not like they can pin this on me if they do find the body. If they *d*o, then it's not like they'll think a sweet and petite little girl, like me, could've done anything like this to a large strapping man like him. You saw him. Who would think it was anything else but an animal attack?" Jamie slapped Asa on the back. "Let's go already. I wanna take a bath."

"Wait… what if they find something of me on him? Like hair, or sweat or something?" Asa said, panicking.

"Than you're pretty much screwed, aren't you?" Jamie dodged when Asa tried to hit him, and then, snickering, ran to the path leading out of the playground with Asa chasing after him.

Even though Jamie played it off as if it was no big deal, he didn't plan on leaving the body there, but with as much noise as he and Asa were making Jamie couldn't afford for them to linger. The park was abandoned, but it was human nature to investigate when something piqued their interest, no matter how dangerous it might be for them. Jamie didn't sense anyone around them right now, but it didn't mean someone—or *something*—wasn't around.

Jamie had been careful not to show it to Asa, but he could have slung the body over his shoulder and took him miles away, dug a deeper grave so the asshole was never found again. Making sure no evidence was left behind too. However, Jamie hadn't wanted to freak Asa out. It was already unnatural, the calmness the boy showed over everything he'd just witnessed.

With the moon gone and the streets void of light from the power outage, getting back to his house went without incident. Jamie and Asa were sneaking into his backyard, the gate having been unlocked and left slightly open from Jamie's earlier departure. They'd just closed the tall wooden gate door when the streets filled with light from the street lamps.

"Good timing," Jamie said, smiling at Asa. Thankfully Jamie's backyard was dark and filled with trees and tall shrubbery, hiding them from any nosy neighbors who might be looking out their windows.

"I don't know about good... I think you need to go and look at yourself," Asa said, his face pale.

Jamie frowned. "Do I look bad?" Jamie figured he'd look awful.

He drained the blood from his victim, but in his haste he'd severed the guy's jugular with his fangs before he'd gotten a good lock on his head, spraying his face and chest with blood before getting his mouth over the puncture marks. Jamie's arms were covered up to his elbows with a mixture of dirt and blood, as was the rest of his body.

"Well... no one would ever vote you to be prom queen with the way you look now." Asa smiled.

Curious, Jamie motioned Asa to come in as he opened the backdoor leading into his family's small humble kitchen. Then alone, Jamie went straight upstairs to the bathroom. Flicking on the lights, Jamie squinted against the brightness, then his eyes widened. He stared at the image in the large mirror hanging over the bathroom's double sinks.

The dye in his hair completely faded away—as it always did when he changed—and the brown contacts of his were also gone, lost somehow, so his green eyes shone unnaturally back at him. Blood, twigs and leaves tangled in his wild mane and, if he looked closely, his eyes resembled more of a cat's or a snake's with their vertical slits.

But it was the amount of blood coating Jamie's face, hands, and body that stood out most obviously against his pale alabaster skin;

blood so thick some of the ghastly trails from his mouth were so dark it appeared black. Jamie's ripped shirt he'd tied in a knot to try and cover his chest, and lack of breasts joined the horrid sight. Some of the stranger's blood had flowed down his chin to his chest, and some of it was still wet. The red glistened frighteningly in the light.

"How the hell could he look at me and not run away?" Jamie whispered, depressed. Jamie had long ago accepted what he was. Not much he could do about it. Just as he accepted the only people who would care for him as his true self would be his mother... and Catherine. Jamie had almost ten years to come to terms with the fact he wasn't human, and whatever it is that he was, his nature wouldn't allow him to deny his hidden beast.

Turning on the shower, Jamie stood there with his hand under the spray waiting for the water to warm before peeling his sticky clothing off his body. "I shouldn't have worn my good skirt," Jamie mumbled.

From the moment he knew the criminal was in the vicinity, Jamie premeditated his hunt. He could have locked himself in his room and handcuffed himself to his bed to keep himself off the streets. He'd done it before, gone hungry until dawn broke and the hunger subsided. But he hadn't and now he'd have to burn his good skirt because of his lack of willpower.

Stepping into the tub, Jamie moaned in pleasure at the hot water shooting over him. Looking down he smiled at the red water that pooled at his feet, knowing it was sick to find enjoyment in thinking about the kill he made, but past caring about those kinds of thoughts. The man he killed hadn't deserved to live. Jamie could smell it in the wind and when he bit into the man. Jamie had gotten a good look at the guy when he'd been held down. It had been the same sex offender from the flyer, down to the scar on the man's neck.

Jamie regretted nothing. Not the kill or

horrible pain he'd inflicted on the stranger before stealing his last breath. Whenever someone evil came near Jamie, his hunger rose to a dangerous level. People said evil doers were rotten to the core, but it was the exact opposite for Jamie. Just like the man he killed, they smelled delicious. Jamie's mouth watered just thinking about those faceless people.

In the beginning he'd been scared and sick of what he was. In the beginning. As the months and years passed, Jamie accepted his 'differences', and even secretly delighted in the change. He considered himself a dispenser of those whom would do harm to the innocent. Okay, mostly it was because his mother kept telling him that. Jamie never hurt someone who didn't deserve it… except the one time he'd attacked his mother…

However, besides that one time, and counting Asa now, Jamie never attacked a clean soul. And it wasn't as if he went out at night and stalked people that needed to die. It was as if

Jamie drew them to him. Just like with the criminal who tried to assault him. The moment his teacher announced someone was roaming the streets, stalking and killing woman and had been seen near their location, Jamie knew he would be seeing the stalker really soon.

Jamie unknowingly called them to him. He didn't know why or how, but it's a problem his family dealt with everywhere they've tried to hide. In those small towns he'd lived in, men and women flocked to him, and trying to hide their bodies became an issue, since in small towns everyone knew everyone, and if one of their own went missing, a red flag immediately shot up.

Larger cities were easier. Murders happened on a daily basis... it was just when Jamie's victims were found, it shot up another red flag, another clue to their location for his father to come find them. How many times do you see 'Wild Animal Attack' in a big city where there were no animals besides poodles and other small household pets?

Grabbing the shampoo, Jamie squeezed a generous amount in the palm of his still bloodied hand, and massaged it on his head. Jamie washed his hair a few times more than normal, as he also did with his body. Scrubbing his skin until the blood, dirt, and grime was gone, and his flesh stung and turned a dark pink.

Jamie turned off the shower and stepped out once the water became cold, wrapping his hair, and himself, in two fluffy black towels. Getting a spray bottle filled with bleach from under the sink, Jamie covered his mouth and nose, spraying the tub and tiled walls. Then unscrewed the top and poured the remaining liquid down the drain.

Exiting the bathroom, Jamie stopped by his bedroom to throw on a pair of pants before heading downstairs. Jamie heard Asa tinkering around in the kitchen as he descended.

"You haven't called the X-Files on me yet, have you?" Jamie jokingly called out at the foot of the staircase, before entering the kitchen.

"Did you know almost all your food in the fridge is bad?" Asa said, standing in front of the refrigerator.

Exhaling the nervous breath he'd been holding, Jamie smiled. "Yeah, I know. We have an account with a grocery store that delivers, so we can call and put in a small order. I don't have very much money, but I have enough to order a pizza for dinner."

"You can *not* still be hungry," Asa said in disbelief.

Jamie rolled his eyes, shaking his head. "It's for you, not me. I'm full."

Jamie finally saw a normal reaction from Asa as the boy looked away from him with a disturbed expression on his pale face. "I can't believe how… callous you are about this. You just killed someone, and you act as if you don't care."

"That's because I *don't* care," Jamie bluntly, coldly, stated. "My 'victim' was the person responsible for killing women in the city, and he'd chosen me as his next death date. If I could kill him over again, I would."

"Have... have you done this before?"

Jamie pulled the towel turban off his head. "A few times," Jamie admitted, scratching the back of his neck. "But they were all *very* bad people."

Asa's eyes widened. "Jonas... Jonas was killed by a wild animal in that park two years ago. Did you do that?"

Jamie nodded. "That was me. Asshole just murdered two innocent girls and was going to get away with it. From the smell and taste of him, it hadn't been his first time doing something evil."

"But they caught the animal that killed him. It was some guy's mean dog. They found parts of Jonas in the dog."

"Ponchi, yeah, he was with me, and we dined together." Jamie grinned when Asa shuddered.

"So you do this all the time? Lure people to a dark place and eat them?"

"No!" Jamie denied. "I've only killed truly bad people. Jonas was my last 'victim', before my mother found a way to stave off the hunger."

"Stave off the hunger?"

Jamie motioned to the containers he'd left on the countertop earlier. "She makes 'tomato soup' for me every week. It used to be every month, but as I got older my… appetite has grown." Jamie watched Asa curiously open one of the containers and then quickly seal it back up.

"That's not tomato soup! It's blood and raw meat!"

"Mother's special chunky tomato soup for her Jamie," Jamie said, shrugging sheepishly. "Mom has a deal with someone at the slaughter mill to give her cow's blood, pig's blood, anything they kill that they don't need, and deliver it fresh to her. Well, not to her personally, but through different contacts and such." Jamie sighed. "It's a lot more hush, hush than I'm making it out to be."

"How do I know you won't kill and eat me later?" Asa asked him with a suspicious tone. "How do I know you didn't invite me back here because you might want a snack later?"

Jamie snickered. "You don't, *but* rest assured, I don't want you in *any way*. You tasted funky, which is the reason why I didn't do anything else but bite you. Don't get all insulted," Jamie said when Asa stiffened. "You should be happy your freaky flavor repelled me and I 'woke up'."

"Why did I make you sick?"

"How about you tell me why you were in the park this time of night?" Jamie didn't want to talk about himself anymore, even as liberating as it felt to talk to someone not in his family about his secret, he didn't have the answer to Asa's questions, or the answers the guy would ask for if Jamie tried to answer them.

"Does the reason have to do with those bruises on your face? I know they didn't come from me tackling you." The side of Asa's face looked painful. The corner of his mouth, cut and swollen, stained with fresh blood.

Poking at Asa, demanding non-stop, Jamie cheered when Asa's shoulders drooped and he began talking. However, the more Asa talked, the higher Jamie's anger rose with every hesitant word that passed the boy's lips. Jamie already knew Asa had problems at home, and getting his ass kicked by his stepbrother wasn't a small thing... but getting sexually abused... was something Jamie hadn't been expecting.

"Ahhh, Jamie? Your *claws* are digging into the table..."

Jamie blinked in surprise. "Oh! Shit, my mom's going to be pissed." Jamie retracted his claws from the now ruined wood.

"You lost the fake ones..." Asa said, pointing to Jamie's claws.

"Umm, Yeah. Whenever I become like

this, I change back to my original coloring, and form. Another reason why we don't use the expensive stuff to dye my hair brown... although Catherine will be pissed when she finds out I lost my contacts," mumbled Jamie, shrugging.

"Change back...?" Asa said weakly.

"So what are you going to do, Asa?" Jamie asked darkly.

"Huh? Oh, ahh, nothing. I promised you I wouldn't say anything, even if my promise was only when I found out you were a boy. I'll hold true to my word though," Asa said quickly. "I won't say anything to anyone."

"I'm not talking about my secret. I already knew you wouldn't say anything," Jamie surprised himself just as much as he did Asa from the startled look Jamie saw flash across the guy's face.

Sure, he'd known to some degree Asa wouldn't say anything, which made Jamie feel comfortable opening his mouth... but only now, after he said it out loud, did Jamie actually believe it.

"I'm talking about your father and stepbrother. What do you plan to do about them, and the shit they're doing to you?" Jamie wanted to help Asa in any way he could.

He couldn't help but feel... responsible for the guy, but Asa's father wasn't a nobody, Clark Jacobs was a high profile businessman, so was the brother. Both were people Jamie couldn't risk confronting, and killing them was out. Hanging out with Asa, Jamie could bring unwanted attention to himself if he killed them and the murders would bring the media. His actions with Asa this morning brought enough attention already.

Asa shrugged helplessly. "I'm... I'm not going to do anything. I can't. If I make any waves I'll lose the inheritance my mother left me, and I'll be stuck under my father's thumb until I finish college, who will probably turn me completely over to Jake so he can 'keep an eye out' on me."

"Kids run away all the time, Asa. Is money so important to you, you'd let yourself be abused?" Jamie shook his head, wondering where the hell the kid's mind was to think cash was so important he'd stay in that house.

"Yes, it is... I'm not greedy or anything, but I know I'll need money." Jamie watched Asa's brows furrow in frustration as he spoke, tried to explain. "If I run off then how will I live? Where will I sleep? How will I buy food? As much as I want to get away, I know I won't last long without funds. I don't have friends I can turn to, and I'm not some streetwise kid who could survive out there in the real world."

Jamie grimly agreed. He'd had nothing but hardship in his life on the road, but he had his mother and Catherine next to him. Asa had no one. "You're right... a pretty boy like you wouldn't last one night out on the streets. *But...*" Jamie grinned wickedly. "You could blackmail your father."

"What?"

Jamie flipped his wet hair over his shoulder. "Think about it for a second. You could tell your dad you'll make a huge scandal about what your brother is doing to you and—"

"*Step*brother—there is absolutely *no* blood relation," Asa stated firmly.

"Sorry. Anyway, you could bluff and say you'll call the press, the cops, whoever, because you're sick and tired of what John—"

"Jake," Asa corrected.

Jamie glared at Asa. "Who cares what the prick's name is, just listen without interrupting me. As I was saying, you can tell your father the only way you'll shut up is if he gives you the same amount of cash your mother willed to you—money you'll sign over to him once the 'cha-ching' your mother left comes to you, the moment you turn twenty-one.

"You can stay with me and my mom... although we probably won't be living in this city for very much longer..." Jamie hated leaving when he was so close to graduating, but the danger if they stayed might be too high.

Asa stared at him in silence for a moment before saying, "You're leaving? Why?"

"I'm not one hundred percent sure but I think more of my 'kind' are at our school... I can't take the chance they know my father." Jamie tried to convince himself what he'd seen had been just a trick of the light, but he would be foolish if he ignored Aidan's eyes. Those pale yellowish-green eyes... they were like his were right now. Not human.

"... I think I'll take you up on the offer to stay with you but as for my father... I-I need more time to think about... blackmailing him. I can't make such a serious decision without..."

"It's cool. No rush." Jamie smiled, stopping Asa from trying to struggle and explain his reasons.

The last thing Jamie wanted was for the kid to start freaking out about his situation with his family, afraid Asa would transfer over to realizing what he'd seen and done to help Jamie.

Jamie waved the taller boy away. "Go take a shower, Asa, there should be hot water now, and afterward I'll bandage up the cut on your shoulder."

"It's a bite, not a cut. You bit me."

"Don't start that again!"

* * * *

"The one destined for me was here. They fed," Aidan whispered, staring down at the blood stained grass of the small secluded playground an hour before dawn, "Returning to the very place that turned my attention to this city two months ago." Aidan looked up to his loyal servant. "Why has no one found them yet?"

Ethan bowed his head. "I'm sorry, your highness, but Mr Leviance has been less than cooperative in helping us locate his offspring. He's yet to even confirm if his child, your intended, is male or female. The only thing he's reluctantly given us is that his child is in this city."

Aidan's pale yellow-green eyes narrowed. "It has been two months, Ethan. Two months I have been forced to mingle with the stench of our prey on my skin."

"What of Janis Yamil? I sensed your interest in her yesterday morning, a reaction you would not have normally expressed physically if she was not the one," Ethan carefully said.

The powerful animal in front of him had been hunting for the alpha's mate. A mate, whom they'd discovered ran away with its human mother, and been missing for nearly eleven years. Once informed of his runaway bride, Aidan began his search... with no success, and they didn't have very much time left before they would be forced to go back home.

Ethan worried Aidan's temper would get the better of the great animal, so Ethan, with the other servants, did all they could to keep Aidan calm.

"She was nothing but a waste of my time." Aidan growled in annoyance. "The human came to me, repeating words I already knew about a certain girl I'd taken an interest in. Even though I knew this, she smelled... delicious."

So much so Aidan had forgotten himself, and pinned the human girl's willing body against the wall, kissing her. However, the more Aidan kissed Janis, the more the tantalizing aroma he'd smelled on the girl faded, and the need which had set his body on fire died. Until the other girl appeared. The scent on Jamie Dexson had been so strong Aidan stood there in shock, and his hesitation allowed the girl to escape his grasp before he had a chance to grab, and test her.

"So she wasn't the one?" Ethan curiously asked.

He'd been serving under Aidan's house, as well as his family, for generations. Born with noble blood, Ethan and Aidan were childhood playmates and for the past seven hundred years, Ethan stood next to Aidan as his highest ranking warrior at the shifter's side. Their personal history aside, Ethan knew better to test the powerful being before him, especially with matters of Aidan's lost mate.

"No," Aidan coldly replied. "Janis fooled me by consuming blood from one of our kind, but where she got the blood is still a mystery."

Aidan failed to comment how he'd smelled the same mouthwatering scent on Jamie. Thinking maybe his wish that Jamie would be the one he had been searching for clouded his judgment. The main reason Aidan and his servants attended the human school was because of his interest in the girl. But no matter how much he wished, the girl smelled wholly human... Except for yesterday morning.

"Unbury the body and dispose of it properly," Aidan ordered, bringing himself back to the task at hand. "It wouldn't do for this little neighborhood to find another human brutally murdered in this area, nor would it be good for us if it was accidentally stumbled upon by one of our kind living in this world, hiding themselves amongst the humans." Aidan wasn't the only one looking for the Leviance child. Other great Houses wanted the baby, be it for ransom or to beget a child from her or him, so the urgency to find his mate was vast.

Ethan nodded and ordered the two silent shadows with them to do as Aidan commanded. "We could be wasting our time here. It *has* been two months, and not once have we found anything to lead us to believe they are here. The kill now, and in the past, could've been from a rogue, the location of this kill a coincidence." Ethan didn't want to leave, not when he had someone who interested him here, but the words he spoke were expected to be said. Being Aidan's friend, Ethan was the only one who could say them without being harmed.

"Aidan," Ethan said, dropping the

honorific once the lesser servants were out of hearing distance. "You've been on this plane too long. Your leadership is being challenged. This is the second passing of the moon sleeping on this world, and signals our time here is nearing the end. We will be forced to depart once it fully appears again, or we will be trapped here for years before we can go home. It might be best, and I am saying this as your friend, if you went back first to handle the whispers before they become more than just rumblings in darkened corners."

Aidan leveled Ethan with a savage look. "They can try to remove me from the throne, Ethan, but they do not have the power to do so, even if all my advisers joined together. If they could overthrow me, they would have done so a long time ago," Aidan retorted as he bent down to look at something that caught his attention in the grass. "Time, on our world, passes slower than the fast pace of the human realm. The next safe passage will not open for another decade in human years. Finding the Leviance child is the only thing important to me right now. He or she will be turning twenty-one soon, so I have precious little time left before Harris can file his request to cancel the marriage contract."

"Allowing him to come in with the full protective power of his own people, this will effectively keep you and anyone else seeking Harris's offspring away." Ethan didn't understand how the seers, who'd seen the Leviance and Montgomery houses joining hands and alliances, hadn't foreseen the child's mother running off... or had they and this was one of their spiteful little games?

"Good things in life aren't free, Ethan. If they were, then I wouldn't be as strong as I am now or have had to fight to keep my throne and kingdom safe." Aidan lifted a piece of cloth off the ground and stared at it. "Tell me, Ethan... you checked out Jamie Dexson's residence... how many times now?"

Ethan shifted from foot to foot; nervous

as he always got whenever *that* girl's name was mentioned. "I've circled her home numerous times, but not once have I seen or felt any evidence she is anything other than what she appears to be."

Aidan rubbed the pleated piece of cloth between his fingers. "So you've never actually been in her home and investigated?"

Ethan began to deny Aidan's question, but slowly closed his mouth when he realized he'd never once actually gone into Jamie's home. He'd never taken a look at her personal effects, or breathed in her private sleeping quarters to see if her scent could be anything other than human.

"No… I've never been in her home." Ethan frowned in confusion. "I don't know why I haven't either."

Aidan brought the small torn cloth to his nose and inhaled, holding the scent in, allowing its flavor to soak into his senses like that of a fine wine, before tucking it into the breast pocket of his jacket. "Time is of the essence. I can't sit back and allow others to search while I do nothing."

"You're not doing *nothing*, Aidan. You cannot afford to be caught if anything goes wrong. You are portrayed as a wealthy young human. Your face and name is known far and wide in this world right now, and if these humans discover you are essentially *hunting* for your mate, the repercussions could be dire." The danger would be toward the human reporters who would search for Aidan's mate, not understanding the wrath which would rain down upon them if they scared the girl or boy, forcing them to go deeper undercover.

The servants with Aidan were gifted with the strongest magic, and placed safe guards around Aidan to contain their lord's powerful aura, but nothing was a hundred percent, and the power contained within Aidan was of a magnitude needed to be controlled at all times, meaning it wasn't safe to allow Aidan to become overly excited. Even hunting, Ethan needed a group of their strongest shield weavers just in case Aidan lost control in a bloodlust.

"As for Jamie, I don't understand why I've never entered her home, but she's proven to be nothing but a regular *human* girl. There is no need to continue watching her." Ethan knew it didn't matter what he said. Aidan had been infatuated with Jamie from the very beginning.

Aidan looked at Ethan. "She smelled like one of us this morning, Ethan. That alone is more than enough reason to seek her out."

"Are you sure? Please, don't misunderstand me, Aidan, but are you sure it's not just wishful thinking on your part that makes you want Jamie to be the one?" Ethan knew all about wishful thinking.

He had Asa Jacobs's cell phone in his back pants pocket, and been harassing the boy every chance he got since he'd seen Asa undressing in the restroom at school after a few human males ruined the boy's clothing with a beverage. Even now, when Ethan knew nothing could come out of the touches to Asa's skin he gifted himself with, because he couldn't take Asa with him when he went back home, Ethan continued finding ways to be alone with Asa. He couldn't help himself. There was something about Asa Ethan couldn't put his finger on, but also made him want to tie the boy to him even more.

"She's not like the rest..." Aidan looked up at the rapidly lightening sky. "Have they disposed of the body?"

Looking behind him, and receiving a nod from the silent servants, Ethan said they had.

"Then come, we are close to Jamie's home. We can put to rest once and for all if she is nothing but an oddity amongst the rest of the prey walking around us." Aidan started off, leaving the blood stained mess on the ground to be dealt with by his servants.

Both walked, with the eerie silent

footsteps of their kind, the short distance to the Dexson residence. Just as before, Ethan saw nothing to lead him to believe everything wasn't as it should be.

"How far have you gotten in exploring her property?" Aidan quietly asked, gazing up at the darkened windows.

"I've..." Once again Ethan couldn't give Aidan an answer. He should have been able to tell Aidan he'd searched every inch of the house, but when he thought about it, all Ethan could say is he had only looked from where they were standing now.

"It doesn't surprise me you can't feel it," Aidan said with a trace of humor in his voice.

"Oh?" Ethan asked, slightly unnerved by Aidan's sudden change in attitude.

"There are wards everywhere, powerful ones, protecting the house. The magic from the wards are great, focused on hiding itself from creatures like us. If it had been anyone else but me, they would have felt nothing and passed by." Aidan brought the torn piece of cloth out from his inner coat pocket. "Do you recognize the pleated design of this material?"

Ethan took the cloth. "No."

"Smell it. Whose scent do you smell?" Aidan asked, smiling.

Ethan brought the cloth to his nose, instantly recognized the scent of the dead man they'd removed from his shallow grave... but it also smelled like Jamie. "It can't be. We've— *I've* been close to her from the very beginning. She's never shown signs of being one of us, and if she's been hiding what she is, we would have seen protective amulets, bracelets, rings, something that would have repelled us from her."

"Unless she is powerful enough that she doesn't need such trinkets while she's awake, but sleeping... when she is at her weakest, there would be a great need for such things," said Aidan, venturing as far as he could onto the girl's property. "Look." Aidan pointed to the mail box, to the painted stones at its base. "Mage symbols written on the rocks warn others away. Orange calcite, from a witch, surrounds the house with protective energy. Even the wind chimes hanging at the porch also have charms keeping us away. They are everywhere." Aidan smiled. "Now, why would a normal human girl have all these protective talismans around?"

Excitement burned through Ethan's veins, and he could also see Aidan was similarly pumped up. "How do we get past her safeguards? If we use brute strength, then everyone within a hundred mile radius will know you found something, and they will all come running." The last thing his lord needed would be a magical siren screaming out, warning others Aidan had found something.

"We will wait until she leaves the property." Aidan took one last look up at the windows before turning away and motioning Ethan to follow.

"This little girl's been keeping secrets,

and I will find out what they are."

CHAPTER 7

September 5ᵗʰ, 2010

Forgive me for skipping out on writing in you, but I've been busy. I spent the week going out with my mother. Every chance I get I try and do something with her, spend as much time as I can with her. I guess you could say I'm trying to do my best to be a 'good' son. Lord knows, with all I've done, I need to do as much as I can to keep her from hating me.

Why? Besides the killing, and turning into a blood crazed monster? Because I bit my mother once... I never, ever, thought I would attack my mother. However, one night under the effects of a new moon, I did.

It was an accident. I was young and couldn't control myself or my hunger in the beginning. You see, people who sin have a seductive, delicious scent and flavor which is unbelievably irresistible to me.

My mother isn't evil; she's a wonderful mom—brakes for animals, and smiles a lot. She's a nice person but she isn't as innocent a soul as I'd tried to convince myself. A slight scent of wickedness came off of her. Older now, I still cannot imagine what kind of sin—not counting my already married father—my mother could have committed to make me see her as a meal. After all, every child comes into this world believing their mother is an angel.

How does that quote go? "Mother is the name of God on the lips and hearts of all children." That's the saying, right?

My mother loved to tell me I'd been given a 'gift' to be able to see evil in people and the power to 'do away with them'. I really don't think she meant herself when she said those words to me.

All people sin, whether it's shoplifting, cheating on their lover, or for the more serious crimes of armed robbery, rape, and murder. Even so, there are 'acceptable sins', but at eleven years old I couldn't distinguish between the moderate and the extreme.

Once we found what triggered my desire for blood and flesh, Catherine trained me, worked with me to overcome my need to feed. Yet it still came as a shock to me when I suddenly lunged at my mother.

The older I get the more the hunger within me grows. It happened on the first moonless night in the first city we moved to. I changed and... hurt her...

The agony I saw in her eyes, the look of... such pain... the shock slapped me back to my senses.

Since then my mother and Catherine have taken a trip, somewhere far away, until the effects of the new moon didn't affect me so strongly. Catherine planned it out so my mother couldn't call me, which she's tried to do in the past. I'm stronger now, but it isn't safe to assume I'll be of sound mind when the moon sleeps. That I wouldn't try and track them down.

I don't think I would... but then I never thought I'd try to kill my mother either.

Mary is *my mother, but for some strange reason I'm not a half-breed... I'm not half-human but a full blooded monster.*

I wrote in one of my entries how one of my fears is hurting my mother. I wrote that because I almost killed her... I'd gone straight for her throat, and if Catherine hadn't been there I would've succeeded.

Catherine hit me and I bit into my mother's arm instead of sinking my fangs into her throat.

There'd been so much blood...

It'd taken almost two months before the wound healed properly. You wanna know the worst part about the whole thing? My mother blamed herself. She said she felt she was to blame because she hadn't put my needs first which led me to attack her. To make matters worse, when I got pissed, I started yelling at her, making her cry...

Guilt sucks. Instead of calming my mother's fears, I added to them by losing my cool. At the time, the horror of being a freak, of hating what I am, I took it all out on her.

Here I am, a monster, something people fear and would try and kill. But to her, my mother, I'm not some grotesque creature. She's blind to the fact I killed people, that I take their flesh into my body for nourishment and drink their blood to quench my thirst.

She loves me, her murderous freak of a child. My mother accepts me as I am, not the person I'm pretending to be, and I'm scared of losing her affection, her acceptance.

I could have left, gone off on my own a long time ago, but I'm scared I will never find the same sort of freedom to be who I really am if I leave home. However, I can't take the chance I'll lose control and hurt my mother again, so after I've fulfilled my promise on graduating, I'll leave.

I take it one step at a time. One day at a

time. I try not to let my fear control my life, but I know I will have to leave as soon as I can, because with each hour the hunger grows, and one day I know I won't be able to keep it leashed.

* * * *

Yawning, Jamie poured himself a glass of orange juice, and gulped it down. They'd gotten groceries delivered last night, so the refrigerator was nicely stocked. Scratching his head, Jamie sleepily poured himself another glass and sat at the kitchen table.

"You're up early. It's still dark outside. Are you going to school today?" Asa asked, shirtless, entering the kitchen.

Grimy eyed, Jamie watched Asa rummage though the refrigerator a minute before answering, "Yeah, I'm going to school. Changing my routine after feeding is never smart. 'People' might be watching, and might get curious as to why I'm absent, doesn't matter if the body of my victim pops up or not. What about you?" Another reason Jamie woke up before the ass crack of dawn was because he needed to move the body before people began their day.

Asa pointed to his face and said, "Go to school looking like this? I don't think so."

"Oh yeah..." Jamie mumbled looking at Asa's smooth, unblemished face. A face no longer marked by his stepbrother's cruelty. "It wouldn't do for you to attend class looking like you did a few rounds in the ring." Jamie lifted the glass with a shaky hand, taking a sip. "Not if you want people pointing and asking you about your wounds." Jamie panicked, wondering what he'd say once Asa saw the discoloration and swelling had magically disappeared.

"And also... I plan on calling my fa-father and telling him to give me the money my mom left me."

"So you really plan to do it? I was just

spewing ideas out." Jamie glared at Asa when the guy took his cup and drank his juice, emptying the glass. "Why don't you get your own?"

"There's nothing left." Asa grinned, handing the empty glass back. "You put the empty container back in the fridge."

Jamie grunted, and laid his head on the table. "I'm still tired... I couldn't sleep on the damn air mattress."

"You offered me your bed," said Asa.

"Yeah, but I didn't think you'd be such an ass that you would take it," Jamie grumbled.

"If you were a girl then maybe I would have done the gentlemanly thing and let you have the bed, but you're not."

"Whatever..." Standing up, Jamie eyed the wide bandage on Asa's shoulder. "We should change that," Jamie said, and patted the chair he'd just vacated, telling Asa without words to take his spot, before going to the cupboard above the kitchen sink, getting the first aid kit.

"Surprisingly it doesn't hurt at all," Asa said, rolling his shoulder.

"Maybe it's because I killed all feeling on your wound when I poured peroxide on it last night. I swear, people may think I'm a girl, but the way you screamed, I'm starting to think you are one too." Jamie laughed when Asa pushed up his glasses with his middle finger, like he did the last time when he couldn't vocally tell him where to shove it.

"Anyone would have yelled like I did," Asa pouted.

"You didn't *yell* out, you *screamed*." Jamie snickered. "Your voice was so high-pitched the dogs in the neighborhood started howling." Setting the supplies on the table, Jamie gently peeled the tape holding the gauze in place and froze at what he saw.

"Tell me when you're done. I don't want to see it," Asa said, turning his head away, closing his eyes.

"Ah, sure. I'll tell you once I'm finished." Jamie tried to keep his voice calm as he possibly could as he looked at the completely healed wound. The bite was nothing but a pink, puckered scar, and Jamie had a bad feeling even that would fade away until nothing but smooth skin remained... just like his skin when he cut himself.

Another thing worried Jamie... Asa's scent had changed... the guy didn't have an earthy tang humans normally had, and Jamie tried not to panic at what that could mean. Jamie wondered when Asa's scent had altered. Last night, he'd been covered in dirt and blood, then after all Jamie could smell was bleach from spraying down the bathtub. Jamie remembered smelling something strange when he woke up, but hadn't thought much about it.

"Are you almost done?" Asa asked.

"Umm... almost..." Jamie didn't know what to do.

Should he say something to Asa now, or

ignore the problem until the boy discovered it on his own, because in all honesty, this was new to Jamie. He'd bitten people before and nothing like this happened. For one, the people he bit never lived, but there'd been the one time he'd bit his mother... although nothing like this happened...

Wiping the scar with alcohol swabs, Jamie taped a new bandage on Asa's shoulder then patted him on the arm to signal he was done. "How does it feel?"

"Strange... but besides the cold of the alcohol it wasn't painful at all." Asa smiled.

I'll bet. Jamie winced. "Good. We wouldn't want the wound to get infected and have to send you to the hospital." Yeah, that would never happen anyway, Jamie nibbled on his lower lip, eyeing the bandage, while wishing Catherine, and what information she had of what he was, were here right now. Jamie had a few days before they came home, and of all the days he needed to talk to Catherine, he had no way of contacting her.

"So are you still planning on going to your house to get your stuff?" Jamie took his empty glass over to the sink.

"I might go later today, if not, then tomorrow. Jake leaves at nine everyday, but with the way I left him last night, I don't know if he'll actually go to work today."

"Do you want me to come along?" Jamie asked turning on the faucet, washing the glass and putting it on the counter. "You might need me... you know... just in case he's still there, even if you don't go today."

"No, I think I got it. I don't know why but I feel good and strangely not frightened at all when I think about Jake."

Jamie turned and looked at Asa. "Seriously?"

"Yeah." Asa grinned. "Not that I want a confrontation with him or anything, but I... I can't explain it." Asa looked at Jamie and shrugged.

Jamie laughed nervously. "Well after what you went through, it would be kind of f-funny if you got scared, right?"

"Are you feeling okay?" Asa peered at him in concern. "You've been acting strange since you changed—"

Jamie rushed Asa when the boy suddenly shot to his feet, grabbing Asa's hand when the guy reached for the fresh bandage on his shoulder. "Dude, I just changed that. You don't want to mess it up right after I fixed it, would you?" Jamie silently cursed at how whiney and completely unconvincing he sounded.

Asa's eyes widened more by Jamie's words and he struggled harder to get his hand free from Jamie's grasp. "What's wrong with it?"

Eating from a fresh source, Jamie's strength could easily bench press a pickup truck, so Jamie could've restrained Asa or popped him softly on the chin, knocking him out cold to keep him from looking at the wound, but instead

Jamie let Asa go and stepped back. The boy was going to find out sooner or later anyway.

"First, I have to say nothing—and I mean *nothing*—like this has ever happened to me before..." said Jamie, trying to sooth Asa just before the boy ripped off the bandage.

"Oh my God! What did you—how did this happen?" Asa shouted, touching the puckered scar.

Wringing his hands, Jamie shrugged his shoulder. "I don't know."

"What do you mean you don't know?" Asa cried.

"It means exactly that! I don't know!" Jamie shouted, then calmed when Asa squatted, holding his head in his hands. "Look, we just need to bunker down here until my mother and Catherine come back. They'll know what to do." Jamie was prepared to tie Asa down if necessary. He didn't know why the guy's wound healed faster than it should, but there could be no way *he* had changed Asa. "You need to stay here, Asa."

"You think I'm stupid?" Asa glared, his eyes glimmering with tears. "Of course I'm staying here! One, I got no money, and two, what if you turned me into a werewolf! What if I end up killing and eating some innocent person tonight because I ran away from here?"

Jamie backed away as Asa shot to his feet and began pressing forward, pointing his finger accusingly at him.

"You're taking responsibility for this!"

"Taking responsibility? I didn't get you pregnant for crying out loud! All I did was bite you, nothing else!" Jamie smacked Asa's annoying finger away from his face. "This has never happened before, okay? You're not the first person I've bitten, and this," Jamie waved his hand at Asa's shoulder, "never happened to them."

"I'm a werewolf…" Asa whined.

"You're not a werewolf, damn it! I'm not a werewolf so that means you're not one either!"

Jamie began rethinking his idea of not knocking Asa out the more the boy opened his mouth.

"Then what are you? If you're not a werewolf, then what could you be?"

"That part is kind of hard to explain..." Jamie muttered, but he saw Asa wasn't paying any attention to him.

"I know... you're some kind of mutated vampire or-or maybe a demented fairy..."

Jamie raised his eyebrows at the "demented fairy" comment. "I'm no fucking fairy," Jamie growled, insulted.

"Then what are you!"

"I'm not a fucking fairy, I can tell you for sure, and you..." Jamie took a step closer to Asa, reached up and grabbed him by the ear, bringing Asa closer to him. "... need to keep your goddamn mouth shut. You're screaming like some hysterical bitch who's just caught her man in bed with her best friend! My place isn't soundproof! People will hear you!" Not entirely true, but Jamie decided to keep that a secret.

Charms and magical stones protected the house from outsiders hearing anything from within.

Jamie thought quickly. "Look, there is one way, a test, which I can do to see if I turned you into what I am."

"How?"

"I met up with my father some time ago. It wasn't a happy reunion. My father told me about it when he taught me how to hunt a few years ago." Jamie ignored Asa's question.

Jamie didn't lie, but he wasn't telling the truth either. His father did tell him if he ever stumbled on a situation where a *human* victim of his became strange, there was a test he could do on the person. Jamie never had to do it before, but he could safely say Asa was strange, as was the wound he gave the boy.

However, being told what he needed to do and what he'd discover when he did the test, were completely different when it came down to actually doing it.

"Then do it!"

Jamie made a face. "You're not going to like it…"

"I don't care! Just do it!" Asa shouted.

"Okay… but I want you to remember it was you who insisted." Jamie reached down and grabbed Asa's wrist.

"So, you never said how you'll do the test," Asa said nervously.

"Oh, you'll find out in a second," Jamie mumbled as he extended his claws. "Now you'll feel just a pinch, but don't worry."

"A pinch?"

Before Asa could blink, Jamie slashed downward, slicing open the boy's arm and quickly brought the bleeding forearm to his mouth, deeply drinking the salty, sweet hotness gushing out. Pulling back, Jamie rushed and grabbed the dish towel hanging on the oven rail, wrapping it around Asa's arm. "Well the test is all done," Jamie said cheerfully.

"Huh..?"

"You look a little pale, dude…" Jamie

barely had time to leap out of the way before Asa fell forward, crashing onto the floor in a dead faint.

* * * *

"You're a vampire... a blood sucking vampire." Asa scowled at the insane, human eating blond as Jamie rolled his strange cat-like green eyes at him, while packing a Ziploc baggie full of ice for Asa's head, which he'd introduced to the table before nose diving it into the floor.

"I walk out in the sun, remember? I'm not a vampire," Jamie replied.

"Edward is a vampire, and he could walk out into the sun," Asa grumbled, swiping the bag from Jamie's sharp nailed hands warily, holding it to his throbbing forehead.

"I'm not a vampire and besides, I'm more of a Team Jacob fan." Jamie suddenly laughed. "Team Jacob, get it? Jacob, Jacobs... ahh, you're no fun."

"Yes, yes, my last name is Jacobs, wow," Asa said dryly.

Not wanting to be labeled as a panicky bitch, Asa tried to keep his fright contained but he was scared. The horror he'd felt when he'd seen Jamie eating the man last night had magically disappeared. Asa's worry came from his easy acceptance of Jamie *not* being human, and how his fear seemed to have vanished *after* being saliva mauled by Jamie.

"I know. You're a mutated vampire-werewolf slash fairy." By the agitated expression on Jamie's face, Asa knew his questions tested the blond's patience, but his *need* to know had little to do with knowing if he was some kind of supernatural being.

Asa admired Jamie. The closer to Jamie he became, the more Asa wished he could become brave like the guy. Because if someone like Jamie could bravely face day after day going to school hiding what and who he truly was, while also living his life with a mad man trying to kill him, then Asa could strap on a pair and face his troubles with that same kind of courage. But the lack of fear he felt now about being different, like Jamie, wasn't normal. Asa's anxiety came from the unknown, his worry that his new fearlessness wouldn't last beyond today.

"I'm not a goddamn fairy!" Jamie growled, snapping Asa's attention back to the conversation.

Asa eyed Jamie's short stature. "You sure?"

"Asshole, you better not say it," Jamie warned. "And if I were a vampire then you'd be my turned child, as would you be if I were a werewolf, which all equals to me *owning* your ass! I'm just... a little different from you, that's all."

"You certainly are a *little* different from me." Asa snickered when Jamie glared at him.

"You want me to slash you again? I can, you know. Just make one more short remark."

"I didn't think you'd be that sensitive about it," Asa muttered, cradling his arm to his chest.

"I'm a fucking bundle of insecurities."

Asa shot Jamie an astonished glance. "Why would you be?" Asa glowered at Jamie when the guy gave him an 'Are you stupid' look.

"Once again I have to wonder how the hell your grades are as high as they are, or are you just book-smart? I dress like a girl, and not only do I get away with it, I get away with it too easily! My voice isn't deep enough, my Adam's apple isn't pronounced enough that anyone would notice, and to top it all off, I'm short!"

"Keebler elf short—I'm hurt!" Asa shouted when Jamie growled inhumanly at him and started forward with his claws extended. "I'm just joking. Haven't you ever had a friend who joked around with you?"

"No… not really…"

Asa fidgeted uncomfortably when he saw the fleetingly sad expression flash across

Jamie's face. "Ah, so anyway, you haven't told me about what the sucking-my-blood thing was about." Asa, not used to comforting someone else since he'd never gotten any growing up, changed the subject quickly. To his relief, Jamie happily took the out he gave him, saving Asa from apologizing for his unwittingly hurtful comment.

"Someone told me if I ever bit someone and they didn't heal normally, then I should drink their blood," Jamie said nonchalantly.

"*And*?" Asa stressed when Jamie didn't explain any further.

"*And* the person I bit, their blood would taste different."

"Couldn't you just have bit me again with your fangs instead of scratching me with your dragon claws?" Asa testily asked.

Jamie chuckled. "Biting you was the start of the problem, wasn't it? What if nothing was wrong with you, and I bit you again and something happened?"

"So you knew something could have happened the first time?"

"No."

Aggravated, Asa said, "But you just said you could have *infected* me the second time if you hadn't the first time aground."

"Did I?" Jamie cocked his head. "I don't think I did, and I don't have the answer you need anyway so there's no point in asking."

"Getting information out of you is like getting your wisdom teeth pulled out without any novocaine," Asa angrily said, as he unwrapped the bloodied towel from his arm and whimpered when the claw marks were already closed up. "I'm a freak..."

"Psh, no, you were already a freak long before I came along." Jamie laughed.

Asa glared. "So do I taste different than I did last night?"

"Do you ever! Last night you tasted like rotten meat, add the image of maggots and that's what your flavor is like. You're not exactly pure—" Asa frowned, confused as to what Jamie meant by that comment. "But you are enough to taste nasty. The flavor of your blood now… it tastes wrong… like family, one of my own, you know? Umm… it's like cannibalism or something. It's hard to explain, damn it!"

"I'm maggot meat…" Asa didn't know whether to laugh or cry

"*Rotten*, maggot meat, don't forget." Jamie cheekily grinned.

"Thanks, I wouldn't want to forget that," Asa muttered, rubbing his woundless shoulder.

"Be thankful," Jamie told him. "Your blood kept you alive so think of it as a compliment."

Asa numbly stared at Jamie.

"If you'd been a bad boy, you would have lost your life. I wouldn't have been able to stop myself with giving you just a little nip. Anyway, I need to get ready for school; let's get your shit from your dad's house later today."

"You want to come? You don't need

to…" Asa planned on going home alone.

Asa was scared of what might happen if Jamie and Jake met face to face. The rage Asa witnessed in Jamie's cat eyes when he'd whispered his troubles with his stepbrother, more than concerned Asa. Asa hated Jake, feared him, but imagining his stepbrother being ripped apart like the stranger Jamie killed last night. Asa shuddered. Despite his antipathy toward Jake, Asa didn't want him ending up in an unmarked grave.

"I can go alone."

"*And I* think it would be best if I went too," Jamie said. "There's no telling what kind of trouble you'll get yourself into if I'm not there to babysit you."

Asa thought fast. "B-but, do you think it's wise? Leaving the house looking the way you do, you're bound to attract a lot of attention." Asa had done his fair share of staring at Jamie's blond locks and animal eyes the night before, thankfully without Jamie noticing. "You look nothing like you did with brown hair. And your eyes… plus, it's still dark outside. Aren't you going a little too early?"

"Not a good idea to stay home after the first night of a new moon, remember? Besides, I do this all the time. I've been doing this for the past ten years—four of them as a girl, Asa. I can't dye my hair until the moon comes back because the dye will just burn away like last night. I have a wig. There won't be a problem," Jamie said, waving away his concern.

Asa cocked his head, trying to picture Jamie in a wig. "I don't know… you might still be noticed. You have this *glow* to you that makes you noteworthy, someone who would receive a double—no—triple glance."

"Aw, are you saying you think I'm hot?" Jamie teased.

"No. Only that your freakiness will be easy to point out in a crowd." Asa could see the mayhem Jamie would cause on the streets.

The way Jamie now looked was

unearthly. While Jamie made a very pretty brunette with brown eyes, he became a hundred times more so as a blonde. And those eyes of his. All a person needed to do would be to look at them once, with their unnatural hue and the first thing that would scream in their heads is 'Alien'! Not to mention the feline slits of Jamie's pupils.

"Don't worry. I've done this hundreds of times. I might not know very much about what I really am, but what I do know how to do is get lost in a crowd," Jamie said.

"Getting lost in a crowd is one thing, but this is school. Our campus isn't very big, so the students always seem to know what you're going to have for lunch before you even know what you're going to eat." Asa shook his head. The guy didn't realize how much of a strong presence he had, or how much people looked at him.

"I very much doubt people care what I eat, Asa, but talking about food, I'm hungry. My metabolism is faster this time of the month so I need to consume a lot of calories."

"And if you don't?" Asa's curiosity ate at him. He'd never been interested in others, but Jamie wasn't just anyone.

"Then I'll be just like you and faint."

"I didn't faint! I just became lightheaded from the sudden blood loss!" Embarrassed beyond measure, Asa's face heated.

Jamie drinking his blood and not being disgusted or showing any kind of human emotion of revulsion had thrown him.

"Sure, buddy, just keep telling yourself that's the case and maybe it'll come true... oh, no, wait a minute." Jamie tapped his chin with his index finger. "I'll be reminding you about this for the rest of your life, so it won't ever come true for you."

Head trauma was the only thing Asa could think he sustained which would make him happy right now. *What nut job would be happy in my shoes?* Yet Asa was happy, and the sad part was he hadn't known what the warm feeling was, until he'd seen the look of enjoyment on Jamie's face.

"You're one strange duck, you know that, Jamie?" Asa smiled. "How can you be so cheerful?"

"Want to hear something funny?" Jamie said, looking at Asa with a serious expression. "I haven't been. Not the happy, jumping for joy kind in a long time. Funny, but the one thing I wanted was for someone to find out what I truly am, and then you came along. Besides your constantly nagging and annoying questions, you're turning out to be a good friend."

Asa beamed. "Looks like you got what you wished for."

"I think I got more than I asked for..." Asa ignored Jamie's mumbled complaint. "And, Asa, I wasn't lying when I said you *had* to stay here because when my family returns we'll probably leave this place... and you'll *have* to come with us. I don't know what I did to you, or what kind of change you might be going through to make you heal so quickly, but from this moment on, I'm responsible for you. Until me and my family can determine what I've done, for your safety and to those around you, you can't stay in this town."

Asa didn't say anything for a minute. "I know, and I'd already decided I would go with you... but... will I have to kill and eat people like you do?" Asa got nauseated just thinking about it.

"I don't know. What part of 'this has never happened before' did you not get?" Jamie said. "But let's say you did have to 'eat' the way I do... then you might not stop like I did with you, and you might end up killing an innocent person... so I'm asking you, Asa, to stay here, just bunker down until I get back. Don't leave the house. Going to school might not be a good idea for me, but I need to confirm something."

"I'll stay here," Asa lied.

Deciding to run home once Jamie left to

retrieve a few of his things was the only way Asa could be sure to bypass the potential danger of having Jake and Jamie meet face to face. But Asa had every intention of returning. Where else could he go anyway? From the way his stepbrother isolated him, he didn't have any real friends. Jamie's house was the only place Asa could return to.

A thought popped into Asa's head. "You said there are more of you out there, and from the tone you'd used they sound dangerous, very dangerous. Shouldn't we leave to find your mom now? Why risk staying here?" If Asa had a psychotic father after him and other non-vampire, werewolves, demented fairies sniffing around, then he wouldn't want to stay out in the open like they were.

"I can't go and find them. Not until the moon's returned. Just stay here. The only safe place *is* here. My family's learned a lot of things while we've been on the run. I've met priestesses and witches who've given us powerful safeguards, and taught us to write spells which we've carved into the wooden gates with protective symbols. Painted holy rocks and other stuff are littering the outside of the house, so if anything, this is the place you should run to if you feel something is wrong."

"What could go so wrong I would need to run back here to hide, and that's if I were to leave the house?" Asa had a bad feeling he wasn't going to like the answer he'd be told.

Jamie looked out the kitchen window. "I'm not the only predator out there, remember? And whoever they are, I don't want to bump into them."

Chapter 8

September 6th, 2010

We never talked about it, about me killing people and what goes on when I... eat them. She—my mother—pretends what I do when I run wild on moonless nights, when the need to hunt becomes too much for me to bear, doesn't happen.

My mother acts like I'm off camping or just off with friends—I didn't have any friends—and I'd pretend, for her benefit, that's where I'd be going when I left. This is before my mother found a perfect blood and meat mixture to keep me from going nuts.

My mother may accept what I am, and Catherine used to say my mother was just trying to give me privacy... but was she? There is only so much a human mind can handle without going insane, and her son eating people could be filed in the "Too Much to Handle" category.

I didn't kill every time the moon disappeared. That would have meant we had to move every month, and the stupidity of succumbing to the need only happened if I went completely cold turkey. And because I hated when we had to pack up and move to a different location, set up a new home, I made damn sure when I hunted, it was only because I understood my choice was either killing a criminal or possibly hurting my mom again.

I remember this one time we—Catherine, my mother, and I—got into a fight because I didn't come home for a full day. Mom had been sick with worry my father had found me, and killed me...

Well, she was right on the first part...

My father is a powerful man in the corporate world. I'd just taken down Mr Huntson—an upstanding citizen who loved to kill hitchhikers and campers as his hobby—when something had me spinning around and there he stood as if he'd always been there.

My dear ol' dad.

I never understood why Catherine and my mother told me my father wanted to kill me. It wasn't as if I had a big role in his silver spoon world. I'm his bastard son. Nothing more, nothing less. Household appliances have more use to him than I ever did. My father has my brother, Joseph, to take over the business, and Joseph is the one who will get everything when father passes on to the next life. I'm nothing but a mistake my father had taken responsibility for.

The only thing daddy dear would want to kill me for would be because I saw him kill Lisa... but even that logic had its flaws... but I'll get to that in another entry.

So I was crouched over the still warm body of Mr Huntson, and I could do nothing but stare up at my father. I instinctively knew I wouldn't be able to outrun him should I try, so I waited. Watching. Hoping I would live to see the next day.

And my subservient attitude might have

been the reason I'm still alive today... but it still left me confused whether my father really wanted me dead like I was led to believe, because that night I hunted again—with him. Not that I had a choice to say no. We stalked for prey farther away than I would have dared to go alone.

My father told me why I killed the scum of the earth, and why I left the innocents alone. He told me why the hunger within is at its highest on a new moon, and he also told me I needed to make sure I was never caught killing. Explained how I could expand my scenes to make sure no one is around, and how to hide my scent so others like us couldn't find me.

Then he told me if he ever found me again he'd kill me... effectively wiping out any confusion I might have had over him wanting me dead.

Greatest father and son bonding experience I ever had. Yay me, right?

His threats hadn't stopped with just me,

but extended to my mother and the "traitorous bitch" Catherine, saying he'd take pleasure in stringing them up by their ankles and skinning them alive while I watched, and once every last drop of blood had been drained from their bodies, then he would kill me...

He even took a swipe at me, catching me on the side, scoring a painful hit.

I don't remember how I got away or how I got home, but we left that town the moment my mom saw my wound.

But why? I still don't understand why my father wants me dead, and if he hated me, for whatever reason, why teach me how to hunt—to hide myself. Why not kill me right then and there? Why warn me?

I also wondered out loud to Catherine once—this is when Catherine and I could speak to one another normally, without fighting—since my mother isn't someone I can talk to about this. About why we never heard anything about Lisa's death. Why no one had said anything about her disappearance when my father was so media popular.

What Catherine said scared the crap out of me.

She said Lisa didn't exist in this world any longer—yeah, I know since she's dead—to the people in this world, it's as if she never was born...

I still don't understand though... Lisa is or was, someone's child. She's someone's mother... she was a fucking beauty queen for Christ's sake!

But Catherine had been right... when I looked up Lisa's name on the internet; there'd been no "Mother of" or "Wife of" etcetera. There'd been nothing about her at all. Just as Catherine said, it's was if she'd never existed.

There's so much about what I am that I have no clue about, and I'm scared my naivety will lead to my capture and maybe even my death. But who can I ask my questions to about this stuff? I know I was told there are more like me out there, but how can I find them to ask?

Catherine and I have a strange relationship where we fight every single time we are in the same room. Yet I rely on her a great deal, and when I have a problem she is the first person I'll go to, but she keeps secrets from me, and will tell me next to nothing about 'what' is out there and 'what' I am. She'll only tell me the things I need to know to survive. And even if I did find one of my kind, how can I know for certain I can trust them?

My father told me a lot of things, and from experience, with every change and every hunt, I've found them to be true... but how can I trust everything else he told me? Just believing anything *my father said is hard, especially after he made it clear he's going to slaughter me and my family.*

Who can I trust?

* * * *

"Jack be nimble, Jack be quick."

Doing a little hop-scotch up and over the neighbors' backyard fences hardly broke Jamie out into a sweat. He'd left the house a lot later than he'd wanted to because Asa suddenly broken out with a fever. It came so unexpectedly Jamie thought about calling for help, but Asa's mumbling of him being exposed to "Vampire cooties" and "Were-Cujo rabies" had been enough to slap Jamie back down to reality. If he called for help, how would he explain what happened to Asa? The hospital would take blood from the boy, and Jamie knew they'd find something wrong.

While Jamie leaped over another wooden fence and dashed to the other side with inhuman speeds, in an attempt to get to the playground before the sun rose, Jamie's mind became consumed with the frightening scene that happened only an hour ago. His playful bickering with Asa faded the moment Asa collapsed after Jamie told Asa there were others hunting the night besides him. Seizures had suddenly racked Asa's tall, slim frame and Jamie had stood there helpless. Once the attack passed and Asa lay on the tacky off-white linoleum kitchen floor, weak and sickly pale, Jamie had watched with growing concern when Asa shakily removed his glasses... and told him he could see better without them.

Jamie's flippant remarks and unconcerned attitude about the taste of Asa's blood came back to haunt him. "It's all fun and games, until your dinner entrée becomes your dinner partner, and your table for one becomes a table for two," Jamie grumbled to himself.

Grunting when he landed on the other side of the last fence, Jamie crouched low to the ground behind perfectly groomed hedges. Fixing his brown wig to stay securely on his head, Jamie peeked over the bushes and scanned the surrounding area. Seeing the coast was clear, Jamie took a deep breath. Pouring power into his legs, he leapt up and dashed across the street into the lush greenery on the other side with such speed everything around him seemed to freeze.

Keeping his pace, Jamie came to a grinding halt and sniffed the air a few feet away from the abandoned park. Cautiously, he tiptoed forward, going down on his hands and knees. Jamie crawled until he got closer to the clearing, ignoring the cold dampness of the earth soaking into his jeans.

Heart thundering in his chest, Jamie narrowed his eyes on the perfectly manicured lawn. The night before, the grass had been ankle high and over running with weeds.

Jamie circled around, slowly, and got close enough to where he and Asa buried his dinner, but saw nothing except smooth earth. No mound, no stench—although only his nose could smell the freshly buried corpse under the dirt—no dead squirrel... nothing.

Panicking, Jamie lowered himself even closer to the ground until his chest pressed against the ground and scanned the park, the trees and bushes, the shadows, sniffing the air, opening his mouth slightly so he could taste the wind better and the scents that drifted in it. Expanding all of his heightened senses to their fullest so nothing could escape his notice... but there was nothing... Jamie swiftly backed up as quietly as he possibly could, his heart racing even more at what he *didn't* find.

There was no smell at all... *The whole park's wiped clean of any fragrances.* Jamie began breathing heavily when he noticed there were no birds chirping happily. No critters scurrying about in the bushes. No sound at *all*!

Jamie clamped his lips shut, cutting off his hiss of pain as a sharp stick jabbed his side, halting his frantic backward scramble. "Think, Jamie, think!" Jamie breathlessly whispered to himself.

He should've ditched Asa at his house the moment he deposited him at his back door last night. Yet he'd blown off going back immediately to clean up his mess, thinking stupidly that he had more than enough time to go back. Jamie tapped his forehead onto the cold moist forest floor in frustration.

Could it have been Aidan?

Jamie tossed the idea. He still didn't know if Aidan really was one of his kind. Jamie thought to clean up his crime scene and get to school, so he could sneak a peek at the stud, and maybe send out feelers to see if Aidan could be more than human. He brought a change of clothes in his backpack and planned to change into them behind a pine tree for this very reason, but now Jamie didn't know if it was safe to even stand up, let alone get buck ass naked in the woods.

Jamie needed Catherine. He didn't know exactly what she was, but Jamie did know Catherine was like him. Not exactly like him, but an 'other'. Catherine normally went back to where he had his feasts to do spot checks to make sure he'd cleaned up after himself. She had the ability to erase scents too, but not to this level. Damn woman would always stamp her scent of disapproval on his kill sites if he hadn't done a good enough job when Jamie went back to double check his work.

She'd also make a point of telling me when I fucked up, too. Jamie scowled. Even so, he hadn't gotten a call from the wench, so Catherine wasn't the one who'd tidied the park up for him... but then, who did? Jamie hid the body so humans couldn't find it... but his efforts wouldn't have been good enough for supernatural eyes...

Any freak within a ten mile radius would've been able to smell the carnage that went down in the small abandoned park. Jamie drained all his victims of their blood before he fed, but there had been enough blood on the ground from when he tore the fucker apart to make a human scared, and to make an 'other' know he's in the area.

Catherine and Mom have only been gone

a day and I've already fucked up. No wonder Catherine treats me like a kid. God, I'm stupid... Jamie banged his head into the ground again.

He needed to make a run for the safe house. A little cottage by the seaside that his mother, Catherine, and he'd been going to during every summer vacation. An isolated, creepy little cottage a friend of Catherine gave them, protected by spells and charms, better and stronger than the ones surrounding their house here.

The question of Aidan being like him would go unsolved forever. Jamie's urgency to move Asa and himself away from the city, like, last night, hammered in his brain. Graduating, and jetting off on his own, died a quick death. Circumstances being as they were, Jamie could only grimly swear silently that he'd start over somewhere else.

Firming his resolve, Jamie heaved up onto his knees, taking the chance no one out there watched as he slipped his backpack off, ripping his sweater and soiled T-shirt up and over his head quickly, shivering at the chill in the morning air, his only warmth came from the heated liquid in the squishy boob bags in his sports bra.

Zipping open his backpack, Jamie took out wet-naps and wiped his hands, and forehead until all the dirt disappeared before grabbing a clean blouse from his bag. Using his dirty shirt to stand on, Jamie took another quick look around, then when it *seemed* like the coast was clear, slipped out of his wet jeans, so he could...

"What the fuck?" Jamie whispered, glaring at the mini skirt at the bottom of his bag.

"Catherine!" Jamie hissed as he swiftly donned on the strip of cloth.

For some reason, the bean pole thought wearing short skirts instead of pants helped make everyone believe he's a girl, but girls wore pants too! Jamie said nothing about hiding an 'escape' bag containing a set of clothing and toiletries in his closet. After Asa's freak attack

Jamie hadn't had time to pack something else, so he'd taken this bag. Catherine always spoke about 'Seduction' and 'Using his feminine wiles to charm his victims or enemies'. He wasn't a fucking girl, for crying out loud! Nevertheless, he should have known the wench would search his room.

Slipping on the tennis shoes he'd kicked off when he took his pants off, Jamie stuffed the clothes he'd removed into his backpack. As much as he wanted to use his 'gifts' to zip his ass back home, Jamie could already hear cars out on the road, and even though they were far away, he also heard people walking and talking on the sidewalk.

Looking over his shoulder to the park he could barely make out through the trees, Jamie kicked himself again for his stupidity before silently jogging through the trees toward the road. The fact he hadn't scented anyone strange when he set out earlier calmed him to a certain degree.

Maybe he was just freaking himself out, and the 'people' who cleaned up his mess thought they were doing him a favor?

"Can't take the chance..." Jamie peeked through the bushes once he got close to the road, making sure no one was around before hopping out onto the sidewalk, but not before taking out a pair of dark sunglasses to hide his green eyes. Stressed and worried about Asa, Jamie completely forgot to pop in his extra pair of brown colored contacts.

Wearing sunglasses shouldn't be a problem, Jamie just needed to walk back to his house with human speed and nab Asa. Jamie would leave an encrypted note saying he'd gone 'swimming' to let his mother know he'd gone to the safe house, grab the cash hidden away then jet. Once they were on the road, they'd be safe.

* * * *

Ethan stood beside Aidan outside the

Dexson residence, waiting and watching for the girl, Jamie, to leave her house so they could see if her appearance changed.

At this time of the month, when the power of the moon disappeared, be it from the human world or their own, it was almost impossible for their young ones to keep up the façade of normalcy. However, time ticked by and Ethan still saw no sign of the 'human' girl.

"Do you think she noticed us and escaped out the back?" Ethan asked.

The humans were waking from their slumber. Ethan could hear them walking around in their homes as the light of dawn slowly began shining its rays, birthing a new day.

Aidan kept his eyes on the house. "It's possible." The words barely left Aidan's lips when Ethan saw a light flicker on in the upstairs window, yet the face which appeared through the glass wasn't who Ethan expected to see.

Ethan's eyes widened when the pale handsome face of his obsession peeked out from behind white laced curtains, his protective instincts taking over, when the rising anger of his king's power manifested, and sparks crackled around them signifying Aidan's displeasure.

"You told me Jamie and the boy's romance was a front, Ethan," Aidan whispered dangerously. "That was the only reason I held back from extinguishing his life."

"A belief I hold still," Ethan said as calmly as he could. "Since the day they announced their commitment, I've been watching them. I've even taken the boy to the side, and questioned him—"

"Your 'watching them' is only because you want to physically join with the human!" Aidan jerked his chin toward the human looking out the window.

Ethan hesitantly nodded. "I will not lie to you... I do feel connected to Asa, and if I could, then I would take him home with me—"

Eyes blazing red with his fury, Aidan

seized Ethan's throat. "I suggest you find out *now* why he is in her home."

Angered himself, but wise enough not to struggle or knock the large hand wrapped around his neck, Ethan took a breath before speaking. "My king," said Ethan respectfully. "Jamie could still be human. The protection wards could have been from another, and never removed after they vacated this hideout and if that is true then she'd be just like Asa. Unattainable."

Aidan's grip tightened around Ethan's throat for a second before being released. "Maybe, but even if she can't be mine, until my curiosity's been appeased, she will stay available."

Stepping away, Ethan nodded. "And if she is one of us?" Ethan couldn't stop himself from asking. "If you desire her this much, why don't you just take her? You don't have to marry the Leviance child—"

"There *is* no *questioning* my marriage,"

Aidan reprimanded. "I will not allow anyone else to have them." Aidan turned back to the house, looking back to the now empty window. "You've been carrying the boy's phone around with you. Call him outside."

Ethan tensed. "For what purpose?"

Ethan knew better than to question Aidan, but Ethan wasn't about to lure Asa out in the open. If Aidan decided to permanently get rid of the competition—if Asa could be considered such—then Ethan would defend the boy… and he'd lose. The balance of power was all in Aidan's favor. Aidan's power was seriously bound being on this plane, and his lord had less than half of his strength to call forth should a problem arise, yet even the amount of power his king harbored was enough to rip him to shreds within a blink of an eye.

Aidan gave Ethan a sideways glance. "Do it."

Grinding his teeth, Ethan reached into the pocket of his leather jacket and unearthed the small silver cell phone. Having access to the school's registry, Ethan knew Jamie's phone number. "What if Jamie is home?" Ethan asked as the line began to ring.

"Then invite her outside as well." Aidan smiled.

Ethan eyed Aidan, noting the rise in temperature around him and the spillage of power seeping out of him, hoping that was all his king would release. Aidan hated to leave their world, since it was agonizing for Aidan to contain his true self, and for Aidan to have kept himself chained up for two months... Ethan could only hope their people searching would find the Leviance child before Aidan snapped. Then again, maybe if Aidan had Jamie in his arms he wouldn't be as twitchy.

Just when Ethan opened his mouth to tell Aidan the boy wasn't going to pick up the phone a shaky, tired, voice answered.

"Hello?"

Ethan barely held back his purr when he

heard Asa's voice. "Asa, baby, I heard you were at Jamie's and had to call you."

"Et-Ethan?"

"Yup." Ethan chuckled at how the boy's voice took on a slightly higher pitch.

"How did you find out I was here? Jamie left only ten minutes ago. She shouldn't even be at school yet."

Covering the phone so Asa couldn't hear him, Ethan looked at Aidan. "Jamie's not in the house."

"Bring him outside," Aidan commanded.

Ethan knew Aidan could hear every word being spoken between him and Asa, and wondered if Aidan had already suspected Jamie wouldn't be home, not when she'd sloppily disposed of her prey, something Ethan just thought about. However, like Ethan had pointed out, there still could be a slight chance Jamie was human. It wouldn't have been the first time they'd been fooled, mistakenly scented something untrue.

If she was one of them, then there wouldn't have been any point in stationing 'watchers' at the park, which is why Aidan had commanded they not leave any. Someone like her who'd been masking her scent so expertly would've sniffed out his sentinels and fled. The last thing Aidan would want would be for the little girl to run away from him.

"Ethan?"

"I'm outside, Asa." Ethan forced himself to say, "And I have your cell phone with me. I'm using it right now to call you."

"You're outside..."

"Yeah, I want to return it to you, and since I'm here I can give you a ride school too." Ethan stepped out in the open when he saw the curtains move, the same time Aidan stepped back, farther into the shadows.

"Um... I-I'm not feeling good, so I won't be going to school today..."

Ethan covered the phone when he heard Aidan start to growl.

"Bring him out, Ethan. I want to see him," Aidan said in a strangely pleasantly tone causing Ethan's body to tense.

If Jamie and Asa were more than Ethan claimed, he would have less than a second to get Asa to safety. Ethan licked his lips when he heard Aidan's knuckles crack as his lord clenched his fists tightly closed.

"Aw, don't tell me you're going to leave me out here, Asa," Ethan said playfully. "Don't you want your cell phone?"

"I do... could you put it in the mailbox? I-I'll get it later."

Ethan looked to Aidan and waited for his nod before answering, "Sure, that's not a problem. I'll see you maybe tomorrow?"

"Ah, I'm pretty sick so... I don't know if I'll be in school tomorrow either."

"That's cool," said Ethan reassuringly. "I'll just see you when I see you then."

"Ah, yeah... um, thanks... bye."

Hanging up, Ethan ran across the street

and, with a big show, waving the phone in the air so Asa, who peeked out the window, could see. He opened the mailbox and placed the phone inside, even flipping up the red metal flag on the side before sticking his hands in his pockets and jogging down the sidewalk, away from the house.

Ducking into some bushes, away from prying eyes, Ethan teleported back to where Aidan stood in the shadows. They waited about ten minutes before Asa opened the front door slowly and stepped out.

"Do you smell that?" Aidan whispered.

Ethan inhaled deeply as the scent of the boy blew toward them from the hidden corner of the house where they watched him. "Asa... he's... how?" Ethan had to restrain himself from marching over and demanding answers from the guy, needing to know how his sweet human scent had become one of their own. "He's human. I made sure of it." Ethan sucked on Asa's tantalizing flesh on more than one occasion, unable to help himself and also to convince himself the guy was human, and couldn't be stolen away.

As Asa started walking toward the mailbox, Ethan noticed how sickly the boy looked. Dark bruising colored under Asa's eyes, and Ethan watched the painful way Asa walked. How unbelievably fatigued he looked. Ethan didn't realize he'd taken steps toward Asa until he felt Aidan's hand gripping his upper arm, pulling him back.

"He has the scent of a babe," Aidan whispered in wonder.

Ethan's need to confront Asa disintegrated with the shock of Aidan's words. "No… not possible…" Ethan whispered.

The last child born to their world happened over three hundred years ago… Asa couldn't have the scent of a child. Their kind weren't immortal, not true immortals since they could die, but because of their long life, their birth rate was low, not even five percent.

Ethan could still remember the sweet taste of Asa's blood on his tongue. The tall, slim, boy *was* human. However, even Ethan smelled the fresh aroma of infancy in the wind, coming off Asa. Yet, there was a strange tinge to Asa's scent. Ethan couldn't place what species Asa might be.

The only explanation—an insane one— Ethan could come up with was someone changed Asa, made him one of them. But who could have pulled off such a feat? Since the percentage of one of their kind being powerful enough to accomplish such a miracle was less than their birth rate.

"A strange girl trying to convince everyone around her she's human. A boy who was once human now has the scent of an undetermined species." Aidan looked at Ethan with a rather smug look. "By looking at this boy, do you really think Jamie is still *just* human?"

Undetermined species... "You do not

recognize his scent?" Ethan asked in disbelief.

"No. I don't," Aidan said with a smile.

Ethan's silent jubilation reached untold heights at the sight of Asa, who seemed to be venturing around exceptionally well, despite the tenderness of his every step, without his spectacles. The oddity of the guy's scent should have Ethan's natural instincts screaming at him to kill Asa where he stood. The strangeness of Asa's aroma posed a potential threat and he couldn't be allowed to live, but Ethan's instincts shouted for him to claim Asa.

Aidan slid a sideways glance to Ethan. "Looks like the rules no longer apply when it comes to this boy," said Aidan with good humor. "It would be a shame to let this opportunity get away from you."

Ethan hadn't seen a transformed human for six hundred years, but he'd never forget how the newly changed person was treated by their maker. The altered female was loved and protected with a viciousness even the most powerful would not trifle against. So, if Ethan took Asa, then his 'mother' would follow.

"Watch the house, Ethan. If the boy tries to leave, I want you to follow him. Make sure you don't let him out of your sight. There is nothing you can do while he is being protected by all those charms, so leave him alone for now. And Ethan?" Aidan stopped Ethan from rushing off. "When I say leave him alone, I mean it. I don't want you doing anything which will have Asa calling Jamie to warn her about us. Take him when I tell you to take him."

Ethan could barely contain himself. The moment Aidan gave the preverbal 'go', he'd wanted to shatter the protective shields which kept him from Asa, but his excitement subsided a tad when Aidan turned and began walking away. "What are you going to do?"

"She is one of us, but it seems like she knows nothing about us. Yesterday at school she made me, she saw my eyes change when I was with Janis, but looked confused. She'll be curious, and I want to be there when she comes seeking answers," Aidan replied, walking away.

"Where are you going?" Ethan asked.

Aidan was already at a distance one could not have a quiet, secretive, conversation, but Ethan knew Aidan could hear him perfectly, he just hoped Aidan would answer before the distance became so great *he* couldn't hear the answer.

"I think it's time to visit Harris Leviance, and this time force him to tell me more information about his runaway child."

Ethan didn't bother asking why Aidan didn't go to school first to find Jamie. He wasn't the only servant of Aidan's in the school, watching, searching. And he also didn't ask to see if Aidan wanted him to go and make sure Jamie actually went to class. Ethan didn't think he could leave even if he wanted to. Nothing could make him leave his current post. Not until he held Asa in his grasp.

* * * *

"Today is just not my fucking day..." Jamie muttered as he glared at the loud redhead yapping her mouth off into her cell phone.

Not three minutes after he'd set off back to his house. A flashy red sports car pulled over with Tiffany behind the wheel. Spewing out excuses did nothing to brush Tiff off his back, the girl had his head so confused with all her ramblings that before he knew it, he'd been strapped into the passenger seat, and speeding off to school—if they made it. With Tiffany's driving, they might not.

"Ever thought of wearing a headset?" Jamie asked, bracing one hand on the side of the driver's seat, one foot on the dashboard, and his right hand clenching the door handle, holding on for dear life as Tiffany took a corner a little too tightly. Horns blared all around them. "Oh God, please save me," Jamie whispered, squeezing his eyes shut.

"Oh *please,* like you can complain. At least I have my license, unlike you," Tiffany huffed at him, putting her phone down.

Jamie began hyperventilating when he opened his eyes and saw Tiffany let go of the wheel for a second to roll up the driver's automatic window.

"You're just lucky I decided to come and pick you up for school today. You should be happy you didn't have to walk."

I think I'm going to puke. Tiffany took another sharp turn, tires squealing under them. "I told you I wasn't going to school today. I thought I would, but I started feeling sick and decided not to go."

"You look perfectly fine to me."

"Seriously Tiffany, I need to go home," Jamie insisted, hardening the tone he used with the girl.

"Yeah, yeah. I'll tell you what. You come to class and go along with our little 'lezzy' show, and after that you can take off."

"One day of not being the center of attention won't kill you." Jamie sighed in relief when their campus came into view and Tiffany was forced to slow down due to the traffic.

"How long have you known me? Seriously. Oh, yeah. I heard what happened with Aidan and Janis yesterday." Tiffany frowned at him.

For someone who just made it very clear the world revolved around her, Tiffany had a funny way of butting her nose into his problems. "It wasn't as big of a deal as you may have heard," Jamie said offhandedly.

His main concern at this point now, was getting out of the car alive more than anything else.

The moment Tiffany parked the car, taking up two spaces, Jamie unbuckled his seatbelt and all but fell out in his rush to feel solid ground under his feet.

"My driving isn't that bad. Don't be such a pussy, Jamie. Grow some balls."

If only you knew. Jamie laughed silently to himself. On shaky knees, Jamie ignored Tiffany's gasp of outrage when he leaned against her sports car, trying to get his bearings. "I'm only staying until you do your 'shock and awe', Tiff," Jamie said firmly. "After that I'm excusing myself to go to the restroom and leaving."

"Yay! You're the best-est friend in the whole wide world!"

Jamie smiled when Tiffany gave him a peck on the cheek. "Let's go." Jamie discreetly straightened his wig and sunglasses when Tiffany turned around to grab her bag, making sure no one saw him either when he shifted his boobs, so he wasn't lopsided.

"You head on up. I need to harass someone before I go to class."

Jamie sighed again as he walked ahead, smiling and waving to students he had classes with when they called out in greeting to him.

When Jamie rounded the corner, his

steps faltered a little, and he cursed under his breath.

"What the *fuck* are you doing here?"

"Good morning to you, too, Janis..." Jamie muttered to the busty brunette who stormed up to him, hissing her question.

"Come with me!"

Jamie tried to pull out of Janis's grip the moment the girl grabbed him, and was floored when he couldn't. He tried again, this time using more strength, his *special* strength, but still couldn't escape the shrew's talons.

Being depressingly shorter than the girl dragging him off, Jamie practically ran behind her or else his arm would have been ripped off for being too slow. It wasn't until they were behind the school, and a connected concrete shed, out of sight and hearing from the rest of the students, that Janis release his arm.

"What the hell is your problem?" Jamie grumbled.

"You! You are my fucking problem! I

swear to fucking God you have a knack of getting yourself into trouble!"

Jamie lifted his brows in question to the brunette who took to pacing quickly in front of him. "And you care because...?"

"All the work I've put into trying to get him off you; and here you come along and mess it all the hell up!" Janis furiously said, looking as if it took all of her control not to shout at him.

"Look, Janis," Jamie said tiredly, leaning against the shed's cement wall. "I don't know what the hell you're talking about—"

Janis stopped pacing to glare at him. "I'm talking about how you came to school after feeding last night! I'm talking about the fact you're wearing a fucking *wig,* and if I were to rip those cheap, ninety-nine cent pair of sunglasses off your stupid face, I'm sure I'll see your eyes are green! That's what I'm fucking talking about!"

Jamie lost his balance, scraping his knuckles in the process of trying to catch himself from falling on his face against the rough wall. *My heart can't take any more surprises.*

Jamie stared at Janis in shock. "I don't know what you're talking about," Jamie shakily replied.

"'I don't know what you're talking about'," mimicked Janis sarcastically. "I've been guarding your stupid punk ass since you escaped with your mother ten years ago! I've had to clean up your crap when you've fucked up on a kill and deal with your fucking impulsive acts of moronism!"

"Moronism isn't a word," Jamie responded numbly.

"You—Wait. Are you fucking bleeding?!"

"Huh?" Jamie's numb brain registered the sting on the back of his hand the second he looked down. Sure enough the skin on his knuckles was scraped off, and beads of blood were forming. "It's nothing," Jamie mumbled.

"It's *not* nothing, you douche bag!"

Jamie snapped out of his haze the moment Janis grabbed his hand and he felt the rough sliminess of her tongue wetly sweeping across his knuckles, lapping up his blood. "What are you doing?!" Jamie yelped, pushing the girl away from him. "Jesus Christ, woman! Are you some kind of freakin' vampire or something?" Jamie grimaced in disgust.

"You know, ignorance is *not* bliss." Janis glared. "Your fucking daddy should've kept your ass locked up instead of trying to give you whatever childhood you had left. If he'd trained you like he should have done, then you would know the smell of *your* blood would attract countless predators. The reason why I licked your wound clean the last time and this time, was to mask its scent from the sexy king warlord who's after your flat ass!"

Jamie watched Janis take a few deep breaths before opening her mouth again.

"I'll admit, even though you've *never*

been properly trained, you are able to mask your scent at a master level. When we found you three years ago—"

"Wait, wait. Hold up a second," Jamie demanded. His brain overloaded with information too unbelievable to be true. "Who the fuck are you?"

Jamie ducked when Janis took a swing at him.

"If you don't fucking remember me, then I'm not going to help jog your memory! Just shut up and listen to me!"

Jamie's quick retort was annoyingly cut off before he could voice it, when a pair of giggling girls passed them without noticing them. Once they were alone again Jamie said, "I don't know what your problem is, and I don't want to. I don't know what you're talking about, and I don't want to hear anymore of your insanity."

Of course Jamie didn't want to leave; he wanted to hear every little bit of information the overly pissed brunette could tell him, but at the same time he knew he had to get away now.

Just hearing his father had known where he's been for two years— "Wait, you said that you found me three years ago," said Jamie, "but I've known you since I started school here two years ago."

"*No*, you only think you do. As I said, you're stupid! Someone like you, *if* you had been properly trained, should have been able to sniff us out before we got within twenty miles of you," Janis said.

"Then why don't you explain it to me since I'm so stupid!" Screw pretending he didn't know what Janis was talking about.

Fuck the fact he should be jetting his ass home, grabbing Asa, and running for the hills. Catherine and his mother never answered the questions he had about himself, but he had someone in front of him who obviously knew him, and what he is. Jamie wasn't going anywhere until he got some, if not all, of his questions answered.

"My father knows where I am? How?" Jamie demanded. "How was he able to find me?" *We've been so careful.*

"Well, beside the fact your daddy is one powerful motherfucker on this plane, he also made sure he had more than just a blood tie to you."

Jamie waited impatiently. "And?" He finally exploded.

"The night he killed Lisa, he *knew* you were watching. The bitch Lisa knew who—and what—you were, yet she still stupidly tried to kill you off. Hell, the bitch couldn't kill you when you were a snot nose brat, but she still tried, even when you killed all the assassins she sent after you."

"No, I never killed anyone!" Jamie insisted.

"*Really*," Janis drawled out. "So you think your skinny ten year old ass was able to get away by sheer luck? There is no such thing as luck in our world. Luck is a blonde haired bitch who keeps stealing my clothes, and make-up back home. You don't remember because—I don't know, it's too traumatizing for your puny brain or something, but the fact is all those times your *aunt* tried to take your head, and mount it on her wall, it was you who mounted her prized killers on yours instead."

Every bad dream he'd had of blood and death… seeing faces he *thought* he'd never seen before. "Shit…" Jamie whispered.

"Okay, I'll admit that impressed me. Just like the last time your father found you and trained you a little. But afterward he didn't want you starting to believe you could let your guard down, so he attacked you. Thinking he'd scare you badly enough you would never walk around without looking over your shoulder. You messed him up so bad—"

"Shut up for a second," Jamie breathlessly hissed.

He needed a minute. Just a minute to

process all Janis said. He might be used to killing now, but to hear he'd been whacking them before he even became a... whatever he was. It was a little hard for him to handle.

He could completely freak out about it later though. Jamie wanted whatever functioning brain cells to focus on what Janis had been about to tell him before he interrupted her. "Go back to the night my father killed Lisa," Jamie said.

"Yeah, fine, whatever. So Lisa had the stupid idea that if she killed your mother, then it might weaken your defenses to the point her last assassin could kill you off... I still cannot figure out how she could be one of us, knowing full well what you are capable of, and still think she could win."

"While I'm still young here, Janis!" Jamie irritably said.

"Do. Not. Take that attitude with me, you little piss ant," Janis growled. "*So*, Lisa tried to kill your mom, and your dad came and saved her. Harris already planned on hiding you away, but because of Lisa he had the perfect excuse of how to get you to run away without getting into trouble himself."

Jamie motioned with his hands for Janis to hurry the hell up.

"Your mom freaked out when your father killed Lisa right before her eyes, and knowing you were watching, he dragged her into the other room, so you wouldn't hear him, and explained everything that was happening and how he needed your mom to run with you. Harris told your mom he'd be watched, so he'd have to pretend to be hunting for the both of you."

"You said my dad did more to connect us," said Jamie. "What did he do?"

"He gave you the thirst." Janis grinned. "Harris compelled you to watch him as he licked the blood of his dead wife off his hand. You remember it, don't you? You can say you felt disgusted, and you thought your father a monster, but even at your young age I bet the main thing you were scared about is how you were more than just intrigued at the sight of your father's fangs. I know you saw them after he lapped up the blood tracking down his forearm, and after when he smiled at you."

How does she know so much? Jamie said nothing, just continued to stare at Janis, listening intently as she talked.

"I'll bet that's when the hunger really started, wasn't it? When you hunt, before you take your victim's flesh into you for nourishment, you drain them of all of their blood. Don't try to deny it because I've seen your kills."

Jamie stiffened when he saw a smug look cross Janis's lovely features. He tried to keep any emotion from showing on his face, not wanting Janis to know how right she was in everything she said to him. But Jamie must have slipped in his control for her to see she was correct. The things Janis said to him, he hadn't even written into his journal, the place where he'd decided to pour all his secrets. But what Jamie hated the most? Janis was right…

"You've suspected what your father is for a long time, haven't you? All those 'family' dinners when all he did was drink red wine, and no matter how long he 'seemed' to be out in the sun, he never tanned. Isn't it time you voiced your suspicions? What you've know to be the truth? Say it. *Say it.*" Janis pressed relentlessly.

"Vampire," Jamie breathed. "He's a vampire."

"Ding, ding! We have a winner!"

Asa's right… Jamie tried to swallow down the lump which formed in his throat. "I'm a vampire…"

Janis laughed. "No, you're not a vampire, Jamie. Sure, your father made everyone believe you're a bloodsucker, but if you were *just* a vampire then your father wouldn't have gone through all this trouble trying to keep you hidden."

Jamie looked at Janis in confusion. "If I'm not a vampire, then what am I?"

Grinning evilly Janis said, "You're something else. You're something which hasn't been seen in over ten thousand years. You already have one creature of unimaginable power stalking you, but if our world knew what you *really* were, the human world would be invaded, the people slaughtered like cattle by the hundreds of thousands just to thin the crowds so they can get closer to finding you."

Janis gave him a pitying smile. "No baby, you're no vampire. My job would be so much easier if only you were…"

CHAPTER 9

September 7th, 2010

You know what the saddest thing is? It's the fact I don't have any friends. Now, I'm not writing this because I'm all depressed about it. Well, not really anyway. But in these ten years the closest people I could call a true friend was a boy I knew back in the second town I lived in. The both of us had a lot of fun, and it hurt when we'd taken off and ran because my father located us. I couldn't even say goodbye to him.

My second best friend had been this calico cat who'd always hung out at the sliding glass door of our apartment in the third town we moved to. The cat was strange at first. It didn't have a problem with my mother, not even Catherine, but whenever I came near it, the cat would start to hiss at me, and always tried to swipe at me with his claws.

It was a beautiful cat though. He had

one blue eye and one green eye, and over time he stopped trying to take a chunk of flesh from my arm. I would spend a great deal of time with him. Called him Kiri from a character in a novel I read once, because of his different colored eyes.

I talked to Kiri as if the animal was a real person. I used to tell him all my worries. Whispered my fears of what I thought I might be. The damn cat would sometimes bite me when I sunk deep into the pit of my own sorrows, but instead of getting pissed at the stupid animal for, once again, making me bleed, I would scratch him behind his ears and bury my face into his soft fur.

It's kind of sad when your best friend is the neighborhood stray... But he never judged me. At night when I was feeling all alone, he'd somehow get into my bedroom, lie next to me, and softly bat me on the head as if trying to comfort me while I was in my darkest hour.

I wonder sometimes if I will find a friend

who I could tell all my secrets to. My fears, my worries, and comfort me like that cat did when I felt as if my troubles were weighing me down, and the weight would sink me farther into the quicksand of who I am.

When we ran, just like the boy in the last town, I left Kiri behind...

In the end... there's no point in making friends. Because sooner or later, I'll leave them all behind.

* * * *

"What do you mean, 'If only you *were* a vampire'? If my father is a vampire and my mother is a human, and I don't take after my mother in regards to my genealogy, doesn't it mean I'm a frickin' vampire?" asked Jamie, more than just slightly confused at the bombshell Janis dropped on him.

"What can I say?" Janis snickered. "You're a freak amongst freaks."

Just breathe. Keep your temper under control. It wouldn't be nice if he slaughtered the bitch and left a mess for the janitor to clean. "Then what am I?" Jamie said through clenched teeth.

"In human words, you're our unicorn. There have only been four of your kind, including you, ever. Hmm... I wonder if you could be considered an endangered species if you're the only one left?" Janis annoyingly shrugged at him.

"Which means?" Jamie snapped.

"Just like the Christian human religion, their God created man, and then later created a woman to be this man's mate. Well, we also have something similar. In the beginning there was a mated pair whom was not just one thing, but all. Every mythical creature you can think of—that was what they were. But their children were not like them.

"If a couple of a different species were to mate and have a child, that child would not be half of what the father is or half of what the mother is. We aren't like humans in that regard. It's one or the other. If the father is a demon, and the mother is a fairy, then the child would be either a full blooded demon or fairy."

"But I'm not," Jamie exclaimed.

"Nope." Janis grinned.

"So you're saying I'm a mutant." *So, Asa was right again.* Jamie didn't know if he should laugh or cry.

"A very *valuable* mutant," Janis pointed out.

"What happened to the couple who were like me?" Jamie softly asked, even though he instinctively knew he wasn't going to like the answer Janis was going to tell him.

"We can live for a *very* long time. The first couple's kids had kids, and those kids had kids, so on and so forth. But it wasn't long before creatures of all species began to envy the power the couple had. In the history books, it said the demons attacked first, thinking they could steal the pair's power for themselves, and after is when the others began their siege. The books say it took two hundred years before the couple was finally brought down."

Jamie gulped. "If they were the only ones of their kind, how could there have been a third? You said I'm the fourth, right?"

"Yeah… well, it's said many tried to protect her, but…" Janis shrugged.

"She was murdered," Jamie whispered.

His fear of being discovered went up to a new level of paranoia when he saw Janis grimace. The only confirmation he needed to know he'd guessed correctly.

"Your father took a huge risk letting you go. But…" Janis shrugged. "I guess you did alright on your own. You were able to protect your mother and that damn succubus for all these years, even if you didn't realize it."

"I did?" Jamie mumbled, his mind in such chaos over what Janis was telling him, his brain felt like it was about to explode. All he wanted to do was curl up in a ball, under the covers, at home. Forgetting any of this ever happened. Maybe it was a good thing Catherine and his mother kept this from him. Despite what Janis said, ignorance *is* bliss.

"There have been a few times Lisa's family tried to avenge her death by killing you, in order to hurt your father. You were twelve at the time, living in this crappy little town, and they sent two teams after you. In a fit of rage you wiped them all out when they tried to hurt your mother. You must have said or did something because they never tried to come after you ever again, nor did they ever speak to anyone about you."

Jamie could only blink at Janis. "You said I've known you for three years—"

"No, dickhead, you've known me longer than that!"

"*But*," Jamie stressed, "I was *compelled* to think I know you longer. Which means you lost me for a year."

"Remembered that, did ya? Guess you're not stupid after all." Janis snickered.

"Just answer the fucking question, Janis. I don't have all fucking day," sighed Jamie.

Janis rolled her eyes. "The connection your father established between you two helped pinpoint your location. If you were just a vampire, your father could have tracked you with ease, and being his son, even better. Harris created another connection because you can change to any creature you want. Four years ago your mother started dressing you and making you act like a girl."

The cool breeze blowing on his bare legs and his boobs were proof Janis spoke true. Jamie motioned Janis to hurry up and continue.

"We knew of your mother's plan, but we never thought you'd use your shape shifting skills or how this act would sever all the connections you had with your father."

"S-shape shifting skills," Jamie slightly stuttered.

"Yeah, you've unknowingly been keeping yourself small and feminine-ish all this time. Your skill is so great you even changed your scent once a month to signify you were going through your menstrual cycle—"

Jamie scrunched is face in disgust.

"You've fooled the most powerful beast here into thinking you're a girl, and all the others who attend this school."

"I've kept myself this short? So, that must mean once I stop pretending to be a girl, I'll go back to normal. Normal being how I would have looked if I never changed myself," Jamie whispered, mostly to himself.

"Nah, you were always short." Janis laughed. "So I don't think anything would change, even if you knew how to quit what you're doing, and it's not like you really *changed* the way you look; you were always a pretty little bitch. You just softened your appearance. The change I'm talking about is within you. By using your shape shifting abilities, you've shoved the vampire part of you behind a locked door, taking it out only when you feed." Janis sighed, checking the time on her pink wristwatch.

"Look, we don't have too much time left. We need to get your punk ass somewhere safe for the time being."

Jamie didn't want to leave just yet. He came this far, listening to Janis's crazy stories, and despite the danger, he needed to hear more. "So, you work for my father?"

"Work for your father? Ha! Like your father would *ever* employ me. That's a laugh. If given the choice, your father would never let one of my kind come a hundred yards—no miles—near of his precious little son," declared Janis, slapping her knee as she laughed.

"The 'person' I 'work' for is your brother."

"My brother…?" It only just then occurred to Jamie that his half-brother, Joseph, had to be a vampire too.

"Oh yeah, all those memories of you playing with Joey, when both of you were kids? All a lie. You were the last baby to be born in over three hundred years. Your big bro's age is in the triple digits." Janis wiggled three fingers in Jamie's face.

Jamie wanted to lash out at Janis for imparting to him this particular information... but strangely, even though her words were harsh, he could see she wasn't *trying* to be malicious. She wasn't purposely out to hurt him by telling him this.

"Why...?" Jamie asked.

"Fucking bleeding heart, that's what the asshole is. Oh, wait, I guess I should say he has a *selective* bleeding heart. Joey is just as much of a cold, deadly monster as your daddy."

The sensation of an invisible person stabbing him in the chest filled Jamie. Thinking his father wanted him dead never made him tremble with the feelings of betrayal, not like hearing Joseph had fooled him into believing they were a couple of years apart.

The things Jamie whispered to his brother, the childish dreams he told him he had. He used to tell Joseph all of his secrets... God, how Joseph must have laughed at him...

"Ah, you're not going to cry, are you?"

"No, I'm not!" Jamie snapped, but Lord did he feel like it. Joseph was the only happy memory he had at that house with the cold, shadowy hallways.

"He... Joseph... ah, he isn't the kind of vamp who... opens to anyone. The person he was with you... it wasn't a lie. He was genuinely happy when you were born, and during the time he spent with you," Janis mumbled, looking to be more embarrassed than he at her attempt to comfort him.

"Joseph pitched a grand ol' fit when it was confirmed you weren't a human, and thus would be subjected to the seers' matchmaking." Janis huffily turned her back on him to hide her reddened face.

"Matchmaking?" Jamie asked.

"As I said, we live a long time. We are extremely hard to kill, which might be why the birth rate is so low it's almost non-existent. Every child born is in danger of being kidnapped, stolen so they can be mated to the strongest of their clan in hopes of birthing new strength into their family. Newbies, when they reach *our* age to breed, have the highest chances of conceiving." Janis looked at him in all seriousness. "It's a dangerous time for everyone."

"You were no exception. Even with the strongest of spells trying to hide you from prying eyes, the seers found you, and a worthy male has been chosen to be your mate—"

"M-male!" Jamie sputtered. "I thought you said the goal when a new brat is born, is to get them knocked up as fast as they can? How the hell is that possible if I'm supposedly being married off to some dude?!"

Janis stared at him blankly for a long

minute. "What the hell kind of bedtime stories did your mother read to you, or more importantly, *not* read to you?"

"Obviously not these kinds!" Jamie growled.

"Well, they should have! Then maybe we wouldn't still be standing here, with me telling you this shit when you should have known about it already!"

Don't kill Janis. All I need to do is breathe, and count to a hundred and fifty thousand, and I'll be okay.

"Well, I don't know, so tell me," Jamie said tightly, choking back his anger.

"Yeah, yeah. Fucking stupid the way they've coddled you," muttered Janis. "All this human crap about only being able to have kids with a girl is shit. Our kind, we all might not be the same, but the one thing which is, is we can procreate with any gender. Boy with boy, girl with girl; it doesn't matter. Obviously the same rules apply when a woman gets pregnant, you know, she holds the kid in her belly and nine months later out pops a baby... or litter, depending on the species."

Litter?! Jamie felt faint.

"Males on the other hand, they aren't made to carry babies... unless they are a special kind of shape-shifter... but if they aren't, then something different happens where they carry the soul of the child within them. Just as a female's belly would grow as the child forms, so too does the soul of a male carrying a youngster." Janis paused for breath before continuing. "Your stomach doesn't get big nor can the soul be seen. A male will just... have this glow about them. They'll bear some of the same trials a woman would go through during pregnancy... sorta."

"You're lying..." Jamie said, horrified. "You're trying to freak me out. None of this can be true. This isn't some goddamn fan fiction where male pregnancies are a normal thing!"

"The succubus seriously didn't tell you

anything, did she?" Janis looked at him with pity.

"This is the second time you said something about a succubus. Who the hell are you talking about?"

"Holy shit, you don't know about that either?" Janis looked at Jamie in amazement. "I'm talking about Catherine! Catherine is the succubus! Why do you think your father wants to kill her? Think about it. What do succubi feed on, huh? Sexual energy!" Janis shook her head at him.

Jamie gagged. His father not wanting him dead. Finding out he was some mystical creature amongst mythical creatures. His brother actually being a few hundred years older and not the kid he grew up with. Male pregnancies, and now this. Picturing his mother and Catherine necking on the couch was his breaking point.

"I think I'm going to be sick..." whispered Jamie, squatting down, lowering his head between his knees. "Catherine has been feeding off my mother all these years?"

"Yuppers." Janis grinned. "Cat wasn't supposed to run away with your mother. Some werewolf or something was planned to take off with your mum and you, but instead Catherine did. Your father mapped it all out ahead of time, and since no human has been found with their 'life essence' sucked out of them, it's only too clear who Cat's been feeding on. Which is why Harris wants Catherine's head on a stick… Your father still loves your mother… or something."

"You suck at trying to make people feel better, you know that, Janis?" Jamie laughed pathetically.

"Not here to make you feel better, ya cumquat. I'm here to save your sorry, *stupid* ass from the bitch who wants to turn you over to the enemy."

"What?" Jamie already had a shit load of 'people' after him. Now he found out there were more? "Who is after me now?"

"Psh, more like who *isn't* gunning for

you. But currently *that* bitch is after you."

Not being able to see who Janis pointed at from the bushes hiding them from view, Jamie had to stand and peek around them. The only person he saw was Tiffany, farther ahead, looking to be waiting for someone.

"I don't see anyone," Jamie whispered, looking past Tiffany to see if anyone might be behind her, and he just couldn't see them.

"Are you fucking blind? Right there! That shape shifting fox bitch who's always hanging on your coattails," Janis hissed, pointing rudely at Tiffany.

"Nah," Jamie denied, shaking his head. "Not Tiffany. No way in hell. I've known her—"

"For two *months*," Janis coldly said. "They came the beginning of this term, and implanted in the minds of everyone they'd started here as freshmen. Tiffany's a servant whose job is to make sure her master is happy. If her king wants something, then she's the backstabbing whore who'll get it for him, not matter what."

Jamie continued to shake his head.

Janis sighed. "Look. You're playing like you're some poor little girl. Why would some filthy rich chick want to hang out with someone like *you*?"

"For my good looks and personality?" Jamie shakily tried to joke.

"Negative. Shit, that redhead's been pushing you to become Aidan's since the very beginning. Again, kinda strange, isn't it? A big time rich stud like him, and she's just going to give him to *you* without trying to bring him home to her mommy and daddy? For that matter, have you ever *met* Tiffany's parents?"

Jamie reluctantly thought back to all the times he'd talked to Tiffany about her parents. The comments he'd made, and the feelings he had, made him think he had a personal, close relationship with her folks. Yet, now that he thought about it, Jamie never actually met them, not in the two years he and Tiff supposedly had been friends.

"You're fucking weak when it comes to compulsion, and the bitch did a fucking number on you—"

Jamie struggled when Janis suddenly tackled him to the ground, covering his mouth and hissing at him to be still and not say anything.

"Look!" Janis whispered.

On his side, Jamie looked from where he lay and froze when Aidan appeared magically from out of nowhere... Tiffany went down on one knee, bowing her head to him.

"Fucking dragon is on the hunt for you, as we thought. We need to run."

Jamie flinched at how close Janis was, her lips literally touching his ear as she spoke.

"My orders are to keep you away from him, to step between you if Aidan gets too close to you," Janis whispered.

"To the extent you'd dry hump his leg by the school bathrooms?" Jamie jealously whispered back.

"Hell, you've seen his face, and that body. I'd do it again even though I'd been ordered not to. But now is not the time to get jealous, Jamie. We are in serious shit. We need to get you out of here."

Jamie hesitated for a split second. His need to keep the information to himself was overruled by his fierce need to protect. Something he couldn't do if Asa wasn't with him.

"We need to get Asa at my house first… I kinda did something to him, and now he's not human any more…"

Janis blinked at him for a second before saying, "Come again?"

"Yeah… umm… I bit Asa, and he's sort of not human any longer…" Jamie's eyes continued to watch Aidan with Tiffany.

He nearly hyperventilated when, before his eyes, they disappeared. "T-they—"

"Yeah, yeah, they both teleported

somewhere else. Plans are still the same. We still need to get your skinny ass out of Dodge, with a slight detour. Shit, I don't get paid enough to deal with this crap," Janis complained, pulling Jamie to his feet.

Slapping Janis's hand away after the brunette helped him up, Jamie looked back at the empty spot where his best friend had stood before turning and following Janis.

* * * *

Walking into the lobby of the hotel his future father-in-law called home, Aidan nodded to the security detail guarding the private metal doors to the elevator. Elevators which would take him to the Leviance rooms on the top floor. Aidan stopped long enough for the guards to swipe their key cards on the scanner, unlocking the elevator.

"Mr Montgomery, I respectfully request while in your meeting with Sir Leviance, you keep your claws retracted at all times."

"Understood," Aidan coldly replied, so the burly guards would step out of his way, and take him to his adversary.

Aidan, his mood already dark from Tiffany's failure in keeping an eye on Jamie, had used a tremendous amount of control not to kill the shape-shifter where she stood while listening to her heartfelt apologizes for losing the girl. It grew darker with every step Aidan took to meet with Harris, who had thwarted Aidan from the day he announced he wanted to take Harris's child into custody ten human years ago. Aidan wanted to bond with his mate before their marriage

Aidan's lip curled as the metal doors opened, revealing two more guards in the elevator. From their scent, Aidan noted they were more powerful than the guards who'd greeted him. Aidan smiled darkly, stepping in. They were no match to his strength, just paper dolls easily cut down by nothing but a look if he wanted them dead.

"Mr Montgomery, I need not ask if you are carrying any hidden weapons on you, do I?" A security guard less than respectfully inquired.

"We don't want an incident if you are. *Your kind* is notorious for their temper."

Aidan revealed a little of his true self, making them cower in the corners of the confined space for their insolent tones when addressing him. The metal walls of the elevator groaned in protest, rippling in his anger. Even the lower animals who spoke to him gave him more respect.

"I don't need any sort of manmade weaponry if I want to cause an 'incident'."

Aidan didn't care if he was frowned upon for exposing a fraction of his already bound power. Fed up with the barricades, the lies, Aidan would start a war to get the answers if he needed to.

Once the elevator doors opened, Aidan walked out, leaving the overly cocky guards behind to recover. He made his way to the only suite doors on the floor, guarded again with more security.

"Mr Mont—"

"I have already been warned, and by repeating, it will only make me angrier," Aidan curtly said, his temper already at its boiling point. "I suggest you open the doors before my mask slips further, and the first person to feel my wrath will be you."

"Let him in, Johnson."

Aidan's temper didn't cool down to hear the calm tones of Harris Leviance coming from the ear piece the guard wore.

"Yes, sir," the guard said.

Aidan growled low in his throat when the guards hesitated in opening the door for him.

"What a pleasant and *unexpected* surprise, Aidan."

"Harris." Aidan acknowledged the tall, blond, handsome bloodsucker who stood by the floor-to-ceiling windows, drinking what smelled to be a cup of human blood. "I would think sooner or later you would have known I'd personally be showing up on your doorstep."

Aidan slowly made his way forward, noting only the two of them were in the hotel room. No guards. Nothing between Aidan and his future father-in-law. Aidan wanted to kill him, but if he did, the precious information the powerful vampire had in his brain would forever be out of his reach, and Aidan needed it.

"You've been in this city for two months and only now you show up? You shouldn't have waited so long. You're here by my approval. It isn't nice to spit on my generosity," the vampire said after taking a sip from his cup.

Aidan chuckled darkly. "Generosity? You and I both know I didn't need your approval to come here, your territory or not. The formality of my people meeting you was only to establish peace so I may find my bride. A bride, your child, who you conveniently *lost* the day you were to hand her over to my house in order to prepare her for our joining of hands."

"How could I have predicted the human mother would run off after witnessing an argument with my deceased wife? I think I've been helpful and very cooperative these last ten years in trying to find them." Harris smiled mockingly at Aidan.

"You've done nothing!" Aidan spat. "The only thing you've done is cause more harm than good in trying to locate them!"

All because Harris didn't want Aidan's house to join with his. If Aidan wed Harris's child, Aidan would have free access to walk on Leviance territory, on their world, and on Earth.

"You need to work on that temper of yours, Aidan. Doesn't look good if you cause a problem," Harris quietly warned.

Aidan's frustration caused his slips, and it didn't help to see the smug expression on the large muscular, blond's face, his green eyes flashing in victory, knowing in a few short days the marriage contract would be voided and

Aidan would be left without a mate. Harris would have full and complete guardianship over his missing child. Able to deny or approve any marriage requests that came for the bride's hand.

Their laws were strange when it came to a newborn. The rare child was paired up at birth by will of their seers. Yet once the child came of age, if the mate chosen did not claim the youth before their twenty-first year, the male or female lost their right to join hands. If such a thing took place then it would prove to all that the parents of the child had the power to protect them.

Aidan's mate was nearing their twenty-first birthday. Right now he had the right to steal her away and mark her. However, if he failed to collect Jamie before her coming of age, Aidan would have to go to war to get her back.

"Don't think you've won, Harris," Aidan said, "I don't plan on giving up, even if the marriage is nullified." Aidan grinned cruelly when the vampire's smile faded. "I still plan on searching, and you and I both know there is nothing you can do to stop me." Nothing Harris could do because out of all the factions of every clan, Aidan was the most powerful.

"Father, don't you think it's time to stop all of this?"

Aidan kept his eyes on Harris as another voice joined in on their conversation. Aidan didn't need to turn around to identify the new party member, recognizing Harris's first born son by the vampire's flare of power he respectfully sent out to notify them of his arrival.

"Keep silent, Joseph," Harris warned his son.

"No, Joseph, don't keep silent." If Aidan were to get any help from this family it would be from the dark haired nightwalker striding toward his father. "It would be in your best interest if you tell me." Aidan didn't need to say out loud why it was in their best interest. He'd just delivered a not so subtle threat to Harris.

"This has gone on long enough, Father.

Your 'protection' is putting my little brother in danger."

Finally Aidan knew what sex he needed to look for, but his relief was mixed with disappointment. Although gender wouldn't be an issue with Aidan, he'd hoped the missing Leviance child was female. The image of Jamie Dexson's lovely face flashed in Aidan's mind.

"He's been out in the world for nearly eleven years with only his human mother watching over him. He needs us, Father," Joseph said calmly.

"No, he doesn't," Aidan said firmly. "What he needs is me, and you will tell me what you know, and where I can find him."

"All I know is he's in this city," Joseph said. "I have yet to find where he currently resides. However, once I discover his location I will relay it to you."

Aidan turned to Harris after a long moment of staring at Joseph… he didn't believe the second part of what the vampire said. Aidan could tell Joseph knew where his brother hid, but starting a fight would only waste his time. "Where is he in the city, Harris?"

"I think what my son told you will be all you are going to get from us, Aidan. I was forced to sign my second child over to you, but that is all I will be forced to do." Aidan stiffened at the sight of Harris's sudden fanged smile. "I made sure my boy knew what would happen if he revealed himself, and he is nothing if not the perfect son."

Out of the corner of his eye, Aidan noted how Harris's first born stiffened at his father's comment. *I might need to watch out for him*, Aidan thought, not liking the barely contained rage he saw in Joseph's eyes.

Without another word, Aidan turned around and swiftly left, needing to get away so he could begin his planning. Per the treaty of peace he'd sighed, Aidan could have no more than seven of his soldiers with him at all times. Not very many eyes to help him search.

However, if Aidan were to unlock the invisible chains he'd willing adorned himself in to hold his powers back, then finding the boy would be easy. The only reason he had not done so, since keeping his wings contained for so long felt like being strangled, was because he'd be forced to leave not soon after. His kind could not be seen by humans.

And it would also send a signal to the vultures—the lowly creatures who escaped to the human realm—in the area, those who sought to feed off the scraps of the more powerful animals. He was on a serious hunt, and they would come flocking in waves to see what was going on. The capture of a newborn would be a prize their world would pay untold amounts to obtain, rare as they were.

Exiting the floor and hotel was easier and faster than entering, and Aidan didn't waste his time going back to his own temporary home, but instead called Ethan for an update on the assignment he had given him, as well as

Tiffany.

Aidan knew following Jamie to be pointless now, but he wanted at least one taste of her before he removed himself for a time to rip the city apart to find his mate. Just one taste was all he wanted.

* * * *

"I have him in my sight right now, Aidan," Ethan whispered in his cell phone.

Whispering because he could see Asa was on his guard, as if Asa knew he was being followed. The last thing Ethan wanted was for Asa to get spooked and make a run for it, back to Jamie's spell protected house.

Only half an hour passed before the guy stepped out of Jamie's house, and the way Asa stopped and tilted his head to the side, listening and sniffing the air in an animal like way, sent a thrill of excitement up Ethan's spine. The sweet tells of one of their kind who were not use to the strange smells, and sounds of the human world.

"No, he stopped at a few shops, but other than that it doesn't look like Asa is headed back to Jamie's house any time soon." Ethan knew, from Asa's direction, he was headed to the Jacobs residence, a place Ethan stalked many nights just to see if he could get a glimpse of Asa.

"Looks like he is headed to his house; he'll be there in ten minutes if he doesn't stop again." Ethan nodded while he listened to Aidan's new commands.

"Wait, can you repeat that?" Ethan asked, thinking he'd misheard what Aidan said.

"Are you sure?" Ethan sighed. "Understood."

Hanging up his phone, Ethan slapped a happy grin on his face and jogged up to the guy. "Hey! Fancy seeing you out and about. Thought you said you were sick?"

Ethan expected Asa to at least smile at him, although he knew Asa would be wary due to their history, and his stealing of Asa's cell phone. When Ethan's charming, rugged smile failed to work its magic on Asa, Ethan threw his arm across the guy's slim shoulders.

"Ethan… I didn't expect to see you so soon…" Asa nervously looked around him, anywhere else than at Ethan.

Hugging Asa tightly to his side, Ethan said, "You know me. I'm not the best student in the whole world. Why spend a beautiful day stuck in a classroom when I can have fun running wild. Besides, you sounded so sick over the phone I wouldn't have been able to concentrate in class." Ethan could see Asa's pupils were slightly elongated, but not enough to draw unwanted attention.

Ethan's curiosity ate at him. How could Jamie have changed Asa without the consequences which have fallen on all the other humans their kind attempted to change? Ethan was impressed Asa could walk with the barest hint of weakness in his limbs. Whoever Jamie was, it was clear she was very strong.

Aidan told him Jamie wasn't the one they were looking for, that their plans changed, but instead of telling him to leave, Aidan gave him permission to take Asa. An order Ethan had no problem obeying.

Aidan's gift to him for following him into the human world, since Ethan never wanted to come. Walking the streets in the human world was like grocery shopping while you're hungry. Every human made his mouth water with the need to feed... but meeting Asa changed his opinion of Earth, and his mouth started watering for a whole different reason.

"Asa... so, what do you have planned that you would leave Jamie's place as *sick* as you are?" Aidan's orders were simple, and better yet, gave Ethan something he had wanted from the very beginning. But before he took Asa, Aidan wanted the guy to continue on his course. Tiffany, the foxy shape-shifter, had fucked up by taking her eyes off of Jamie.

Ethan felt for Tiffany and the position she found herself in. Having Aidan pissed off was never pleasant. Aidan's decision for Ethan to wait to take his prize home, to keep him walking around, was only so Asa could leave a trail of his scent for Jamie to follow.

Aidan might now know the girl wouldn't be his mate, but it didn't mean Aidan didn't still want her. Ethan liked the girl, and if he ever had the chance, he'd thank her for what she'd done to Asa.

"Nothing special." Asa gulped.

Ethan held back his grin, seeing how badly Asa wanted him to take his arm off of his shoulders.

"I just wanted to buy some medicine. And, ah, I'm now on my way home so..."

Ethan kept his stupid playboy persona in place, ignoring Asa's subtle hint he wasn't wanted. Nothing Asa could say or do would make him leave. Ethan just needed to get Asa to keep walking.

"Ah, where is Aidan? You two are never very far from one another..."

Ethan carefully answered Asa's question, not knowing if Jamie told the boy about Aidan. "It's not like we're attached at the hip, Asa, baby. We have our own lives."

"Really? It always seemed Aidan... well, controlled everything you did." Asa looked up at him, then ducked his head quickly down.

Ethan could hear Asa's heart rate increase. "The A-man. He had some family business he needed to deal with, so he's not around." Without meaning to, Ethan leaned down, inhaling deeply Asa's fresh scent.

A rumble of pleasure vibrated from his chest. Not a bit of human was left lingering on Asa's skin. Unknowingly Ethan accidentally squeezed Asa's shoulder harder than he meant to.

"Ow! Let go!" Asa yanked away from Ethan's hold.

Startled, Ethan quickly let go and watched as Asa massaged his shoulder. "Did you hurt yourself?" Ethan watched as Asa's lovely eyes darted up to his then quickly away.

"I pulled something that's all..." Asa slowly backed away from Ethan.

Ethan allowed Asa to retreat, seeing the guy's panic by the way Asa's nostrils flared and how his body trembled as Ethan's scent circled around him. However, when Asa made a move to dodge his comforting touch, Ethan threw his arm back around the guy's shoulders, this time pulling Asa closer. "Well, stick by me and I'll take care of you." Ethan wasn't lying either. He had every intention of making the ex-human his.

"So, where are we off to?" Ethan asked.

"We?" Asa shook his head vigorously. "Ah, I think it would be best if we parted ways here..." Asa trailed off.

"Aw, come on Asa, don't be such a stick-in-the-mud. Why can't I come along?" Ethan whined prettily.

"I'm sorry, but no," Asa said.

Ethan raised a brow at the firmness in Asa's voice. "Is it a secret you can't tell me about?"

"Why the sudden interest, Ethan?" Asa asked stiffly. "Why can't you go away?"

Ethan chuckled. "My interest in you has never been sudden, Asa." They were only a couple blocks away from Asa's house, and Ethan hid his smile at Asa's attempts to remove his arm and get rid of him before reaching home.

"Why the harsh vibes, Asa? I just want to hang out with you." Ethan pretended to grumble when he let Asa remove his arm from around his shoulder, allowing Asa to escape his arms only because he felt his phone vibrating in his pocket.

"Sorry, Ethan," Asa said, stepping away. "I need to go… so… goodbye."

* * * *

Walking quickly away, Asa looked over

his shoulder and saw Ethan still standing in the spot he'd left him. Ethan smiled and waved, but worried Asa about who Ethan spoke to with such a serious expression... and what scared Asa more? He could have sworn Ethan's eyes glowed slightly. Not the freaky Ghostbuster kind of glowing from the dog lady at the end of the movie, but Ethan's eyes glowed... like Jamie's eyes did. Asa gave himself a little mental slap. Telling himself that just because Jamie said there were more of... well, whatever Jamie was out there, didn't mean Ethan had to be one of them. Besides, Jamie would have warned him.

Abandoning all thoughts of taking any roundabout ways to get home, Asa forced his sore body to go faster. Heading straight through his neighborhood to his house, Asa couldn't stop feeling paranoid. Jamie's words made him see monsters in every shadowy corner.

Reaching his house, Asa unlocked the door and entered. Throwing the deadbolt, and the door chain, only then did Asa breathe a sigh of relief.

Asa grimly gazed at the Spartan like décor of his family's home. The only humor to come bubbling forward, was imagining what Jamie would have said if he had been with him right now. *"Your family's not much for pastels, are they?"* Asa could hear Jamie's whisper, commenting on how everything was gray, white or black; even the art lacked color.

"Father likes things to be… clean looking…" Asa whispered to himself, walking toward the stairs, wanting to take the steps two at a time, but after one step up Asa's muscles screamed in protest.

Jake beating him, Jamie attacking him, and his strange sickness, added to the stress of Ethan hanging on him, and on top of it all, the fearful anticipation his stepbrother might come back earlier than expected, Asa didn't have the energy to rush anyway.

In his room, Asa rummaged through his

closet and threw clothes on his bed. Pulling a duffle bag from the top shelf, Asa shoved as much as he could in the bag, along with a few precious items he refused to leave behind. Tripping over a pair of jeans on the floor, Asa cursed as he crashed into his bookshelf next to his desk.

Grimacing in pain, Asa grabbed his external power cord for his laptop from the top drawer of his desk, and stuffed the cord and laptop into his bag. Wiping the sweat from his brow, Asa hesitated as he looked at his phone on the nightstand. He told Jamie he was going to contact his father... but now that it came for him to do it, Asa's courage faltered.

Sitting down on the edge of the bed, Asa stared at the phone. It wouldn't take much to contact his dad, Asa just needed to reach out and grab the receiver...

"Ball up, Asa." Licking his lips nervously, Asa shakily leaned over and picked up the cordless phone, dialed and waited, his breath getting harsher with every ring that sounded over the line.

"Hello?"

"Fa—" Asa cleared his throat when his voice broke, and started again. "Father, it's Asa."

"Asa? Why are you calling me?"

"I'm leaving, Father, and I want money." Asa winced at his choice of words. "I mean, I want the money mother left me," Asa clarified.

"You won't get the money until you turn twenty-one and that's if you can behave yourself."

"No, Father, you don't understand me." Asa exhaled a shaky breath. "I want the amount I would have been given transferred into my account now. Once I'm gone, you will be given everything back when I turn twenty-one, so it's not like you'd be losing out on anything."

"What makes you think I would do something like that for you? Your selfishness knows no bounds, does it?"

Asa became silent, too stunned to speak for a minute. "I'm selfish? *I'm selfish!* You are one to talk! Having an affair with a married woman while still married! All you have ever done is think of yourself, and what you want! Think of me for a change!" Asa shouted on the phone.

For years Asa tried to justify what his father had done; ignoring his mother and him, wanting nothing to do with either of them. Yes, his parents didn't have a happy marriage. But once upon a time they did.

Asa's mother told him how she'd acted out in a moment of weakness, and forever turned his father against her. How, after his birth, she'd done everything she could in hopes her husband would once more care for her. Asa had done everything he could to help his mother win back the love of his father, but all Asa ever felt from the man was indifference. Asa's father didn't just ignore them; it might have been better if he had.

Clark, his father, pretended they didn't exist. And it crushed his mother. Killed her, and killed Asa slowly to watch his mother try so hard to win the affections of a man she knew to be unfaithful. Asa didn't want to turn out like his mother; he wanted to be free of being a burden in his father's eyes. He didn't want to continue to be the unwanted child from an unhappy marriage.

Making sure Asa got good grades, had clothes on his back, a roof over his head, and food in his belly. Asa counted himself lucky his father thought about him to that extent. Asa wanted to leave before his view of the world became completely jaded.

"You don't want me in your life, and I don't want to be in yours. I want out of this family, and to do that I need money. Money I worked hard for, that I earned." Asa swiftly wiped the tears from his eyes before they rolled down his cheeks.

"You'll get nothing from me. If you leave,

then you leave with nothing."

"I don't think you quite grasp what I am saying." Asa gripped the phone until the hard plastic groaned in protest. "I'm not asking you for the money, I'm *telling* you to wire the money into my account or else."

"Or else what, boy?"

"Or I'll tell everyone about your affair with a married woman while you were still married to Mom, and not just that—" Asa tried to swallow the lump in his throat so he could say the next part. "I'll humiliate myself by telling everyone how you've allowed Jake to not only beat me, but rape me for almost four years."

"No... Jake wouldn't do something like that; he's a good boy!"

"Like you didn't know," Asa sneered, his voice shaking, "Jake told me you said for him not to overdo it, how he could use me like a bitch because that's all I'll ever be good at." Even now, recounting those words Jake said while he loomed over him, while he lay on the floor in pain from his stepbrother beating him, still hurt.

"The beatings, yes, I knew, but—"

"I don't want to hear your excuses! You allowed him to do it to me! How could you give him your approval?" Asa's mind reeled at his father's acknowledgement. "I knew you hated me because you think I'm like Mom, but to do this to me… I tried to hold on until the end, but no more… I can't take it anymore!" Asa turned his face toward the breeze from the open window.

"Asa… we'll talk about this when I get home in a few days. The three of us will talk and sort this whole thing out."

"Asa? Are you still there?"

Asa could only stare at the figure grinning at him, who squatted on his windowsill acting as if it was the most natural thing in the world to be doing.

CHAPTER 10

"E-Eth—ommhf!" The phone dropped from Asa's hand when Ethan tackled him backward onto the bed, his mouth covered from shouting out.

"Shhh, don't want papa bear to hear you scream." Ethan grinned.

Asa struggled to free himself, to remove the hold over his mouth. Asa could hear his father's voice calling his name from the phone he dropped by the side of his head, and began thrashing wildly when Ethan picked it up.

"Calm down, Asa," Ethan whispered.

Asa did calm down, but only because Ethan pressed his body down on the bed, and he felt the larger boy's excitement in his lower extremities by his vigorous movements.

Smiling, Ethan held a finger over his lips, before speaking into the receiver, "Mr Jacobs, this is Ethan Martins. Do you know who I am?"

Asa strained to hear what his father would say to Ethan, but gasped and settled back down when Ethan grinded his hips into him.

"No, no, Mr Jacobs, I'm asking if you *know* who I *am*. Good!" Ethan laughed darkly, "Saves me the trouble of explaining. Now what I'm going to tell you will remain between us. The Montgomery family will be taking guardianship over Asa. Some of my people will be showing up at your hotel in a few minutes with papers you will be signing. And as for Jake..."

A shiver slithered up Asa's spine at the sudden change that came over Ethan, the way Ethan's blue eyes glowed and body seemed to grow just a little bit larger. Asa began his struggles anew, trying to claw the hand over his mouth off so he could call for help.

"As for your stepson," Ethan continued, "it would be best if you kept him hidden from me, for touching what is mine."

Asa whimpered when Ethan hung up the

phone, and smiled down at him.

"Sorry for coming so late. I needed to take a call from someone who couldn't be ignored, or else I would have helped you pack. I'll take my hand off your mouth, but if you scream I'll have to hurt you, even knock you out. You don't want that, do you?" Ethan asked.

Glaring up at Ethan, Asa shook his head.

"Not one sound, Asa," Ethan warned, lifting his hand away.

"What are you?" Asa gasped once his mouth was free.

"Didn't Jamie tell you?"

"She won't say just yet." Asa's eyes darted to his closed bedroom door, hoping Jamie returned to his house, saw his note about where he had taken off to, and would come storming over to save him.

"Tell me, Asa, how did Jamie change you and make you one of us? How did she do it?" Ethan coaxed, tucking an errant brown lock from Asa's forehead behind his ear.

Asa refused to answer, and instead began asking questions of his own, "Why did you ask my father if he knew who you were? Does he know you're a mutated werewolf?"

"Mutated werewolf?" Ethan barked out with laughter. "I've had people whisper fearfully I was a werewolf before I killed them, but never a mutant."

Asa turned his face away from Ethan's seeking lips, and pushed at Ethan's broad shoulders. "You haven't answered any of my questions."

"And neither have you," said Ethan. "Then again, it's better than the same ol', same ol' of hearing 'Why Grandma, what big teeth you have', not that it matters to me right at this moment if you tell me. Aidan will find out from Jamie; but don't worry. He won't hurt her. He just wants a little taste before he leaves her in peace."

"Taste?" asked Asa, stiffening when Ethan shifted his body, pushing his legs apart so he could lie between his thighs.

"Mmm… just a little taste, he won't take more than that. Aidan's looking for his mate, a boy who has run away from his father with his mother and nanny."

Asa's heart stopped in his chest for a few seconds before beating again. "Aidan… his m-mate ran away from him?" Asa slightly stammered.

"Nah, from what we've been able to piece together, Aidan's intended's father killed his wife and the boy saw him, so Harris, that's the boy's father's name, used the incident to scare the boy and his mother, making them run so he didn't have to turn the boy over to Aidan. Harris and Aidan's people have always been at odds with one another, so when it was discovered Harris's union with a human bore fruit, and the seers matched his child with Aidan's house, Harris did everything he could to stop the mating." Ethan shrugged. "It isn't as if we didn't know something like this would happen; only that it had worked so well."

"If they are being forced to wed, then shouldn't the boy running away be a relief for Aidan?" Asa pressed his lower body down to try to get it away from touching the relentless hard length of Ethan's body.

Asa flinched as Ethan pressed him deeper into the mattress. "Nah, you see, Aidan has always wanted to marry Harris's kid. I don't know all the details, but I *do* know Aidan won't stop until he finds him, even with the attraction he has for Jamie."

"And me?" Asa finally asked, "What did you mean when you said Aidan is taking guardianship over me?"

"You are one of us now, Asa." Ethan grinned, flashing just how un-human he was by showing off his abnormally long, large, and sharp canines. "You're the first human to be changed in six hundred years. You're coming home with me. Remember what I said when I whispered in your ear yesterday before I took your cell phone?" Ethan leaned down, looking Asa in the eyes. "How if you were like me, then nothing would stop me from taking you? Well, you are like me now, and I don't plan on letting you go. I'm taking you home with me right now."

Asa's eyes widened, his mouth falling open to the sight appearing above Ethan's head.

"Say goodbye to this world, Asa, and hello to your new one."

* * * *

"For crying out loud." Jamie panted as he and Janis rounded the last corner to get to his house. "Was it really necessary to run all the way here without stopping?" Jamie glared at the annoying brunette smirking over her shoulder at him.

"Maybe if you worked out once in a while, you wouldn't be feeling this fatigued when running like a human," Janis shot back.

"We wouldn't have needed to rush if *you* told me from the very beginning you had changed Asa. Stupid punk."

"Tell me again why I even decided to trust you?" Jamie grumbled to Janis's back.

"Keep your trap shut, will you? I need to make sure the streets are secure. It wouldn't do if Aidan's people caught you just before you got to the safety of your house."

Jamie bristled at Janis's tone.

"As for you deciding to trust me? Hell, who could you put your trust in, huh? The fox bitch who's been lying to you and pretending to be your bosom buddy? Or maybe the hot, 'Sacrifice the virgins!', fire breathing king, and his moon howling henchman?" Janis smirked. "Face it, *sister*, I'm the only one you could have turned to now that mommy is off on vacation."

An arm… it would be okay if he just ripped her arm off, right? After all, Janis had another one, so it wouldn't be like he'd be leaving her completely helpless. He'd even make sure it was her driving hand the damn chick kept.

"You go in, grab Glasses, and come back out. If you need to, then grab only the most important things, no crap. And if anything happens. Do. *Not*. Leave the house under any circumstances."

"Anything else, your majesty?" Jamie sarcastically asked.

"Yeah, stow the fucking att—"

A tornado of wind whipped around Jamie, blinding him and slamming him against the siding of the nearest house. As suddenly as the wind came, it disappeared and once the dust settled Jamie found himself alone. Janis had magically disappeared.

Spinning around in a circle, Jamie so badly wanted to shout out that Janis's joke had gone too far, but the ten percent of his brain still thinking rationally silenced his tongue. Whatever the wind had been, had not been natural, and Janis had just been swept away in it. Problem was Jamie didn't know if it was the good or bad guys who'd taken her. Were there even any good guys who had his back?

"Shit," Jamie cursed. Whatever happened to Janis, Jamie couldn't stand outside like an idiot, waiting in hopes the annoying wench came back. Wiping his sweaty palms on his skirt, Jamie peeked around the corner to see if the coast was clear, even though his nose already confirmed it was.

Taking a deep breath, Jamie closed his eyes for the briefest of moments before opening them back up. Stepping out into the open, Jamie plastered as much of a normal, carefree, smile on his face as he could, before casually walking across the street, all the while his brain screamed at him to make a run for his front door. The last thing he wanted was for whoever was out there to think they had been found out, and come out at him all at once.

Jamie might not know how many were out there, but he did know that by them thinking he knew nothing, he had the advantage. Jamie didn't know what kind of creatures he would fight against… or what they could do… or what they could change themselves into… or for that matter what exactly he was or could do, but the thing he was damn sure of was he could take them all down if he needed to. Because the one thing Jamie knew how to do, and do damn well, was hunt.

With his height, stalking his prey and taking them down from behind, regardless of his superior power against humans, became Jamie's biggest strength. The exhilaration of his quarry not knowing he's behind them until it was too late. Jamie shivered in pleasure. Yes, it would be to his advantage they didn't know he was aware about them.

Running and hiding had been the first thing he'd been trained to do by Catherine and his mother. Never letting them find him… but it was different this time, because they *already* knew where he was, and they were closing in. If they attacked, Jamie needed to hurt the opposing team badly enough so they'd back off to regroup, but not so badly they couldn't follow him. Then he could safely get Asa out of the city without worrying they would be on their heels.

And when his unseen foes regrouped, Jamie was confident they would come after him, and leave his mother and Catherine alone. If Janis hadn't been lying, then his mother had his father's protection, and if luck was on his side his old man would have found a way to warn his mother not to come back.

At his front door, Jamie frowned when he realized he didn't have his house key. Rushing out the door this morning all he'd grabbed was his backpack... "Son of a bitch," Jamie muttered with a stupid smile still on his face.

Pressing the doorbell, Jamie tapped his foot, waiting impatiently for Asa to get his ass up and come unlock the door. "Open the fucking door, Asa!" Jamie hissed, all pretense of being calm and cool disintegrating the longer he waited. Ringing the bell repeatedly while pounding on the door with his fist, Jamie cursed when Asa still didn't appear.

"It won't matter if I break it," Jamie mumbled as he took hold of the door knob, turning it with unbelievable ease, and grunting in satisfaction when the lock broke. Luckily Asa hadn't locked the deadbolt, or else he'd have to do more than just destroy the door handle.

"Asa!"

When Jamie couldn't find Asa downstairs, he literally felt like he flew up the stairs in his need to find the damn kid. "Not the best time to be fucking playing hide and seek, asshole!"

Jamie panicked as every room he checked turned up empty. Leaving Asa after he'd tucked him in his bed had been almost impossible to do. Jamie tore himself away only because the corpse and the evidence on the man's half-eaten body had been a danger to Asa he couldn't allow.

"Where the fuck are you?!" Jamie shouted. "This isn't funny, Asa! We have to go now! The things that go bump in the night have come out in the day to grab our asses!"

"Damn it, Asa!"

Running back downstairs, Jamie went into the kitchen. It was the first place Jamie checked when he'd entered the house, but this time actually looking around for anything out of place. Anything that might suggest where Asa went.

On Jamie's old fashioned refrigerator, amongst the god awful amount of tacky magnets, a note lightly fluttered. Jamie ran forward, ripping the bright pink paper off the icebox, sending heart-shaped magnets flying.

After reading the note quickly, Jamie cursed. "Stupid fool. I told you to wait for me!"

Jamie crumbled the missive, and threw the paper to the floor. Asa had gone back to his house to get his crap; back to the house where his stepbrother might be lying in wait for him. Jamie's vision turned red, and his fangs dropped, piercing his lower lip. He didn't know where Asa lived, but that didn't really matter. He'd been trained to track things down.

Ripping the stupid wig off his head, storming out the back door, Jamie used every trick he knew. Pushing his body to the limit, running faster than he'd ever run before, Jamie followed the trail of Asa's scent, which lingered on the pavement from every step he took and everything he may have touched.

* * * *

"—itude!" Janis sneered… only it wasn't Jamie she spoke to anymore.

"Is that any way to talk to me?" a cool voice answered.

Janis glared at the vampire standing in front of her. "Not the best of times to summon me. I was with your little brother. You know, helping him escape discovery and all."

The vampire, Joseph, narrowed his deep blue eyes. "You know better than to be in my presence in this deceptive form."

Smoothing her hands down her sides, making her ample breasts strain against the thin cloth of her red tank top, Janis lifted a dark brow and whispered seductively, "Aw, come on. You can't tell me that seeing these," Janis crossed her arms under her breasts, leaning over so the fearsome vampire could take in his fill, "doesn't turn you on? Admit it; you like them."

"Change. Now," threatened Joseph softly.

Growling, Janis stomped her foot, but did as Joseph ordered. Taking in a swift breath, Janis held her tormentor's eyes as the change took hold of her. The shifting of bones making her grunt in pain and discomfort, but she'd been doing it for so long the transformation, and the agony which came with it, was easily brushed off. In the end, Janis turned back into the form she'd been born in.

"Outfit isn't nearly as impressive now," Janis muttered, looking down at his now flat male chest. "You happy now? Can I go back to Jamie?"

"Jamie is safe for now," replied Joseph as he walked forward, inspecting his special shape-shifter from head to toe. "Aidan met with my father not long ago. To turn his gaze off Jamie, I told Aidan the sex he needed to look for is a male, not female."

Janis laughed. "That's not going to do anything! I've been hanging around and watching the badass. Aidan might not know Jamie is really his mate in disguise, but he'll still go after him. You haven't seen the way Aidan's looked at Jamie, but I have."

"Such disrespect…"

Janis stiffened when the vampire circled him, stopping behind him.

"If memory serves me, I said you were

only to verbally interfere, never physically. But my spies tell me you were engaged in a sexual situation with Aidan."

"You had someone watching me?" Janis growled.

Janis stilled as Joseph brushed his long multi-colored, shoulder length locks away from his neck. "Someone as wild as you needs to be constantly watched. Who knows when you'll try to escape?" Janis shivered as Joseph leaned down and placed a feathered kiss on his shoulder, stifling his moan at the vampire's touch.

"Running has been ineffective against you." Janis swallowed audibly.

"And yet you continuously try."

Janis panted as Joseph inhaled, feeling the vampire's hot breath on his neck, no doubt dining on the scent of hot blood flowing beneath the thin layer of Janis's skin.

"Yeah, I get it, so don't fucking bite me," Janis grumbled, licking his lips, wanting to step forward and away from those fangs but knowing better than to try. "I'm wasting time being here. Jamie needs me whether he knows it or not."

"Remember, Alia; your job is to protect my brother from harm. Keep Aidan away from him. Jamie turns twenty-one in just a few days. We need to keep him hidden until he turns of age, and then we can bring him home," Joseph whispered into Janis's ear.

Janis flinched hearing his real name uttered from those dangerous lips. "I know already… you've been hammering it in my head since the damn kid was born…"

"I won't have him be sacrificed to the dragons just because a few seers imagined a pairing between the two. I don't want that kind of life for him. I love my little brother, Alia. Tell me, what exactly are your feelings for him?"

Janis turned, looking the vampire in the eyes. "I'm pissed at the little shit for leaving me behind, but I don't want him hurt." Humor flashed in Janis's different colored eyes; one blue, one green. "If anything, I like the bastard."

Joseph trailed his fingertip down Alia's cheek. "Just make sure your feelings for him do not go further than 'like'."

Janis backed away from Joseph. "We're wasting time. Jamie isn't the kind to just stand back and wait for me to reappear."

Joseph bowed his head. "Then go back to him, and Alia… don't get caught."

Janis curled his lip, his answer to the bossy vampire even as he shifted, turning himself back into the voluptuous, brown-eyed, female brunette Jamie knew.

"Yeah, tell me something I don't know," muttered Janis as he felt wind gather around him, consciously aware of the magic filling his body, sending him back across town to where he'd been before being summoned.

Only when Janis finally got his bearings he found he wasn't alone.

"I was wondering who was showing up.

Never did I think it would be you."

"Tiffany!" Janis growled.

From all sides appeared the dragon king's soldiers. Boxing Janis in.

"I always knew there was something not quite right about you," Tiffany said to him. "You didn't smell right."

Janis stood tall, and put his hand on his hip. "Well, I've always known what you were. Foxes have this stench you just can't get rid of, no matter how much air freshener you use."

Insults aside, Janis knew he was in deep shit. At first he had thought the animals closing in on him were just regular warriors… but the closer they got to him, the quicker Janis realized they weren't normal grunts, but Aidan's personal guards. *This is going to hurt like a bitch.*

"Who do you work for?" demanded Tiffany.

Janis laughed. "You're not serious, are you? You think just because you got me backed up in a corner I'll bare all my secrets? *Please,* you don't know my boss like I do."

Tiffany sneered. "Take her."

Growling in rage, Janis transformed, his muscles twisting and rippling with new power as black stripes and orange fur covered his skin. However, Janis kept his human form, not completely converting into the great predatory cat. He also sprouted wings, which shot straight out, six feet on either side of him, knocking the sentinels attempting to cage him onto the ground.

Flashing his fangs in an evil grin, Janis looked at Tiffany. "Bet you weren't expecting me to do that, were you?"

"Y-you're a cast out."

Janis bared his fangs in a deadly smile. "That's right, bitch."

Tiffany shot him a calculating glance. "I heard Aidan's chosen mate has a vampire brother who uses a Forbidden One as his servant..."

Cast out. Forbidden One. The

Condemned. Offspring of shape-shifting parents who willingly abandoned their people, and decided to keep themselves isolated from any other clans. The rare children of these couples were born with no ties and so were able to shift their shape to any creature they wanted to be, instead of the base form of their clan.

Oh, this is not good. Joseph is going to be so *pissed at me.* Janis winced, but then shrugged.

Only one way to make sure this little tidbit didn't get repeated. "Time to play, mother fuckers." Janis grinned, rushing Tiffany.

* * * *

Using his unnatural speed to get to Asa's house took no time at all. Jamie would have reached Asa's home in less time if he hadn't been sidetracked by the scent of Ethan mixing with Asa's not far into the little market area. Jamie would have passed it off as Ethan skipping class and bumping into his friend, *if* Ethan's scent had been human.

Jamie had stumbled to a stop, shocking a few people with his sudden appearance. But luckily enough humans had a way of explaining the unexplainable. Making excuses for him at his magical appearance without him having to utter a single word.

Once again Jamie had been royally bitch slapped with the knowledge Ethan was a creature like him. A stupid mistake, considering he knew how close Ethan and Aidan were. He should have known better.

Testing the door to Asa's house and finding it locked, Jamie didn't bother ringing the bell or knocking, but kicked the door in. He didn't want to waste any time to see if someone would answer… of course he might have used a little bit too much strength as the door flew inward, crashing into the hall, knocking glass and other whatnots in its path all over the place.

Stepping over the threshold, Jamie

followed the powerful scent of Asa up the stairs, his heart speeding up in concern. While Asa and Ethan's scent had parted for a moment on the road, Jamie smelled Ethan around, and in the house.

The pungent smell of wolf filled Jamie's nose... werewolf? Jamie shook his head. He was letting Asa's comments affect his thinking... or could it be true? Janis told him many things, things he hadn't had time to ask about. He was supposed to be some being who harnessed every creature that made humans go running screaming in the streets. Why would Ethan being a full moon Scooby come as a surprise to him?

"Maybe because I've hung out with the bastard for God knows how long, and never once had an inkling he was anything other than human," Jamie muttered, panting by the time he reached Asa's bedroom, where the trail ended.

Jamie stepped curiously inside the wide open door of Asa's bedroom, his heart beating furiously at the sight greeting him. The room was torn apart. The stuffing from the mattress still fluttered in the breeze blowing from the open window... clothes littered across the floor. What used to be a computer was smashed into pieces under an equally destroyed desk...

"Asa..." Jamie whispered.

Rage quickly replaced Jamie's fear. "They took him," Jamie growled. "They fucking took him!"

Storming out of the room, Jamie retraced his steps, stopping at the staircase. Never had he felt the amount of fury he felt right now. Not even when he had murdered the man who hurt his mother, his very first victim. Killing was only to sate his hunger, never for anything else... not out of anger or revenge. Of course, just about all his meals were, to a point, revenge kills. His victims' screams of terror and last gasps of breath were Jamie's way of giving justice to all those poor souls who'd fallen under their evil heels.

But the feelings filling him now… Jamie couldn't shake them, even if he wanted to. They consumed him, and Jamie needed to tear into something, anything, to release some of the intense emotions locked in his chest. *They took my only friend!*

"Who are you and what are you doing in my house?"

Just what he needed, Jamie bared his fangs in a frightful grin. "You must be Jake, am I correct?" Jamie asked, still at the top of the stairs. The stench of the human reached Jamie before he saw him.

"I asked you a question!" The man sporting a bandage around his head shouted.

Jamie stalked down the stairs. "Me? I'm a friend of Asa's… and Asa has told me *so* much about you."

The man laughed, pushing Jamie closer to the edge. "Asa doesn't have any friends."

Jamie continued to smile until he reached the bottom of the landing. "Oh, Asa has friends alright," Jamie snarled just before he attacked, slashing his claws across his foe's chest, delighting in his cries of pain.

Jamie tried hard not to feel pleasure at being the cause of this man's pain, but he couldn't help it. Just like it had been impossible not to enjoy everyone else he had killed before him. The taint of darkness that sprayed in crimson joy across his face was just the same as all the others. Evil. Impure. Murderer.

Delicious…

Asa's stepbrother may not have literally killed anyone, but the acts he had cruelly inflicted against Asa, were the same as if he had. The words Jamie's father told him the last time he'd seen him repeated in his mind as he dispassionately watched as the larger, more muscular man tried to crawl away from Jamie, pathetically pleading for his life.

"Kill or be killed. Doesn't matter the situation. Protect those you care for or watch them die."

Jamie had snickered at the hypocritical words his father had told him at the time, but now he understood. He'd always been the one protected, never the protector. And until now he hadn't realized that, by his actions, past and present, every kill, he had been following what his father said to him. But he had also tried to live up to what his mother tried to impart in him.

He grew up with humans. Loved what they loved. Treasured what they treasured. But one thing never stuck, what his mother tried so hard to teach him, humanity. To forgive those who had wronged him, and others. To Jamie, those who preyed on the good, the ones who tried to live in peace, and tried to pass that bit of harmony to others, they were free game to him. They were his to kill, and feed off of.

"Not so fun now, is it?" Jamie growled. "What's the matter? You like hurting those weaker than you, right?" Sneering, Jamie planted his foot in the middle of Jake's back, stopping him in his sad attempt to escape. "Not so fun when the tables are turned."

"Crazy bitch."

Jamie grabbed a fistful of Jake's hair, yanking his head back. "Lights out, Jake," Jamie purred as he forced the larger human's head to the side, exposing his neck, and with a clean strike, savagely bit down, casually breaking Jake's arms when he tried to protect himself.

Releasing him, Jamie spat a mouthful of blood onto the ground. "Normally, I'd be dining on your liver right about now, but I don't think Asa would think kindly of me eating one of his family members, no matter how much of a prick you are. You should be happy."

Jamie wiped his mouth with the back of his hand. "I give you ten minutes, max. Ten long minutes, to dwell on the fact no one will be coming to help you, and with every second that passes, you'll be much closer to death." Jamie snickered, grunting when the only answer he received was wet gurgling sounds from Jake's mangled throat.

"I don't think he can hear you any longer, Jamie."

Spinning around, Jamie tripped, his hip hitting hard on the edge of a nearby side table on his way down. "A-Aidan…" Shocked, Jamie could only stare at the man who appeared behind him without making a sound.

Unlike the time when they were in the school, Jamie could feel Aidan's aura; his power emanating from him. Aidan's appearance also changed, his face more angular and eyes more slanted; pale yellow-green irises taking over so the whites of his eyes disappeared, his pupils nothing but reptilian slits. And fuck, if Aidan wasn't larger than before!

"What do you want?" Jamie stood shakily, bravely lifting his chin.

"I want a kiss." Aidan smiled.

"A kiss?" asked Jamie in disbelief. "You stalked me all the way to Asa's house—" *and probably watched as I tortured, and ultimately killed, Asa's stepbrother*, "just to try and steal a kiss from me?"

"A kiss is all I can take." Aidan growled. "I'd entertained thoughts of taking you with me… but reason has made me see I cannot. I'm to be married, and that is a vow I will not taint, even if it is without love."

"And if I don't want to give you a kiss?" Jamie sure as hell didn't want Aidan's lips touching his. He wouldn't be able to control the reaction in his lower anatomy if the sexy stud and he engaged in a little tongue action. Not the best thing to happen, especially when Aidan, the all powerful one Janis claimed the 'man' to be, still thought he actually was a she.

"I didn't ask you for a kiss, Jamie; I said I *want* a kiss."

The faster you give it to him, the faster you can escape, thought Jamie taking a hesitant step closer. "Just one kiss and that's it, right? Nothing more?"

"Nothing else," Aidan said in a smooth

tone.

So not a good idea, but Jamie still nodded in agreement. "Okay… but you are not to touch me." Standing in front of Aidan, Jamie flinched when a large, and sharply clawed hand caressed his cheek.

"Tilt your head up and look at me," Aidan commanded.

Jamie did as ordered. "Be quick about it. I want to go home." Jamie began to panic the closer Aidan got, because for the first time one of his wicked little fantasies was coming true. All the days Jamie wondered what it would be like to feel Aidan's lips on his own, and now he would.

Jamie's heart raced as one of Aidan's strong arms circled his waist, pulling him close, and how Aidan rested the hand, which stroked his cheek, at the base of his throat. Jamie's complaints of where Aidan's hand lay evaporated the moment he breathed in Aidan's intoxicating musky scent. Sighing as Aidan leaned down, capturing his lips gently in a long drawn out kiss.

As if of their own accord, Jamie's arms wrapped around Aidan's neck, pulling him closer, deepening the kiss as he pressing his body fully into Aidan's for the barest of moments, then pushed him away before Aidan could feel his growing erection.

"If only you were the one."

Jamie froze when Aidan grabbed him by the throat, not in a threatening way, but to caress the spot where Aidan could feel the rapid beating of his pulse. Jamie tried not to swallow for fear Aidan would feel his Adam's apple bobbing.

"So sweet. Thank you."

Jamie remained silent, concentrating on trying to control his physical reaction to Aidan's kiss.

"Have you nothing to say? You also seem to be unresponsive to the fact I took your friend, and don't plan on ever returning him."

Jamie shook his head, stifling his snarl, trying to be as unconcerned as possible as he lifted his hand to try and remove Aidan's hold from his throat.

"Give me one more second," Aidan whispered, "and I'll leave you alone, I swear."

Jamie tried to stay calm as those pale eyes seared into him, but as the minutes passed Jamie began to panic, and in his nervousness swallowed. Jamie's breath caught as Aidan's strange reptilian eyes narrowed, his hand tightening around his throat, and a large thumb pressed into his throat, searching.

Knowing in his gut the gig was up the moment he saw clarity enter Aidan's eyes, Jamie slashed out, and thankfully Aidan jumped back to protect himself from being harmed, letting him go in the process. Running to the front door Jamie barely got a foot out the door when he was pulled back by hands he couldn't see, from a force he didn't understand. Before Jamie's eyes, the destroyed door magically lifted up in the air by unseen hands, fixed, and slammed back to where it used to be, effectively cutting off his closest escape.

Trembling, Jamie hissed, baring his fangs, and backed up as Aidan began to stalk him.

"Tell me, Jamie... your school registration says you live with your grandparents, mother, and an aunt, but is that even true?"

Jamie refused to answer him, continuing to back up, stepping over Jake's body, and what he hoped was the direction to the back door, raising his claws defensively when Aidan got too close.

"You live with your mother and a nanny, don't you?" Aidan demanded.

"Look, Aidan, you had your kiss, so why don't you leave me in peace like you said you were going to?" Jamie didn't dare take his eyes off of Aidan, seeing how every step Aidan took toward him, the angrier he became.

"Tell me, Jamie, do you know who Harris Leviance is?"

Jamie paused for just a second in his retreat, his eyes widening. "O-of course I know who he is. He's some elite businessman; everyone knows who he is." Jamie's back hit the dining room table, and he quickly moved around it and backed up quicker now to what smelled to be the kitchen.

"How very clever of your brother to tell me the sex of his sibling so I'd turn my attention away from you. Even so, I'd hoped you were the one, even after my meeting with Harris," Aidan said.

"My thoughts so consumed with you, I didn't stop to think of your appearance when I saw you standing over the human, of the color of your hair or eyes. How their hue matches perfectly to those of the vampire—your sire. After all, what boy would pretend to be a girl?"

"I don't know what you're talking about, Aidan. I've been dressing like a girl, not because

I've been hiding from anyone, but because it's fun," Jamie said, his voice breaking due to his nervousness. "Girls have all the fun, you know. They have pretty clothes, shoes. People hold doors for you, and guys buy you drinks. What can I say? I like the attention, and my family lets me do whatever I want. Just because the shade of my hair and eyes are like someone you know is pure coincidence."

"No… I don't think so. You know, there have been a lot of questions asked about you." Aidan laughed, making Jamie shiver. "Like how you never shower after working out and things of that nature, which would make sure you were never fully unclothed in front of them."

"Some people are shy," Jamie said, panicking when he entered the kitchen and couldn't find a back door. Jamie continued to back up in hopes the farther he went in, the more likely he'd bump into a door. He couldn't look behind him; unable to take his eyes off Aidan.

"I would say it was more than shyness," Aidan replied darkly.

Jamie's back hit the wall by a window, nearly toppling the small table and a flowered vase.

"If you are looking for a way out, the door you're seeking is in the dining area which leads to a sunroom, and from there, the entrance to the backyard."

Jamie took the chance of taking his eyes off of Aidan, and frantically looked around the kitchen, cursing when he saw Aidan didn't lie. His only exit, the door Jamie had entered, now blocked by Aidan's big body. "We can work something out, right? I don't know what you want, but..." *But what?* Jamie hysterically thought. He had nothing to offer Aidan as payment to let him go.

Flattening himself to the wall, Jamie dug his claws into the drywall as Aidan closed the distance between them, placing his hands on the wall just above his head. "You think to buy your freedom?"

"I'm sure my father will pay you *anything* you want if you let me go. And if you don't want money, I'm sure we can work something else out," Jamie said, his voice trembling.

"So Harris is your father, and you are his lost son?"

Jamie lifted his chin. "Yeah, he is. Are you going to take me to him now?"

Jamie didn't expect to get French kissed again. In fact, it was the last thing he thought Aidan would do when the giant yanked him into his arms. Hell, he'd been sure he'd get a punch in the gut for letting Aidan kiss him and not telling Aidan about being a male.

Jamie could feel his panic subsiding, his eyelids closing at the heat and gentleness Aidan gave him. The taste of ambrosia filled his mouth, and Jamie was helpless not to swallow the intoxicating flavor. Jamie continued to drown in Aidan's embrace, and kiss, until he felt those strong hands lifting his shirt up and Aidan touched him under his bra.

Tearing away his mouth, Jamie panted, "That's enough, Aidan." When Aidan didn't stop as he requested, Jamie shoved at broad shoulders, then shoved harder when the first time did nothing. "Stop! It wouldn't do if my father found out you were messing around with his kid, his male kid!"

"You're correct on so many levels, Jamie," whispered Aidan. "Your father wouldn't like knowing you were with me since he's been trying to hide you from me; trying to keep you away, scaring you to keep you running until you turned twenty-one."

Jamie flinched when Aidan caressed his chest, his real chest, pinching his nipple, sending a shiver of need down Jamie's spine. Shaking his head, Jamie pathetically attempted to shake off the web of desire Aidan cocooned him in which threatened to fry his brain.

Jamie licked his dry lips. "Hide me?"

Jamie huskily asked.

Some of what Aidan said to him, Jamie knew from Janis... but there had to be something else Jamie was missing... something important which kept slipping from his grasp. Something Janis told him he needed to remember.

"From me. Your father tried to hide you because he doesn't want me anywhere near you."

Jamie suddenly screamed when Aidan ripped his shirt open, biting him hard on the chest and began sucking. Struggling, Jamie tried to pull Aidan's head away, feeling as if Aidan was branding his soul with every pull of his mouth, every drop of blood he drank from him, making Jamie feel as if Aidan were... marking him.

His hands free, Jamie dug them into Aidan's biceps, ripping deeply into his flesh, and when he was finally released from Aidan's teeth, Jamie sank his own fangs into Aidan's shoulder, taking great pains to make sure the bastard holding him captive felt every inch of his canines tearing through his skin.

However, Jamie's plan backfired. With a roar, Aidan jerked Jamie's head up and crushed him to his chest, smashing his mouth over Jamie's. Struggling to break from Aidan's hold before he fell under his spell once again, Jamie dug his claws into Aidan's chest, dragging them down and jumped away when Aidan released him, slamming into the wall behind him. Pressing his hand over the burning bite mark, Jamie panted in fear, pain, and mortifyingly enough, pleasure from Aidan's rough hold.

"Shit... if my day isn't bad enough already," Jamie rasped. "Why did you do that?" Jamie demanded.

"I marked you, twice, so your father can do nothing if he tries to save you." Aidan grinned with satisfaction.

Marked him! Taking his hand off his pec, Jamie looked at his fingers, coated in blood, grimacing at the intensity of the sting. "You said he hid me from you. Why?"

"Your father wasn't as big of a bloodsucker as he is now, so when commanded by the seers to betroth his child to me, he could do nothing but obey. He believed 'they' would not see he'd fallen in love with a human woman, or that the human would bare him a child, a non-human child. Harris tried to keep his lover's pregnancy a secret, but the seers see everything, and while you were still in your mother's womb, we became engaged," Aidan imparted.

"That was, what? Twenty years ago? You're telling me you're going to obey some engagement forced upon us two decades ago?" Jamie laughed. "I never thought you would be such a stickler to the rules, Aidan."

"You have it all wrong, Jamie," Aidan said. "I don't do anything I don't want to."

"Then why?" Jamie cried out desperately. "Why the hell are you so dead set on continuing this if you don't have to?"

"Because *I'm* the one who chose *you*," Aidan announced. "I went to your father's house, here on Earth, to meet with Harris. Even though the seers chose you for my mate, I was not about to bend to their will. I'd planned on refusing the mating... but instead, when I arrived at your father's home, and entered, I became drawn to your father's lover who'd been seven months pregnant. You called out to me, and my soul answered. From that moment on you became mine."

Jamie gaped at Aidan. "I refuse," said Jamie, dread filling him. "You expect me to marry you? I'm only twenty, and not ready to ruin my life," Jamie attempted to joke.

"Refusing is not an option," Aidan replied coldly.

Jamie glared at Aidan. "I said I don't want to marry you. Besides we're boys—"

"Gender doesn't matter."

Jamie gulped. Right... Janis had told him. "Well, then I just don't want you. I. Don't.

Want. You. Not in the permanent way with a ring chaining me down to you forever."

Jamie never saw anyone as angry as Aidan, and began to think maybe telling Aidan he didn't want him wasn't the brightest idea he ever had.

Jamie tried to reason with Aidan. "Look, it's been a bad day. You kidnapped my friend, and then told me my daddy's basically been the good guy this whole time." Something Jamie already heard about from Janis, and he still found it hard to believe. "It's a lot to process. How about we call it a day and talk about this tomorrow?"

The words were barely out of Jamie's mouth when Aidan, bleeding from the 'scratches' he gave him, tried to grab him. Feinting to the left, Jamie tried to make a run for the door, and landed hard on the cherry wood floors when Aidan tripped him.

Jamie's claws dug into the floors, gouging out long chunks of wood as Aidan dragged him backward. Flipping onto his back, Jamie kicked at Aidan's hand around his ankle, but his victory was short lived when Aidan grabbed a fistful of his shirt, picked him up, and slammed him painfully back into the wall.

"As I told you, refusal is not an option," Aidan snarled.

"Okay, okay." Jamie grimaced, holding up his hands. "Can you let go of me and back up? You've already proven I can't get away from you," Jamie pleaded when Aidan didn't look like he planned to back off an inch.

"I've waited a long time for you, don't make me hurt you. I have a *very* short temper. You *are* coming with me."

"So I see." Jamie in no way planned on going with Aidan to God only knew where, but he stayed still, not attempting to run again when Aidan let his feet touch the floor, releasing him.

"Come with me."

Jamie looked at Aidan's out stretched hand... and slowly shook his head.

"Jamie!"

"I'm not going anywhere until I talk to my mother," Jamie stalled.

"We shall see."

Jamie glanced around the room, trying to find another way to escape.

"There is no other way out, Jamie, and someone of your… *size* has no chance of taking me down."

"I don't like it when people talk about how short I am," hissed Jamie, picking up the small vase on the little table by the window. Jamie threw the vase at Aidan then the table itself, before jumping out a closed window, crashing through the plate-glass, and hitting the grass already running to escape the psycho stalker shouting his name.

* * * *

Hiding was the one thing Jamie knew how to do well. Getting away from Aidan had been difficult as hell, but he'd managed to do it. Jamie wanted to run straight home but with the gashes all around his body he had to stop and rest so he could heal, thanking God his freakiness gifted him with accelerated skills.

Taking refuge in his abandoned park, he stumbled to where he and Asa had buried the man he'd killed last night. Jamie went to the softened dirt where the body should have been. Throwing the problem of the missing corpse aside, Jamie dug until a hole was large enough for him to crawl in, and covered his body.

Even though Jamie left a trail of blood behind him, the park, with the absence of smell, even now, was the only place Jamie could think of as the best hiding spot for him. Blanketing his grave with leaves, Jamie pulled a small branch over to use as cover for his head. Hoping no one could see the arm he couldn't carpet with shrub, Jamie promptly passed out.

Jamie didn't know how long he slept, but something forced him to wake up. Slowly, and as quietly as possible, he pushed the shrubbery off of him and un-dug his body from the damp earth. Night had fallen, and with the moon still gone the world around him was pitch black, but with his animal like eyes Jamie could see everything clearly.

Sniffing the air, scanning the area, and seeing no one, Jamie stepped out of the bushes. Safety being the number one thing on his list, Jamie didn't waste any time, cutting across the park to head straight to his house. Once he got home, Aidan wouldn't be able to get to him.

Running... Jamie concentrated only on the burn in his thighs, and the sound of his feet pounding on the pavement. Chest heaving, Jamie pushed his tired, hurting body forward with everything he had in him, but even after his long nap, his body strangely didn't feel one hundred percent, his speed almost... human. Burning pain rippled up Jamie's legs, and he tried to force himself to go at full speed. Jamie knew he couldn't keep up his pace for much longer. But very soon he wouldn't need to. The alley he'd turned down, led straight to his house, the narrow passageway so dark Jamie could barely see farther than a few feet ahead of him. But all Jamie needed to do is get there and he'd be safe to rest.

Forcing his tired legs to go faster, Jamie didn't see the dark figure in front of him until he slammed into him. Shouting out in fear Jamie did his best to get away, fighting with all his strength. Jamie could see the light shining warmly in welcome on his front porch.

"Let go of me!" Jamie shouted, biting the warm flesh of his attacker until he tasted blood.

Pain filled the side of Jamie's face, dazing him, and in his weakened moment he was heaved over a broad shoulder. Lifting his head, the last thing Jamie saw was the light over his front door burn out, leaving him in the dark...

"You belong to me now."

Twisting his body to see what had caused the sudden ripping sound to fill the air, Jamie shouted when the world split in two, and in the middle of the split another world shined back at him. Jamie screamed and bit Aidan on the shoulder, clawed at his back, anything to try and get Aidan to release him, but nothing he did stopped Aidan from advancing forward.

Jamie's last scream for help echoed throughout the alleyway before it disappeared from his sight.

EPILOGUE

September 8th, 2010

There you have it, eleven sad entries of my screwed up life. I bet no one has ever had growing pains or went through puberty like me.

Killing my first victim—who deserved it—before getting my first pube. Growing fangs before my wisdom teeth came out, and claws... well, it took awhile before my mom would put sheets back on my bed that's all I'll say about that.

There are so many other things I could write about my childhood, but I don't want to. It would be just more of the same thing, and I think I've already gotten the main facts written in my previous entries.

If I lose this journal, and it ends up in the hands of some stranger, then don't bother looking up information on who Jamie Dexson is because it's not my real name, just an alias I've clothed myself in for the past few years. And seriously, after reading what I have written, would you want to find me? Who knows what kind of hornet nest you'll disturb?

Just with every other name I've used since we ran away, it's easily discarded and just as easily replaced.

Anyway.

Summer break is over and tomorrow starts my second year of college, and even though it means I'll have to put my boobs back on—vacationing the whole summer far away from anyone we know—I don't care, not really.

I predict this year will be the same as the previous year. Boring.

They say living in the city, or like us close to the city, excitement is always around every corner... What a load of crap. Nothing ever happens here, and I guess it's a good thing for me... I guess... but in a way, I just can't help but wish something heart pumping would happen this year, something besides the same ol', same ol' shit that's happened year after year...

Maybe this year I'll cause a scandal and go out with a girl or French the hottest guy in school—Aidan Montgomery. Maybe I'll strip and streak the hallways. I can just imagine the look on Aidan, and everyone else's, faces if I were to do that.

Best thing about wishes is I have a better chance of stepping in dog shit than any of them coming true, and I'm a pro at stepping in crap. But as much as I want to have at least one person know who I really am, it's a good thing I don't. In this time of my life, it's best to be alone, especially with a killer on my heels.

Despite what I just said, I pray for another ordinary year. I guess the best thing I can look forward to would be my friend Tiffany getting caught going into the men's locker room like she did last year.

With the way my life has been up to until now excitement is the last thing I would want, *right?*

Right...?

THE BEGINNING...

CPSIA information can be obtained at www.ICGtesting.com
Printed in the USA
BVOW030127010612

291541BV00001B/25/P